D0235576

Lincolnshire
COUNTY COUNCIL

COMMUNITIES, CULTURAL SERVICES
and ADULT EDUCATION

**This book should be returned on or before
the last date shown below.**

MO 3

Metheringham Library

2 2 FEB 2013

Tel: 01522 782010

NA 4 ,0/14   31. MAY **14**

13. 12. 14.

Bracebridge Heath Library

SEP 2013

Tel: 01522 782010

2015

BURGH

Washingborough Library

MAR 2014

Tel: 01522 782010

27/10/17

To renew or order library books please telephone 01522 782010
or visit www.lincolnshire.gov.uk
You will require a Personal Identification Number.
Ask any member of staff for this.

EC. 199 (LIBS): RS/L5/19

04796858

RATTLESNAKE MESA

RATTLESNAKE MESA

Peter Dawson

GUNSMOKE

First published in the U.S. by Five Star

This hardback edition 2011
by AudioGO Ltd
by arrangement with
Golden West Literary Agency

Copyright © 1997 by Dorothy S. Ewing and
Golden West Literary Agency.
All rights reserved.

ISBN 978 1 408 46319 2

British Library Cataloguing in Publication Data available.

LINCOLNSHIRE COUNTY COUNCIL	
AudioGO	2 1 DEC 2012
	£9.95

Printed and bound in Great Britain by
CPI Antony Rowe, Chippenham and Eastbourne

RATTLESNAKE MESA

Chapter One

The man on the black reined off the trail a hundred yards below the big dead cottonwood. The wind was blowing, and the air here off the mesa was cold. A large, dry branch from a nearby tree was blown down, crashing in front of his shying horse. It had come upon him suddenly that something was not right, was in fact quite wrong and out of order. Strange powers were out tonight. The feeling was so strong and distinct that it was as if a frozen hand had passed for a moment across his face. His hair rose a little on his head beneath the flat-crowned Stetson.

For a few moments he was more than cautious. He was genuinely afraid, struck by an extraordinary terror. In the weird turbulence of this night, he could feel the wild life of dead things all around him, especially there before him, the silent, shadowed body, swaying slightly in that terrible wind. The kerosene lantern in the buggy illumined with a flickering light a figure in the bed, a cape whipping about its form while it was reaching upward and sawing on the rope from which the lifeless body was suspended. The light glinted for a second on the knife the figure was holding, with which it was sawing at the rope. Then the strands must have given way finally, since the body collapsed and plunged downward into the wagon bed.

From where he sat his horse, he could see the figure in silhouette, now discarding a placard that had been attached somehow to the lifeless body. Thus cast aside from the wagon, the wind whipped the placard aloft, before it cascaded against the great dead cottonwood tree whose grotesque, barren branches were like savage claws, striking into the soul of the night.

Now the figure was at the reins. The wagon was moving in his direction. He bent forward, clamping one hand to the nose of the black so the gelding would not nicker to the other horses. The wagon passed close enough for him to see that it was a woman on the seat, but her face was indistinct, covered by the surrounding darkness and the hooded cowl of the cape she was wearing. Had her features not appeared briefly in the lamplight, he would not have been able to see that she seemed old.

He remained, keeping his horse quiet, until the wagon creaked and rumbled out of sight. The lantern was in the bed, below the sideboard, still lit and winking dimly. A few moments later he urged the black forward at a slow walk. Without the light from the lantern, it was now so dark that he could see very little, just a darker shadow in the darkness where he knew the tree stood. Dismounting, he walked toward the bole of the cottonwood, holding onto the reins of his horse. Probing with his boot around the base, he located the placard. Picking it up, he dropped the reins, holding them fast with his boot long enough to fetch a match from his shirt pocket. It was difficult, shielding the match from the wind which was so oppressive, but he only needed a brief moment to see what was scrawled on it.

LUKE BARRON BEWARE

Casting the match aside as well as the placard, the man drew up the reins and again mounted the black. It must be near midnight. There was almost no light at all, except for a dim starshine, and the memory of the ghostly, hooded figure in the wagon with the lantern and the grisly burden. The wind continued to sweep around the clearing. Pulling his sheepskin-

8

lined coat more closely around him to shield him from the wind, he knew he must now find a suitable place to camp for what remained of the night.

Eagle Cañon was still several miles to the north. Even had all the lights in the boom camp been illuminated, they still would not have been visible to the rider on the trail beyond Rattlesnake Mesa. The trail looped some distance from the mesa in a gradual curve, wending its way into the timbered reach of this country, piñons and cedars mostly, until it merged with the main thoroughfare leading up from Stirrup Gap to enter Eagle Cañon. As it was, only a very few lights were burning in Eagle Cañon, one of them at the back of the jailhouse. It was one of two brick buildings in the relatively new town, the other, directly adjacent, being under construction. A wooden, painted sign in front of the construction site proclaimed it to be the Bank of Eagle Cañon. Across the main street from the jailhouse was the wooden Temple of the Redeemed.

The light from the jailhouse came from two windows in the rear of the building with glass panes behind iron bars, each window opened slightly to let in the night air. Inside was the area known as the bullpen, easily occupying half the floor space of the cell area. There were four cells along the north wall, the one that faced the left side of the new bank building. A four-foot wooden crucifix was suspended from the south wall in the bullpen. At the back of the bullpen was the witch's chair, its back fastened to the brick wall by iron screws mounted in iron plates, its front feet similarly fastened to the cement flooring. The chair was made of hollowed iron with leg and arm braces, also of iron, that could be locked. Beneath the witch's chair was a square, open-faced oven that circulated intense heat throughout its seat, arms, legs, and back.

A short, compact, thick-bodied man, gagged, with his hands

9

tied behind his back was being secured to a strappado by two burly men dressed in white shirts and dark trousers, the uniforms worn by the Avenging Angels, as the deputies in the service of Sheriff Samuel Ingalls were now called in Eagle Cañon. The rope, being tied to the man's bound hands, coursed through a pulley bolted to a crossbeam in the ceiling, strung along the beam, and down the rear wall of the bullpen until it was anchored by a metal lynch pin mounted in that wall about three feet from the cement floor. Ingalls himself, a wide-chested man with a heavy, black beard and black hair that hung shoulder-length, stood with his back to the interrogation table and the barrel chair, the only real furniture in the room. He alone was dressed all in black.

When the two deputies stood away from the bound prisoner, Sheriff Ingalls directed: "Ray, close them windows in case the prisoner starts screaming." Once the deputy had done so and returned to stand beside the other deputy, the sheriff ordered: "Elevate him."

It took both of the deputies to draw up the rope, hand over hand, until the prisoner's face was at eye level with the sheriff's.

"Ed Tyler," he said, "I am now going to loosen your gag. If you cry out, you will be raised all the way to the ceiling, and then dropped. The rope stops short a foot from the floor. Both your shoulders could be dislocated at one drop. Therefore, I advise you to speak softly and truthfully. You have already heard Yokum Bos in the witch's chair confess to being a member of Luke Barron's gang. Recently two miners were killed and robbed by Barron's gang. I do not need a confession from you. Your identity as Ed Tyler, a member of the Barron gang, has been proved to our satisfaction on the dodger I received through my office in Stirrup Gap. What we ask of you is to tell us what you know about Luke Barron and his whereabouts. If you do not tell us, your arms will be broken,

10

slowly but surely, until you do tell us."

He stepped forward to loosen the gag.

There was also light coming from two hanging Rochester brass harp lamps in the assembly room of the Temple of the Redeemed. It was here that Father Matthew was holding a special convocation for three recent novitiates into the Faith of the Redeemer. All were women. Ilse Jeliff, wife of mine owner Fred Jeliff, was rotund with faded orange hair tucked beneath an equally faded bonnet. Rebecca Summers, the store-keeper's sister, also wore a bonnet, her austere face made more trenchant by her thin, slightly pursed lips. Nancy Steele, lacking a bonnet, wore a handkerchief over her light blonde hair. She was the youngest of the three, the only daughter of mine owner George Steele, working now as a volunteer nurse with Dr. Royal Logan at the Eagle Cañon tent hospital. Dr. Logan had been one of Father Matthew's earliest followers, accompanying the wagon train of the faithful on the trek to the West in search of religious freedom.

The wind had brought with it a terrible chill, and Father Matthew wore a dark cloak about his shoulders and over the black cassock that was so familiar. Despite his age, which surely must have been nearly seventy, his high forehead was clear except for the deep crow's feet on either side of his long, thin nose. His white hair was in wisps around the bald dome of his head, and his narrow face and penetrating eyes only added to his riveting appearance.

"I have found," he was saying, addressing the three women who were seated in straight-back chairs in a semicircle around the small lectern he used for religious instructions, "that, as we grow older, we come slowly to believe that everything will turn out badly for us, and that human failure is in the way of things. I rather imagine that this is the way our poor, misguided

11

brother, Yokum Bos, must have felt when he betrayed himself and all of us to Luke Barron. That man . . . as Dr. Logan observed . . . had seen the cloven hoof and shaken the wooden hand. I do not doubt for a moment that Yokum Bos felt much as did Saul when he asked the Witch of Endor to conjure for him the spirit of Samuel . . . that he was sore distressed because the Lord 'is departed from me, and answereth me no more, neither by prophets nor by dreams.' Yet, this man could have come to me. He did not. Even though he had been the first to discover gold here in Eagle Cañon, he did not wish to share it with his brethren. Instead, he went into league with the right hand of Satan, robbing and killing. He left our good sheriff and his archdeacons no alternative but to invoke the extremity of the law. As you know, he was fairly tried before me, confessed his sins, and even begged for punishment."

Father Matthew suspected Nancy Steele might be too strong-headed and outspoken to befit a proper woman in the eyes of God. She confirmed him in this suspicion with her suggestion that her father felt the charge against Yokum Bos to have been totally preposterous and his death a brutal fraud.

"It is well that you should bring that up, Nancy Steele, in the presence of these two sisters in the faith." The priest smiled benignly at Ilse Jeliff and Rebecca Summers. They beamed at the acknowledgment. "Our concern, as faithful followers of the way of the Lord, is not with saving the souls of those who are destined to be outcasts, from whom the Lord has hidden Himself. Our concern must be the well being of the faithful. A person committed to the dark works of Satan has already declared his guilt before the community. Extreme measures sometimes may be necessary before such a soul, possessed by a demon, has had his resistance broken, before he is willing to admit how he has sinned against God's community of souls. Believe me, Nancy Steele, any punishment he received here

12

on earth will pale before Divine Justice. Yokum Bos will be damned for all eternity, thousands upon thousands upon thousands of centuries filled with tortures more keen and more agonizing than any devised by the faithful here on earth. Believe me, the Lord has more imagination than any of His creatures."

He could see that Nancy Steele was not satisfied with this and was ready to speak again in protest, so he hurried forward to anticipate. "You are not yet one of us. Like Yokum Bos, your father was one of the early prospectors to discover the Lord's bounty here in Eagle Cañon before the arrival of the faithful in the Redeemer. Your father, George Steele, has been known to imbibe alcohol and to use tobacco, even though they are strictly forbidden among the Redeemed, as are all forms of gambling and carnal excesses like dancing and preening in fine clothes, temptations to which women of all ages are particularly inclined. The day will come, I am sure, when our faithful will be so strong that these things will be forbidden by the laws of the land in all the States and Territories, so that this one nation can unite under God in the path of righteousness for all the world to see what has flowered where men and women have been free to practice their faith. Doctor Logan smelled liquor on your father's breath the last time he saw him. I warn you now, though such tools of Satan are not forbidden outside Eagle Cañon, they are forbidden here, and the price you both shall have to pay will be banishment."

The wind outside the high windows clawed against the panes, as if the terrors of the night were threatening to enter even the haven of this sanctuary. Nancy Steele, though seated, in her plain, gray, gingham dress was tall and graceful. Her deep blue eyes, so dark sometimes as to appear almost black, dropped now to the floor in what Father Matthew interpreted to be chagrin. His religious training in the Church of Rome, from which he had separated himself at some time in the past,

13

was still sufficiently strong in him that, as he made the sign of the cross, signaling that their gathering was at an end, the Latin words that for so long always accompanied this gesture sounded silently within him.

Chapter Two

The man on the black reined off the trail a hundred yards below the post with the sign. The sprawled litter of tarpaper and board shacks, the brick jailhouse, and the impressive assembly hall, lining both sides of the cañon beyond the wooden post, took his momentary attention. The camp would be Eagle Cañon, he knew, for all along the trail below, after the junction with the road to and from Stirrup Gap, he had ridden this morning amid the traffic of freight wagons and lighter rigs, of men in the saddle and men afoot, going in both directions. Almost as many were on the way out, true, as were on the way in, not quite the telltale sign one would expect of a boom camp that offered the promise of gold.

After that first brief inspection he ignored the town that was his goal in preference for the post with the sign. There was something about it that held the eye, like that cottonwood tree of the night before near the mesa. The weather-whitened surface of the post showed plainly against the pale brown monotony of the sandy, piñon-studded slope beyond. The sign nailed to the post read:

LUKE BARRON BEWARE

The lean face of the rider on the black turned grave for a moment. Then a broad smile eased the severe planes of his features, and he drawled under his breath: "Now, should I?"

The wind had abated, and there was little terror in the bright sky or the brilliance of the powerful sunlight. He slowly looked at the tent just beyond the signpost and the man who stood before it. Alongside him was a high rectangular board lined with rows of spikes. From this distance the man on the black could see that an odd assortment of weapons hung from those rows of spikes. There were six-guns, of the cartridge and the cap-and-ball variety, both long-barreled and short, a few carbines, a pair of long rifles, and a partial row of wicked-looking Derringers and similar belly-guns. At the very top of the board was another painted sign:

Check Your Guns
Sheriff's Order

The tent beyond the signpost marked the place where traffic along the trail uniformly slowed and stopped. The man outside the tent, a deputy evidently because of the star he wore, was dressed in a white shirt and black pants. He was inspecting wagons and riders before waving them on. In the five minutes the man on the black watched, he saw several guns handed across to out-goers, several others taken from those on the way in.

He was faintly irritated by this show of authority. He had a week ago turned twenty-nine, and for ten of those years it had become his habit to keep a gun within reach, both sleeping and waking. The prospect of now having to surrender the short-barreled .38 Colt that hung low in a holster along his right thigh wasn't especially welcome. Finally, when he moved on up the trail toward the tent, he decided he wouldn't surrender it.

He waited patiently while the deputy checked each passenger of an in-bound stage, collecting four six-guns and the driver's carbine. Then, being his turn, he reined the black in abreast the tent, looked across at the board where the guns hung, and queried: "Why all the trouble to dehorn the camp?"

"Luke Barron," the deputy said, as though the mention of that name should be answer enough.

"Who's he?"

"You ain't heard?" The deputy regarded the stranger as though he was half-witted. "You don't know Luke Barron? Hell, that's the name of the biggest murderer and robber this side of the Snake! Him and his wild bunch are operatin' around here." He gestured in the direction of the mesa. "One of his understrappers was hanged yesterday. The sheriff's got another one in jail. He was caught hijackin' a claim night before last and'll be hung at sunup tomorrow" — he grinned quickly and coldly as he said it — "after his trial today. Ed Tyler's his name. Hand over your iron. And, remember, no drinkin', smokin', chewin', gamblin', or dancin' inside the town limits."

The deputy was all at once impatient, scanning the line of riders and wagons that had already formed behind this rider who seemed to be in no hurry. He was obviously not very fond of his job, which required that he stand out here in the full blaze of the sun. His face was glistening with perspiration, and his shirt stuck wetly to his thick-muscled shoulders.

"Why should I?" the man on the black queried.

The deputy's face took on a dark, ugly scowl. "See here, stranger! I ain't in the habit of answerin' damn' fool questions. How do I know but what you're a Luke Barron man? How do I know but what you're mebbe Luke Barron hisself?"

"What if I am?"

The deputy moved his boots apart and stood with hands on hips. "Salty, eh? You goin' to hand that iron across, or do I take it off'n you?"

"I reckon I'll keep it," the stranger drawled.

The deputy suddenly made a stab to snatch the stranger's weapon from its holster. The stranger's right arm, idly bent across the horn of his saddle, straightened and seemed to move

17

slowly. Yet the gun slid out from under the deputy's reaching hand with a half second to spare. The stranger, tossing the weapon across to his left hand, rammed it through the waistband of his denims out of the deputy's reach, stating: "You can get along without mine."

"Like hell! Hand it over!" All his patience gone, the deputy hastily made a grab for the black's reins. The animal jerked his head away, reared, and settled placidly onto all four hoofs again as the deputy scrambled wildly out of the way, tripping on a tent rope and sprawling on his back. He rolled over quickly, hat falling into the dust. When he sat up, his right hand was swinging a gun up from his holster. But his arm froze in the act of lining the weapon. For he was staring into the round bore of the stranger's .38. He dropped his gun as though it had been scorched too hot to hold by the pitiless glare of the sun.

"No offense taken," the stranger drawled. "Now, if you'll kindly step wide of that hogleg and walk off there a few steps, I'll be on my way."

The deputy, his face gone purple with rage, picked himself up, then his Stetson, and beat the dust from it. He was careful to stay away from his gun, lying nearby. He had enough sanity left in him to recognize a quality of warning in the stranger's smooth tone and so walked ten feet out from the tent, his look ugly as he caught the raucous laughter of the driver of a freight wagon loaded with bricks who was waiting his turn down the line. Others immediately joined in a derisive demonstration against him and, when the stranger said — "A bit farther" — the deputy swore obscenely as he doubled the distance between himself and the tent.

"Just wait there till I'm clear," the stranger said, sheathing his weapon in a swift, effortless motion of practiced ease. He lifted his reins and put the black on up the street.

As he entered the lower end of the camp twenty yards beyond, the stranger looked around to see the deputy run to the gun rack and lift down a carbine. He reined the black in behind the protection of a passing buckboard and went on, ignoring the threat of the rifle back there.

Eagle Cañon appeared brutal and cruel under the sun's pitilessly hot midday glare. There was nothing permanent about most of the shacks that lined its narrow street, actually the bed of the cañon on which the camp was built. A third of the dwellings at the upper end were tents. At first the presence of the filth and mud and stagnant pools of water along the street puzzled the stranger. Then he thought of the sluices of the diggings up beyond the town limits and knew that they must be leaking badly or that their owners were careless of the water. Up the gradual slope of the east wall of the cañon a ditch had been dug, a ditch that he rightly concluded must carry the scant water of the stream around the town. High on the rim of the west wall stood a huge, red-painted water tank and, alongside it, a windmill slowly creaked in the light breeze that blew along the cañon rim.

The walks at the camp's center were crowded, jammed with a restlessly moving assortment of rich and poor, a mass of seedy-looking and rough-shod men and, occasionally, one who was immaculately outfitted. There were only a few women to be seen walking the street, and all of these were plainly, even austerely dressed, utterly without the profusion of powder and rouge, the most obvious sign of the lusty bawdiness of a new boom camp. There were no saloons or gambling houses but only various kinds of stores, and they were all doing a full-out business. The street was glutted with a varied collection of light and heavy rigs and of saddle horses, wading fetlock deep in the mud. Eagle Cañon definitely did not have that wide-open look of other boom camps. The check point at the foot of the

19

street was evidently a very effective deterrent. Not a gun was in sight.

The man on the black reined into a narrow, vacant space at a tie rail before a mercantile, witnessing the strangest of all the sights Eagle Cañon had so far offered. Forming a long queue out into the street waited perhaps ten men with a few women and children, all carrying pails or buckets or any receptacle that would hold water. At one corner of the store's flimsy frame wall stood a gun-belted man, wearing a badge like the one the stranger had seen on the deputy back at the tent, and he was similarly clothed in a white shirt and dark pants. At knee height on the wall beside this second deputy protruded the stem of a pipe. At the pipe's end there was a thick valve. The ground close by was viscose with sticky black mud. Against the wall sat a nail keg with a slit in its top.

The stranger saw the deputy fill a woman's pail, collect a coin from her, drop it through the slit in the keg, and then hurry her on her way so he could serve the next customer. He was selling water. Curious, the stranger looked beyond the general merchandise store and up toward the rim where he'd seen the water tank. Down from the tank, following the natural line of a gully, he could clearly see the pipeline that ended here at the walk. More than curious now, he reached down and tapped the shoulder of a peak-hatted figure passing his stirrup toward the walk, asking: "What's going on here?"

The head lifted, and the stranger was looking into a girl's pretty oval face. He was surprised, for the Stetson and the man's waist overalls and the plain cotton shirt had given him no warning that he was addressing a woman.

She told him, her face touched by a wry smile: "You must be new here. This well belongs to the Temple of the Redeemed. The Temple . . . actually, one of the elders, Doctor Royal Logan, sells the water to everyone. Twenty-five cents a pail, two dollars and a half a barrel. Cheap, isn't it? Doctor Logan is a public benefactor. Without this well, we might all have died of typhoid long ago. I work part time as a nurse for Doctor Logan. There hasn't been a single case of typhoid since the Temple came here and supervised the building of the town and the working of the claims by the faithful."

Her tone might have held sarcasm. The stranger couldn't be certain. Yet, if it was sarcasm, or just skepticism, he was more alert to the contradiction of her tone and her finely molded features, the pale blonde hair that framed her delicately boned face, and above all her very direct eyes that were the deep blue of a mountain lake and seemed lit by some inner sparkle of the spirit.

He reached up to touch the brim of his Stetson, smiling now, drawling: "I reckon that answers my question. Are you a member of this Temple?"

"I'm taking religious instructions, if it's any of your business!" the girl flared, unamused by this effort to match her tone. Suddenly her glance took in the gun low along his thigh. He saw her face lose some of its color. Then she was saying, in a biting voice: "No one is allowed to carry guns within the town limits or at the claims except Sheriff Ingalls and his archdeacons."

"Beggin' your pardon, ma'am, but what was that about archdeacons?"

Her glance showed sudden alarm. "How did you manage to get into town wearing a gun?"

"Because I've toted one for a long time."

She glanced quickly toward the walk, as if wanting to make sure she wouldn't be overheard. Then, low-voiced, she said: "You'll be arrested unless you hide it! I told you, it's against the law to carry one."

With that, she turned and left him, going hurriedly to the

21

walk and along it until she was lost in the crowd. The stranger sat, watching her, until she was out of sight. She held her carriage erect when she moved so that he was aware of the slim straightness of her back, and yet there was a gliding quality to her gait that was at once airy and supple. Only slowly did his glance come back to the man who was waiting on the customers. With a shrug he swung lithely down out of the saddle and looped the black's reins over the hitch rack and sauntered through the crowd into what a wooden sign over the covered porch roof declared to be the **Eagle Cañon Mercantile.** He was thinking mainly of the girl, wondering who she was and if he'd ever see her again.

Once inside, he ambled leisurely amid tables piled with the paraphernalia of placer mining, blankets, canned goods. He was pausing before an array of jugs, jars, and large canteens for transporting water when he felt the jab of a gun's hard snout along his backbone. Behind him, someone snapped: "Hold it, stranger! You're under arrest!" The weight of the .38 eased off his thigh as the voice said again, even more crisply: "Reach! Turn around . . . slow!"

The stranger's hands lifted to shoulder level. With the gun still ramming his spine, he started turning to the right until he could feel it no longer. In a brief instant he had a glimpse of the tent archdeacon, gun holstered, and before him a massively built man outfitted in black broadcloth, a white shirt beneath his buttoned black vest. This man was holding the gun.

Lazily, but with the same swift sureness the archdeacon had seen earlier in his draw, the stranger brought his right elbow back and down in a hard stab. The point of his elbow caught the man in broadcloth full in the face. The blow viciously knocked the man's head sideways. Before he could recover, the stranger's hand had swept on down and caught his wrist a slashing stroke that spun the gun from his hand. The stranger caught the gun in mid-air, threw it quickly into line with the archdeacon, raised a boot, and put all his weight into its thrusting drive.

Just as his boot took his victim in the pit of the stomach, the stranger saw the sheriff's badge pinned on the man's vest-pocket. Then the boot struck. The sheriff staggered backward, then fell, and slid across the puncheon floor. Pushing himself up on one elbow, rage plain on his bearded face, he ignored the gun in the stranger's hand and snatched out the stranger's .38 he had a moment ago thrust into his belt.

The stranger arced the .45 around and thumbed one shot. The sheriff gave out a grunt of pain as his hand opened, and he dropped the .38 onto the floor. Across the outside of his wrist was a red line where the bullet had scorched him.

He snarled: "Get him, Tiny!"

But the deputy to whom he'd spoken kept his hand carefully clear of his gun. Then a voice coming from the rear of the store said: "Sam, I have need of a man like this!"

The stranger glanced quickly behind him, still holding the six-gun on the prostrate sheriff and his deputy. The man was tall, with white hair forming a nimbus around his high forehead. He was dressed in a simple black cassock without a clerical collar, a black hood behind his head.

"Please," said the old priest, extending his hand outward toward the stranger, his long fingers without intimacy but, strangely, with a promise of security.

Most of all it was the light blue eyes that held the stranger, and the expression behind them, wise, celibate, and lonely, eyes that seemed to observe life from a safe distance, with sympathy, but implying by an intangible impression that an exorbitant price had been paid for the exaltation, burning deeply and silently within their depths.

Without speaking, as if it were the most natural gesture in

the world and even though it was the sheerest folly, the stranger twirled the big .45 on his index finger until he held the weapon in his palm by the chambers and extended it to meet the outstretched hand of the old priest.

All at once, as he took the proffered revolver, a smile broke warmly on the austere features. "I am Father Matthew," he said.

Sheriff Sam Ingalls came awkwardly to his feet, pointedly ignoring the gun lying near him on the floor, still standing hunched over from the pain in his stomach where the stranger's boot had taken him. He gave the man in the cassock an uncomprehending look, saying flatly: "This man is a fugitive, Father."

Father Matthew walked over to the frustrated lawman, placed the .45 in his empty holster, then bent deftly and retrieved the stranger's .38. Only then did he speak.

"He may seem a fugitive to you, Sam, but he bears upon him the mark of the Lord's grace. I wish to speak to him in my sanctuary." He nodded toward the back of the room. "Please, let us talk this matter over between ourselves," he suggested and nodded again, this time toward the stranger. "Just the two of us."

He turned without saying more and started back toward the rear of the general store, ignoring the bystanders who had watched the swift happenings of the past few moments, mostly with surprise and awe but also on a couple of the faces unmistakable satisfaction.

Sam Ingalls eyed the stranger levelly for a moment, rubbing his miraculously unbroken wrist. When the stranger turned to follow Father Matthew, the sheriff said curtly to his deputy: "Let's get back out there!" The sheriff's face colored deeply because his anger was returning, but he thought better of saying whatever was on his mind and without a word followed his deputy out the front doors.

The stranger walked after the old priest through the space that divided the long counter that otherwise ran the entire length of the rear wall of the store and into and through the storeroom in the back, piled high with wooden boxes of air tights, barrels, bins for recently received produce, and out the heavily paneled back door. The general merchandise store was directly adjacent to the wooden building that housed the Temple of the Redeemed, all of the buildings on this side of the street abutting the steeply inclined cliff on the rim of which stood the great water tank. Father Matthew, without once looking around, led the way through a wooden door at the near edge of the back wall of the Temple.

There were only two small windows located high up on either of the outside walls and below which there were crude bookcases of wood, housing what must have been several hundred books. The titles of the few at which the stranger threw his glance had titles in languages he did not understand. There was a flat library table in the center of the room, covered with a few open books and what appeared to be blank manuscript paper on which there was handwriting in black ink. On either side of the table were tall wooden candleholders with candles for illumination. Against the wall at the head of the room, on the right side of a door, was a cot, neatly made, beside it a small pot-bellied stove on which had been placed a blue-speckled metal coffee pot, and on the remaining wall there was suspended a great wooden crucifix but no body was nailed to it as the stranger remembered seeing in mission churches in which he had been in the past. Before the crucifix was a great chair of polished wood with a rawhide seat and back.

Father Matthew placed the stranger's six-gun on the library table near the inkwell and then brought one of the chairs over to stand near the great chair beneath the crucifix. Like it, the seat and back were made of rawhide, deeply tanned a dark brown, but it was without arms.

"Please," said Father Matthew, making himself comfortable in the great chair.

The stranger sat down cautiously. He appeared restless, his eyes wandering about the relatively compact room with a nervous intensity.

"That cross for me," Father Matthew said, and his eyes ascended toward its stark, ominous simplicity, as it leaned outward from the foot to the apex suspended by a wire affixing it at the crossbeam to the wall, "has the same significance as the Penitential Psalms of which Saint Augustine had a huge copy hung upon a wall before which he meditated the day he died. It was during the siege of Hippo, a city in Africa. The Vandals had invaded, and around the city's walls they had piled the bodies of their victims to putrefy. I am certain Saint Augustine did not see the wall as he gazed upon it, nor even the Penitential Psalms, but rather what existed beyond that wall, the meaning in those psalms. He once wrote . . . 'as it is in Africa, so it will become in the whole world,' and I could say the same of our community here in Eagle Cañon . . . as it is now in Eagle Cañon, so it will be in the whole world." Seeing the perplexity in the stranger's face whose eyes were now fastened on those of the old priest, he smiled gently. "I have spent much of my life in contemplation of the Holy Ghost. If a man is fortunate enough to be inspirited by the Holy Ghost, for that brief time he, too, becomes a son of God."

"I'm afraid I'm not a very religious man, Father," the stranger confessed in a voice so dry it involuntarily cracked.

"Would you care for a small glass of claret?" the old priest then asked, a benign smile flashing across his austere features.

"I'm not much of a hand for drinkin', either," said the stranger, "but thet coffee you got on the stove is something I

26

could use, and be grateful."

For a few moments the old priest busied himself finding two blue-speckled metal cups from a narrow wall shelf near to the small pot-bellied stove. After he had served the stranger with a cup about half full of hot coffee, he paused at the library table to bring back with him a box of matches and a large-bowled briar pipe. He set his coffee cup on an arm of the chair while he fired up his pipe.

"They told me when I rode into town that smoking and drinking were forbidden in Eagle Cañon," prompted the stranger, his forehead furrowed as he clutched his coffee cup in both hands.

"And so they are," confided Father Matthew. "I fear the strong advocates of this policy are Sheriff Ingalls and Doctor Royal Logan . . . I presume you have not yet had the good fortune to meet Doctor Logan. The doctor has been a member of my flock since the early days in Centralia, Illinois. The sheriff is a more recent convert. And they are correct, as far as they go, for it is human nature to do all things in excess. Personally, in moderation, I regard tobacco and alcohol in the form of wine as splendid vices. Open abstention from them is among the highest of social virtues, yet they possess a real value in their own order if we indulge them with strict moderation. Yet, it is far more important to focus the soul on what is eternal. When you do that, you come to realize that the disorder, confusion, even chaos of human events are only apparent because God has ordered all events in the form of a universal harmony . . . only it is beyond the ability of a created mind to grasp that harmony. The best way to put it, I suppose, is what I told my small class of novitiates last night. God has more imagination than any of His creatures."

The stranger was at a loss to understand this, and his hands, holding the tin coffee cup, trembled now with a mute palsy.

"Does that mean you will allow me to roll a cigarette?" he asked, his voice still dry and croaking a little. He knew he wouldn't dare to touch tobacco to paper, so pervasive was his nervousness, but he made the inquiry anyway.

The old priest merely nodded, his head wreathed now in silver-blue wafts of smoke from his pipe. "You have me still at a disadvantage, young man. Tell me, what is your name?"

"Luke Barron," the stranger said, still in a croak, although he had lifted the coffee cup to his lips. As soon as he said it, he drank, the taste bitter but somehow pleasant.

The old priest's eyes were piercing and intent, as he spoke, although a smile almost brash in its good humor played at the edges of his thin, ascetic lips. "All right, Luke it is," he said, "but it can not be Luke Barron. Not in *this* camp. Luke Barron has every one of us fast in his lawless grip. The miners, whether among the faithful or the few pagans who remain, haven't been able to ship out any ore because he and his gang will be sure to attack the stage carrying it. He seems to have spies everywhere. Maybe you heard about the reign of terror he brought about in Colorado. Now he's doing the same thing here. That's why Eagle Cañon needs law so desperately . . . and why firearms are not permitted within the camp or further back in the reaches of the cañon where all of the placer claims are located."

The old priest made a gentle gesture with his right hand before he picked up his own coffee cup from the arm of the great chair. "As I said in the store, because of Luke Barron, I have need of a man like you. Do not ask me how I know. I never question the inspirations from Providence. They have always come to me, often in the most mysterious ways. I have learned to heed Providence."

He smiled again, very gently, and the stranger felt himself drawn to this old priest, fascinated by him in a way he could

28

not even begin to explain to himself.

"While it is possible for two Luke Barrons to be co-present in Eagle Cañon," Father Matthew resumed, having drunk now delicately from his own coffee cup, "I do not believe it. Sheriff Ingalls and his Avenging Angels have gathered surmounting evidence, including two confessions, one from a known cohort of Luke Barron's, that Barron and his gang are behind all of these robberies and murders." He paused to affix his intense glance on the stranger. "Yet, I take it that you do not believe this is true . . . that Luke Barron and his gang are responsible?"

"No, Father Matthew, I do not," the stranger said, noticing as he spoke now that his trembling had all but ceased.

"I thought not," the old priest responded, nodding his head gently. "Will you accept this assignment? To find out for me, for the sake of this whole community and its welfare, what is behind these terrible depredations? I shall not ask you to wear the uniform of one of Sam's archdeacons, but you will be permitted to retain your firearm. In fact, it cannot even be known that you are under the protection of the Temple or that you are to report directly to me, but I shall tell Sam that I wish no harm to come to you from his men, and I am sure he will abide by my word, as he always has. What is it to be . . . ah, Luke Ashford . . . for that will be your name here in Eagle Cañon? Am I right about you? May I count on you?"

The stranger drank what remained of his coffee, then he smiled before he answered. "Yes, Father, I reckon you can."

Chapter Three

George Steele had arranged to rent a wagon from Timothy Kamu at the livery stable. His daughter, Nan, had gone to inform Dr. Logan at the tent hospital that she wished to accompany her father out to console Neele Bos and then had gone to Frank Summers's Eagle Cañon Mercantile to pick up a few items. George intended to dig the grave for his friend and fellow miner. He had brought in with him from his claim the necessary tools to build a coffin and had bought sufficient lumber at the lumber yard. Nan presently came out of the store. George gave her a hand up onto the seat and then climbed up himself.

Taking up the reins from where he had tied them, George gently urged the team into the street that, as always, was crowded with incoming wagons, miners or their wives lined up to get their water ration, and outgoing traffic, empty wagons returning to Stirrup Gap or disappointed gold-rushers finally convinced that all the available or likely claims had already been staked, mostly by members of the Temple of the Redeemed.

It was not often that the grizzled, bearded George Steele, with his slouch hat and his miner's clothes, had a chance really to look at or be with Nan these days. He was inordinately proud of his daughter, of the easy grace with which she moved, and yet her upper body was more prominent than her slim hips. Years ago he'd had his moments of wishing she'd been a boy, but that feeling was long gone now, even though the way she was dressed today, she could readily have passed for one. He had noticed the way she carried her head at a tilt that was almost proud as she came out of the store. It was the one thing in her that reminded him of her mother. Aside from that, and her pale blonde hair, she might have been another woman's daughter. Louise hadn't been especially pretty, but Nan was definitely so. Nan's eyes, however, were like his own, deep blue, and had a direct way of looking at a person that met with his approval. There was no guile, not even shyness, in Nancy Steele. All in all George had to admit she was a powerfully appealing woman. "To me, at least," he said half aloud.

"What's that, Dad?"

"Nothing, nothing. It's just that I gotta stop now at that check point to pick up my six-gun on the way out. Damned holy rollers!"

"Please, Dad, you have to admit Sheriff Ingalls's policy on weapons is working. There haven't been any shootings in Eagle Cañon the way there have been in Stirrup Gap, and this is a boom town."

"Some boom town, Nan. And some sheriff! I don't see him stopping the Luke Barron gang from robbing and even killing. I haven't been able to send any dust down to Stirrup Gap in three months."

"I don't think you've been working your claim all that much, either. You've been too busy sampling what you brew in that still of yours."

"Now, Nan, that jest ain't the truth, an' you know it. I take a nip now an' then, shore. An' why not? There's not much else for me to do if I can't ship what I pan."

"I'm sure the archdeacons will bring the law even to the Barron gang."

"Hah!" George Steele dismissed her statement as he drew the team to a halt, looking over at the gun board in front of the tent at the outskirts of town. "Look at that line comin' in, Nan, an' nary a one of those deputies around to tend to business. They're jest sittin' there."

"I think I know what this is about, Dad."

"I don't care what it's about, Nan. I'm goin' over there an' claim my six-gun."

As he spoke, he tied the reins to the base of the empty pipe that served as a whip holder on the rented wagon, climbed out, and made his way across the rutted, dusty road. A group of men had congregated around the check point where the deputy was supposed to be positioned to check rifles and hand guns. Steele, when asked, told the bystanders that he had no idea when the archdeacon would return or where he'd gone. He was taking back his gun because he was leaving Eagle Cañon. It was a long-barreled Colt Double-Action Army revolver, Model 1878, and easy for him to recognize.

"I wouldn't wait, if'n I was you," Steele called back as he walked again toward the wagon. "Jest go on in totin' yore guns." He laughed.

"Dad!" Nan said as he resumed his seat beside her. "That's irresponsible. I already saw one stranger in town who'd refused to give up his pistol. He said he was too used to it to give it up."

"Smart man," was her father's curt reply, as he touched the reins, and the horses resumed the journey down the road. "I told you afore, Nan, the only ones this gun-checking business is protectin' is Ingalls and his danged white shirts. The rest of us is jest at the mercy of Luke Barron and his gang . . . if there even is a Luke Barron."

"What d'you mean by that?"

"Jest what I said, honey. No one's ever seen this Luke Barron and his gang, but we've all seen Ingalls and his crowd a-plenty. You mebbe can believe old Yokum was in with Barron, but I don't believe it for a minute. Hell . . . excuse me fer sayin' that . . . but old Yok an' me spent two, three months prospectin' together afore we hit the pocket in this cañon, an' even though he moved out near the mesa, we kept in touch. He warn't no more a killer and robber than I am."

Keeping one hand on the reins, her father turned toward Nan and placed his left hand on her right knee. He gazed at her keenly, urgently. "I'm tellin' you, Nan, Yok had the best claim in Eagle Cañon other than the Nan Steele. He didn't need to steal from anyone, least of all from those holy rollers who're less well off than he was."

"I wish you wouldn't call them that, Dad," Nan protested.

Steele took his hand away and brought it back to join the other holding the reins, turning his eyes again toward the road as it stretched before them. "An' why not, girl? It's the God's own truth. Now, listen, listen, honey, I'm not a-tellin' you all I know. I can't. But that Father Matthew's not all he's cracked up to be. Yok knew him back in Illinois." He hissed the "s" when he said it. "Mebbe, if she's of a mind, Neele can tell you more. I won't. Jest let it go at what I said. Father Matthew ain't no saint." He reached into his shirt pocket for his sack of plug cut, worked the plug out one-handed, and chomped down on a corner of it.

"Dad," Nan protested, but more softly than before, "you know chewing tobacco is against the law."

"It's not against my law, darlin'," George Steele said emphatically. He flashed her a grin, and he was pleased to see she returned it. "Mebbe there's hope fer you yet."

"Dad," Nancy said, her blue eyes dark and serious, "I want to hear what you know about Father Matthew."

"Nan, your old dad may be a lot of things, includin' a tobacco chewer and pipe smoker and a drinkin' man, but he ain't no gossip. Neele Bos knows a heap more about it than I do. I only know what Yok told me about his days back in Illinois. She'll tell you, if she has a mind thet way, more'n

33

likely. Knowin' her, and knowin' what Yok told me on a couple of occasions, I reckon she'll hold Father Matthew to blame fer what's happened."

"But, Dad, Yokum Bos confessed. Sheriff Ingalls has a signed statement. Yokum Bos was acting as a spy for the Luke Barron gang."

"There's lots of ways that you're right smart, girl. Your ma and I felt thet way enough to send you East to school so you could learn to be a nurse. We saved outta what I was makin' them days as a teamster to do it, and I'm right glad about it, but you're not so savvy when it comes to human bein's. That Doctor Royal Logan's makin' a heap of money, sellin' water to those dumb believers of Father Matthew's, an' Sheriff Sam Ingalls has old Yok's claim, I hear tell, now that Yok's dead. That'd be enough to tell me a thing or two about that crowd."

"Have you ever talked with Father Matthew, Dad? I mean, really talked to him? He's the wisest man I've ever met. Royal says he's been touched by the Holy Ghost, and Royal has been with him since the days in Illinois" — Nancy Steele did not pronounce the "s" — "since before Father Matthew broke with the Roman church and before he brought the faithful out here to the West."

"I don't reckon I know much about the Holy Ghost, girl," said her father, leaning sideways to spit tobacco juice onto the side of the road, "but I know a snake in the grass when I see one, an' Father Matthew's got all the earmarks."

"Dad, please let's not argue about religion."

"I'm not arguin' about religion, Nan," her father said, his tone no less earnest than hers had been. "I believe in God as much as the next man, mebbe more. Many was the time I prayed when you was growin' up that the Lord would look after you, and 'specially when you was took sick that time. It was only after the Lord took your ma an' you was through with your schoolin' thet I quit drivin' for Warbow and Morgan an' went off prospectin' with Yokum Bos. I figger the good Lord has watched over me a-plenty, or I wouldn't have such a beautiful and smart girl sittin' right here beside me on this here wagon. But I don't need no Temple to talk to God an' nary Father Matthew to tell me all that I can't do if I want to be saved. Never did need no Temple. Look around you, girl."

They had turned into the cut-off now, leading toward Rattlesnake Mesa. The stands of tall trees stretched beside and before them, pines, alders, spruces, and an occasional oak. George Steele motioned with his right arm.

"Thet's always been cathedral enough for your old man. The Lord is right here, girl. He's a-walkin' right alongside us, and I can speak to Him whenever I've a mind thetaway. I wouldn't trade places with nary one of those as has been redeemed by Father Matthew."

He fell silent, and Nan did not speak in return. But as they drove on, she did reach over and touched him firmly on his left arm.

Nancy Steele loved her father. She knew that some of his ways were questionable because Dr. Logan condemned alcohol, gambling, dancing, and tobacco as inventions of Satan and felt it was imperative that those whom God had chosen as His elect here on earth must enforce their prohibition if there were to be any hope whatsoever that weaker human souls, naturally inclined toward these temptations, were to have any possibility of redemption. The fact that her father had a still out at his claim was in defiance of one of those prohibitions. And, what was worse, her father had been rather clumsy in concealing this defiance. So far, although Dr. Logan suspected the existence of the still, there had been no raid on it by the archdeacons. That was because of the reign of terror Luke Barron and his gang had brought to the miners in Eagle Cañon. Yet, only

35

yesterday Dr. Logan had dropped a hint to Nan that, following Yokum Bos's execution, Sheriff Ingalls might well now turn his attention to other criminals in their midst. He hadn't mentioned George Steele by name, but the implication had been unmistakable.

In fact, Nan's strongest reason for accompanying her father on this mission of mercy was her determination to persuade him that, if he would not convert to the Temple of the Redeemed, he must at least abandon his still so there would be no chance of his arrest and conviction for undermining the spiritual well being of the Eagle Cañon community. Nan had lived enough in the outside world as the only child of a stagecoach driver and then freighting teamster, moving from town to town, but always farther West, and then the time she spent in the East to know how eccentric by other standards in the States and even in the Territories was this zealotry of the Avenging Angels, but here in Eagle Cañon they were a law unto themselves and must be obeyed. When she had questioned Dr. Royal Logan on the severity of the consequences of flaunting these prohibitions, the medical man gave her what he believed were irrefutable arguments. Satan had been very wise, indeed, in devising these temptations. It was human nature, seeing someone drinking alcohol, for example, or dancing, to want to join them. Therefore, the punishments had to be severe to make the prohibitions permanent and universal.

Dr. Logan had admitted that this question of punishments had been raised at a meeting of the board of elders, consisting of Father Matthew, Sheriff Ingalls and two of the Avenging Angels, Ray Cune and Mart Kemp, as well as the doctor. Logan had even admitted to Nan that Father Matthew had proposed banishment as opposed to execution, but he had been voted down four to one. Banishment did not really solve the problem. A criminal like Yokum Bos would not willingly surrender his claim if he were banished for collaborating with Luke Barron and his gang. No, the only way to deal with evil was to eradicate it completely. As a physician and surgeon and as a believer, Dr. Logan knew the truth, he insisted, of God's law. If gangrene developed in a leg, the leg had to be amputated, just as the Bible says, if an eye offends you, it must be plucked out. So it has to be in all aspects of life. A community such as that in Eagle Cañon, should it be threatened by gangrene developing in one of its members, as had been the case with Yokum Bos, must react in the same fashion — that member must be *cut out* in order to save all the others from contamination.

Nan was so frustrated with her father's stubbornness and terrified for him at the same time that she was beside herself and feared she couldn't find the words to persuade him of the danger looming over him. His belief in God was so different from that of the Redeemed. Her father said he felt the Lord's presence beside them, even now as they rode together in the rented wagon. On the other hand, Dr. Logan had stated, and Father Matthew seemed to confirm the view, that, while God can be loved, He *must* be feared. George Steele's belief that the Lord would protect those who loved Him as He loved them — a belief she knew her father had held dear as long as she had known him — was very likely now to be his undoing, unless she could convince him otherwise. This journey to see Neele Bos and bury her poor husband's body would be, Nan was convinced, her last chance to intervene in what would otherwise be her father's inevitable destiny.

"Dad," Nan said, breaking what had been their protracted silence, her tone desperate, "after you bury Yokum Bos, let's just keep going."

"Where to, girl?"

"I don't know. Back to Stirrup Gap, maybe. Or some place

else . . . any place that's not Eagle Cañon."

"Now, Nan, thet's jest foolish talk. I must have ten thousand dollars in dust hidden up at the Nan Steele thet I ain't about to throw away, an' I shore can't get it out, not with Luke Barron and his gang preying on us miners. An' what about you? I reckon you think a heap of thet doctor. I know how you defended Logan's sellin' water to the faithful, the way he does, when I railed against it. Water should be free, thet's what I say."

"Royal isn't selling the water, Dad, the Temple is," Nan disagreed.

"Who gets the money, girl?"

"The hospital does. That's how Royal can afford to provide his services for free to everyone."

"He never gave me nothin' fer free."

"Have you ever gone to him?"

"Girl, you know I don't trust medicine men, white men or Injuns. Besides, if I get sick, I reckon you'll look after me. You told me, growin' up, you wanted to be 'a doctor yourself some day. I didn't stop you, did I? Your ma and I saved fer years so you could go back to Lawrence to doctor school."

"Nursing school, Dad."

"Same thing in my mind. What do doctors know that nurses don't, 'cept doctors wear britches and nurses don't . . . least ways most of the time." George Steele smiled and winked at his daughter, glancing toward the Levi's she wore.

Nan realized this stratagem hadn't worked any better than had their earlier conversation. She had one more thing to say to her father, something she had sworn she would not bring up unless all else failed.

"Dad, Royal Logan asked me yesterday afternoon if I would marry him."

The smile vanished from George Steele's face. His mood

became as serious as her own.

"What'd you tell him, Nan?"

"I said I'd have to think about it."

"When does he want your answer?"

"Soon, Dad, very soon."

"What do you reckon you're gonna tell him, Nan? Is thet why you asked me to keep a-goin' after we stopped at the Bos place?"

"Yes," Nan lied, and now there were tears in her eyes.

"Girl," George Steele said, "no man . . . an' no woman . . . ever licked any problem by runnin' away from it."

That did it! Nan could no longer contain herself, as much as she had been trying to do so. The sobs now burst from her in a torrent. Her hands rushed to her face, and her shoulders began to heave.

"Hold on, girl," her father insisted, deeply concerned. "Whoa, there," he said to the team, pulling back on the reins.

"No, Dad, don't stop!" Nan, through her sobs, screamed the words at him. "Whatever you do, don't stop."

"Now, now, honey, you're all upset," her father said gently. "We can stay here fer a spell and talk this out some. If you don't want to marry thet doctor, it's all right by me. You don't see me tryin' to tell you to go a-runnin' into anything. Far as I'm concerned, thet doctor's not a whole lot better'n Sheriff Ingalls, that old hypocrite of a priest, or the rest of them holy rollers."

"Please, Dad!" Nan said, placing both her hands on her father's shoulders and gazing at him intently through the tears in her luminous eyes. "Please, just drive to where we're going. Will you just do that for me? Just keep moving?"

"You shore, girl?"

"Please, Dad, just drive! Let's not say another thing. Please . . . ?"

She dropped her hands, but her eyes and voice kept their urgency.

"All right, Nan," her father said, and clucked again to the team.

The wagon began moving again. Nan turned her face off to the side, looking at the phalanxes of trees, marching down to the sides of the trail. She kept her eyes averted from her father, not wanting him to see the tears that would not stop now, not wanting him to talk any more.

Her father was silent for a long time.

"Nan," he finally broke in, "I'm only going to say this. If'n you still want me to keep a-goin' after we bury old Yokum and pay our respects to his widder, I will. I'll take you anywhere you want to go, do whatever you ask me, as long as I'm still kicking. Your ma and you followed me around plenty of years. Lord knows, she backed me all our time together, as she backed you when you wanted to go to school to become a nurse. I figger, if'n you want me to pull out now, I owe that much to the memory of your ma and to you. This here is my word on it."

She turned toward him when he said that, hugged him, kissed his grizzled, bearded cheek, but did not answer.

Yokum Bos had been a builder of houses in Centralia before he came West. What passed for restlessness with many who left the East, or the Midwest for that matter, to seek their fortune in the Territories was in Yokum Bos's case was more an urgency created by the scandal that had developed at the Church of the Sacred Heart where his wife, Neele, had worked for some years as housekeeper for the parish priest. He had built the cabin and small barn in the shadow of Rattlesnake Mesa himself with logs he cut from the forest on his homestead and finished lumber he had secured in Stirrup Gap. He had long had the yen to seek his fortune by prospecting. With no job any longer to hold him, and a wife who preferred only privacy for the rest of her life, he had taken the occasional odd job in Stirrup Gap, shrewdly conserving his money until he had a stake. As destiny would have it, he met George Steele who had also long had the urge to try his hand at prospecting and whose wife had recently died of consumption. Together they combined their grubstake to buy food, equipment, and pack animals. George had had the considerable advantage of having worked as a teamster around mining camps and had learned a good deal about mineral exploration and placering in general.

There was, according to Steele, given natural conditions and geological formations, a good possibility of finding some color near the source of Eagle Creek, and so that was where they set out to prospect. They had been out for over a month when Bos had found the first lode in the creek bottom, near its source, at the head of what was now called Eagle Cañon. Steele had located a second lode downstream from Bos's claim. They had agreed to keep the location a secret until they had filed on their claims at the federal Land Office in Stirrup Gap. By that time George Steele's daughter had returned from nursing school in the East. Yokum Bos, of course, had shared his knowledge of the strike with his wife, and George Steele had told Nan about their good fortune. Although Nan never informed her father about it, she had confided the secret to Dr. Royal Logan with whom she was working in Stirrup Gap where he was practicing medicine. Nan had come to suspect, however, that it had been due to this inadvertence that Father Matthew had learned of it and decided to move his congregation to Eagle Cañon. Sam Ingalls, sheriff at Stirrup Gap and a recent convert to the Temple of the Redeemed there, had taken a core of his assistants with him in the move to Eagle Cañon, and immediately outsiders were discouraged from entry into the gold fields, not only for the obvious reason of protecting the claims of the faithful followers of Father Matthew's, but also because most of the stampeders who came, seeking to stake a claim, ran afoul of the local ordinances against bearing arms of any kind, alcohol, gambling, dancing, and tobacco.

In this sense Luke Barron's observation was absolutely correct. Eagle Cañon resembled no other mining district in the West, from the placer claims of the 'Forty-Niners in California to, more recently, the claims along the Vasquez outside Denver City or the rich lodes at Virginia City and Alder Gulch in Montana Territory. Eagle Cañon was utterly devoid of the saloons, gambling halls, prostitution, and murderous claim jumping that characterized such places. Sheriff Sam Ingalls was inclined to state, rather emphatically, that the only serious crime problem plaguing Eagle Cañon from the outside was caused by Luke Barron and his gang. The righteous execution of the law in Eagle Cañon would soon put a stop to this pillaging, just as prosecution of evildoers found guilty of engaging in forbidden vices would assure that Eagle Cañon would remain a model community, one that might well inspire others both far and wide to follow their example.

All of this meant nothing to Neele Bos. In losing her husband she had lost the very last thing that she held precious in her life. Their marriage had been far from what she had hoped when, as a young woman, she had married Yokum. Her father had abandoned her mother when Neele was still a young girl on the farm her parents had had outside Centralia. She was told he had gone to California to seek his fortune in 1849. She wasn't certain that was true, but it was what her mother had believed. Her mother had tried to keep the farm together, but finally the mortgages on it had become overwhelming, and the bank had foreclosed. Neele had heard it said at the time that

42

there were more mortgages than farms in what was called the Middle West, and she believed it. Yokum Bos had a good trade as a carpenter and builder, and Neele had felt at the very least a marriage to him would offer her a degree of security her mother had never had, especially after they had moved into Centralia and her mother had gone to work in a shoe factory.

All her life Neele had believed in God and had tried to do His will and to follow His teachings. When Yokum had experienced a desperate time, plying his trade, she had taken the position of housekeeper to Father Matthew who had newly come to the Church of the Sacred Heart. All his life, Father Matthew had said, he had studied the works of the Holy Ghost and believed his life was guided by Him. Neele's fall into what she since had come to regard as sin had begun innocently enough, but now even in retrospect it shamed her to think about it. Had the move West with Yokum been able to free her forever of the memory of what had happened in Centralia, her prayers to God for forgiveness might have been answered, but God had not listened to her pleas. Father Matthew, too, had come West, and now here on the kitchen table was the naked body of her husband, his neck broken, his face without expression. The terrible burns visible on his back, his buttocks, his thighs showed how great must have been his physical suffering before finally he died.

Neele would bury him. Then, as surely as her desire to form a pact with God had failed her, she would now do all she could to form a pact with Satan. In exchange for her immortal soul she would ask only one thing of the Prince of Darkness: to see Father Matthew damned for all eternity. The exchange would be worth all the suffering she herself had endured and would continue to endure. Gaunt to the point of appearing emaciated, her hollow cheeks, sunken dark eyes, the moles that now grew on her face and body, she realized in her anguish and despair,

43

were but the preparations to make her fitting for this final marriage in her life.

It was with definite irritation — she was long beyond fear of anything on earth — that she heard the approach outside of a wagon, the squeaking of the wheels, the jingling of the harness chains, the sounds of plodding hoofs. Going to the oil-papered window, she found she could see only indistinctly. There was nothing to do for it, then, but to throw open the door. When she did, she still had to gaze for some time before she finally recognized George Steele and a younger man beside him, approaching in a wagon.

Chapter Four

Dr. Royal Logan's makeshift hospital was an elongated tent building with wooden half sides and wooden flooring that squatted on a wide rock shelf at the foot of the sheer east wall a few hundred yards beyond the first downcañon tar-paper shack — the café operated by Lee Hop — and well behind the tent where the Avenging Angels collected firearms from everyone entering Eagle Cañon. The inside of the hospital consisted of a single long room and a curtained side alcove that served as a combination office and operating room. Half a dozen cots lined each side wall. Only two of the cots were occupied. Taking a break after his rounds and having set a broken arm, Dr. Logan, wearing a white cotton jacket with a wooden stethoscope still hanging from his neck, was seated at a rolltop desk. Medical books lined the top shelf of the desk, and what papers he had, including correspondence, were neatly ordered in piles at the rear of the desk top or appropriately pigeon-holed. The medical man was well past middle age with a craggy face in which the sockets of his eyes appeared darkly circled and sunken as if from exhaustion. The brown eyes that might be kindly and warm under other circumstances now had a forbidding glint of suppressed rage. There was about this man at once a look of reassuring competence and a strong willfulness.

Logan had graduated from medical school in Chicago a few years before the Civil War and for almost a decade had practiced medicine in Centralia prior to becoming the principal elder in Father Matthew's parish who had joined him in coming West in search of religious freedom. The astute physician had also long been a student of the political process. He had been particularly impressed with the manner in which the late President Lincoln, another citizen from the state of Illinois, had used adept political rhetoric to keep the focus of the conflict between the States on the issue of slavery rather than on what Logan conceived as the true purpose of the war — the economic and ideological subjugation of the southern States in the deliberate abridgment of any rights individual States in the Union might claim to govern themselves. Especially appealing to the doctor were those moving words in what became known as the Gettysburg Address concerning "a nation conceived in liberty and dedicated to the proposition that all men are created equal."

The very notion of a nation conceived in liberty, while certainly ennobling rhetoric, had been precisely what had been wrong with the old order. Liberty was a most precise term for the disease that continued to infect the nation as a whole and its territories. Liberty must not be allowed to guide the lives of men, but rather conformity to the principles of righteousness, codified into the strictest laws to govern all human endeavor and enterprise. The doctor had spent more than one session stressing this very point to Sheriff Sam Ingalls, who had been one of Father Matthew's most ardent converts in Stirrup Gap and who was a no less vigorous ally of the faith of the Redeemed here in Eagle Cañon. The only problem Dr. Logan could detect in the lawman's zealotry was his inclination to disparage peripheral members of the faith, such as Timothy Kamu and Lee Hop. The physician had done his best to redirect this very zealotry to more evident sources of human wickedness like alcohol, gambling, dancing, and the use of tobacco. These vices appealed to all men, not merely to those from inferior races.

In his heart of hearts Dr. Logan knew that as long as a single person engaged in *any* of these vices, even in the seclusion of his own quarters, he was placing the entire community in mortal danger. He knew that Father Matthew was secretly addicted to tobacco, as once he had been addicted to carnality. In the case of the latter he had urged the priest to forsake his order and bid the faithful in his parish to follow him in the path of truth revealed to him, as Father Matthew had confessed to the doctor, only after a lonely journey of the soul in which he had sought divine inspiration and had received it from the Holy Ghost. Dr. Logan had been the first forcefully to urge the priest that he must act upon that revelation or lose his immortal soul for all eternity. The priest had consented to follow the dictates of the Holy Ghost, and it was clear now for all to see what wonders had been wrought.

The war against all vice, however, was now being threatened not merely by clandestine sins, such as that of the old priest, but by the more obvious presence of this Luke Barron and his gang. Originally it was Dr. Logan's hope and belief that sinners such as that besotted George Steele might be permanently banished from the earth by holy execution, thus removing from the sight of all men the obvious temptation of the false gaiety promised by fraudulent spirits of any kind. But how could you muster the support of a righteous community to execute those guilty of other forms of viciousness when an outlaw and murderer like Luke Barron was cutting them down at their claims and robbing them of their gold? The gold that continued to come Dr. Logan's way through his control and sale of the drinking water was intended to be only the beginning of a means of financing a political movement to outlaw throughout the entire nation the vices now prohibited by law in Eagle Cañon. On a couple of occasions when the medical man had raised this issue with Father Matthew, the old priest had only smiled and rendered his opinion that the Congress of the United States would never outlaw alcohol and tobacco, much less dancing or gambling. Such matters would remain always within the province of a person's own free will.

Were it not for Luke Barron, Dr. Logan was certain that even Father Matthew could be forced through enforcement by the Avenging Angels to surrender his addiction to tobacco. God knew the Mormons — although in matters of theology clearly heretics, idolaters, and fornicators — had been able to stamp out these vices among their followers. Why should it be different in Eagle Cañon? Why, indeed? There was only one answer to that question. Luke Barron. Sheriff Ingalls must find this desperado and hang him, just as he had hanged the pagan non-believer, Yokum Bos, following his confession of iniquity.

Dr. Logan's free moments for reflection were cut short by the arrival of Lee Hop with his mid-morning tea. The medical man rose from his desk and smiled warmly as the Chinaman entered through the curtain screening the alcove from the area of hospital beds after having tapped softly with his slipper three times and being bid to enter by the medical man. In contrast to Dr. Logan's white coat, Lee Hop was dressed in black, light-weight, slick trousers and a black three-quarter robe. Incongruously, his sandals were of leather dyed a shade of vermilion. On his head was a plain black skull cap, sufficiently big to keep hidden from sight the pigtail that some like Sheriff Ingalls found deeply offensive and, if anything, a proud badge of Satan.

Bowing discreetly, Lee Hop padded into the alcove. He carried the tea as always on a small teakwood tray in a china pot, with cup, saucer, and a small china vase in which there was a single wild flower that the Chinaman had obviously picked for Dr. Logan's pleasure. From experience, Lee Hop knew to place the tray on the desk before the doctor's swivel chair. He bowed again, a grin lighting his broad face.

"Tell me, Lee," the doctor asked, "was that a gunshot I

heard earlier? It sounded as if it came from somewhere up the street."

Lee Hop nodded. "Tlouble at Mercantilee. Mellican man no wantee give up gun, so sheriff men come to knockee hellee out of him."

"And did they?" the doctor inquired, chuckling softly.

"No," replied Lee Hop, gravely shaking his head. "Mellican man shoot at sheriff, knockee sheriff man's gun out of his han', and Father Matt' save him."

"Father Matthew saved whom?" the doctor asked, now suddenly concerned.

"Mellican man. Father Matt' send sheriff and his man away and save Mellican man."

"Let me get this straight, Lee. Sheriff Ingalls and a deputy tried to disarm this outsider. Instead, the outsider shot at the sheriff's deputy, and Father Matthew is protecting this stranger?"

Seeing the obvious consternation on Dr. Logan's face, the Chinese café owner shrugged his shoulders. "Not sheriff man but sheriff. Eengalls."

"Is the sheriff badly hurt?"

"Not thinkee so, not so much, but he comee here fo' shure, mebbe soon."

"Is this gunman still with Father Matthew?"

"Mebbeso. Don' know."

"He shore as hell is!" an irate Sam Ingalls announced from where he now stood, holding open the curtain to the alcove. "Get out of here, you damned heathen. The doc and me has got to pow-wow."

Lee Hop ceremoniously again bowed to the medical man, then merely nodded his head at the sheriff, before scurrying around him and through the curtain. Ingalls stepped aside to let him pass, and then, before he was out of earshot, spoke again to Dr. Logan.

"The only good thing I can say about that Chinaman is that while he's in Eagle Cañon not even the mice'll stay around. You know what they do with his kind in other mining camps? They hang 'em."

"Are you hurt, Sam?" the doctor asked solicitously, having risen and approaching the lawman.

"Ain't no more than a scratch, Roy," the sheriff replied, dismissing the question with a flourish of his right hand, wrapped in a white handkerchief. "Bullet just grazed the back of my hand. I'm here about somethin' more pressin' at the moment. We got us another of Luke Barron's gang what needs hangin'. Let's tend to that first, and then we'll see about this stranger."

"Has the man finally confessed?"

"You bet he has, Doc. He's been workin' with Bos, relayin' information to Barron and his gang. He confessed last night, told us the whole dirty, rotten deal."

"Still, Sam," the doctor said, nodding his approval at what he had heard, "you'd best let me examine that hand. Even seemingly mild gunshot wounds can become serious."

"Oh, all right. But it ain't nothin' worth squawking about. Soon's Father Matthew's done with that stranger, I'll have him in jail, and then things'll be different."

While speaking, the sheriff was clumsily tugging at the knot in the handkerchief. Dr. Logan reached out to assist him. Letting the makeshift bandage fall to the rough pine floor, the doctor turned the palm downward and examined the bright red stripe of the burn running across the back of the hand.

"Better let me put some disinfectant on that burn, some salve, and then bandage it for you."

"I don't like bein' without the use of this hand, Doc," the sheriff affirmed gruffly. "It's my gun hand."

50

"All the more reason for you to take proper care of it."

The sheriff was told to sit up on the operating table while the doctor went to the cabinet against the back wall of the alcove where he kept his medical supplies. Returning with carbolic acid and bandages, the doctor lowered his voice.

"I would suggest, Sam, that what is said between us should not be overheard by any of the patients."

The sheriff nodded as he extended his injured hand. The doctor then went to the wash basin and brought it over to a stand beside the operating table. He next poured hot water in the basin from the kettle kept on the small stove against the back wall.

"Let me cleanse that hand before applying disinfectant," he said quietly. He lightly scrubbed the hand. "Are you aware that George Steele is believed to have a distillery up at his mining claim."

"I've heard a rumor to that effect from more than one source," the sheriff replied.

"I would suggest that you seize that still, destroy it, and arrest George Steele for breaking the law against the sale of alcoholic spirits."

"I'm not sure he's selling the stuff, Doc."

"Merely possession of a still would be sufficient grounds, I'm sure."

"And if I find the still, smash it like you say, and arrest him, then what?" The sheriff winced involuntarily as the physician scrubbed the area grazed by the bullet.

"Then we can put him on trial before the board of elders for breaking our community laws."

"We ain't ever tried that kind of case."

"All the more reason to make an example of him, Sam. Ordinarily I would say he could be given a sentence of banishment, but, since I have asked Nan to marry me, banishment

51

might prove inconvenient."

"But, Doc, if we don't banish him, what are we gonna do with him?"

Doctor Logan paused to gaze intently at the lawman. "Let me explain something to you, Sam. If we have laws against alcohol, gambling, tobacco, and dancing, and if innocent people see others engaging in these activities, they will want to imitate their behavior. Evil is like an infectious disease. Sometimes, for the common good, you have to treat a man who engages in evil activities the way you would an arm or a leg that has become infected with gangrene . . . the way you yourself might become infected from a bullet wound such as this, were it not properly cared for. In such a case there is only one thing left to do. Amputate."

"You mean cut off the arm or leg, like they done during the war?"

"Precisely."

"But Doc, drinkin' ain't like murder and robbery."

"No, Sam, it's not. It's worse. A person who drinks is not only destroying himself, but he is also destroying the souls of others who are inspired to drink because they see him doing it." The doctor turned to the carbolic acid and poured some on a clean white cloth. "Have you thought about what will happen to Yokum Bos's claim, now that he's been tried, sentenced, and executed?"

"I was gonna talk to Father Matthew about that. I don't see as how it should rightly pass to his widow, seein' as how she ain't one of us. For that reason I took it over."

"I agree with you, Sam," Doctor Logan said, applying the cloth to the injured area. "His claim should rightly pass to one of us, and I propose that it should pass on to you. I intended to bring that up with Father Matthew when I see him later today."

Sheriff Sam Ingalls nodded solemnly. "And don't you worry none about George Steele, Doc. I reckon I savvy what you've been sayin', and I'll see that your name is kept out of it."

"You're a good man, Sam," the doctor told him cogently, beginning the bandaging process. "The Temple of the Redeemed is most fortunate to have the benefit of your devotion to righteousness. Evil is all around us. It requires constant vigilance, and, to be truly effective, justice must be swift and certain."

The doctor tied off the bandage. His expression was still overcast, but the sheriff felt a great reassurance in his presence.

"See you later at the hearing of that Barron man, Doc," the sheriff said, slipping off the operating table and straightening his holster.

"You certainly will, Sam. I'll have discussed the matter of Yokum Bos's claim being passed on to you prior to the trial before the board of elders."

The sheriff thanked the physician for tending to his hand and then passed through the curtain of the alcove. Dr. Logan then adjourned to his desk to pour himself a cup of tea, hoping that it had not cooled too much during the time he had spent with the lawman.

Chapter Five

Luke Ashford did indulge himself, because of Father Matthew's graciousness, to roll and smoke a cigarette before the old priest rose and led him over to the library table. He had two rolled maps, one of plots on either side of the single street of the township his parish, as he called it, had founded, and the other of the various mining claims located along Eagle Creek as it wound its course through the deep cañon. It was this latter that the old priest presumed would be of the greatest interest to the special deputy for the Temple.

It was Father Matthew's plan that Luke should spend the rest of the day riding out among the claims, familiarizing himself as well as he could with the actual physical terrain and possibly striking up an acquaintance with any of the miners he chanced to meet at their claims. After dark he was to return to town, putting up his horse at the livery stable. Father Matthew would by that time have informed Timothy, an ex-slave who acted as the hosteler for the Temple which owned the stable, to expect him. Luke could have the small room with a cot located at one side of the loft.

The afternoon promised to be rather eventful for the old priest. There was to be a trial and sentencing to take place at the Temple, and the next day, inevitably, there would be another hanging conducted by the Avenging Angels at the old cottonwood near what Father Matthew called Rattlesnake Mesa, a name given the place because of the infestation of reptiles reputed to be found there. Although Father Matthew would speak to Sheriff Ingalls, it was his request that Luke try to avoid being seen on the street and to avoid all the accepted prohibitions if he were seen outdoors, above all not to wear his Colt in open sight. Luke agreed to carry it hidden in his right Justin boot when in camp. The only thing Luke learned about the hanged man whose body he had seen the previous night is that he had been the one who had originally discovered the gold in Eagle Cañon and, apparently out of resentment of the incursion from the followers of Father Matthew and the disciples of the Temple of the Redeemed, had associated himself with the thieves and murderers who were presumably following a man calling himself Luke Barron. Once construction on the Bank of Eagle Cañon was completed, the free-wheeling activities of this gang would be further impeded. However, the problem of shipping gold dust from Eagle Cañon down to Stirrup Gap by wagon or stage would still present a danger. Father Matthew hoped that before that time his special deputy would be in a position to name names of other culprits and possibly even locate the headquarters of the thieves.

For the most part and as well as he could, Luke Ashford stayed out of sight as he explored Eagle Cañon, and he was able to avoid meeting or talking with anyone. The claims were located all along Eagle Creek, although it was Father Matthew's intention to develop farming in the verdant earth of the cañon once the gold played out. He also hoped some day for the disciples to expand into communal ranching in the area around Rattlesnake Mesa.

Timothy Kamu was a black, raw-boned hawk of a man with a face like a mahogany mask, tightly curled, steel-gray hair, and a thin nose that flared into wide nostrils. He was quite voluble, possibly because of the faith Father Matthew had in the stranger, and spoke openly about himself and his past over a late supper he fetched Luke from Lee Hop's café while the latter tended to his black in the stable. Timothy had his own room at the rear of the livery stable. It was here that Luke ate.

Timothy supplied the coffee. He liked to chew tobacco, which he could do in the privacy of his room, and he even had a penchant for sour-mash whiskey — supplied, he told Luke, by George Steele who had a small distillery hidden out on his claim. George, of course, was a notorious drunk and not one of the disciples, having been the original partner of the unfortunate Yokum Bos.

The hosteler was certain that Nancy Steele, who was presently taking religious instructions from Father Matthew, would eventually bring her father into the fold. Timothy's only hope in this matter was that George Steele's conversion, when it came, would not cause him to close down the distillery. Then he shocked Luke by speaking what sounded like gibberish: *"Steuete eis tin Theon, kai eis eme pisteuete."*

"That one of them languages they spoke where your ancestors come from?" Luke asked, forking up some fried potatoes as he sat at a little round table against one wall with a coal-oil lamp on it for illumination.

"No, suh," said Timothy proudly, sitting across from Luke but not eating. "Dem's the words of Saint John hisself . . . I mean, himself. On Saturday afternoons I have my weekly lesson with Father Matthew. He's teachin' me to read old Greek. It's a matter of special pride for me 'cause my people weren't allowed even to read English. It means . . . 'in my Father's house are many mansions.' And like de Lord, Father Matthew is preparing a place for us, for me an' Lee Hop an' others who want to be disciples. Dere's some, like Sheriff Ingalls, who thinks dat whites is . . . are . . . more equal den coloreds in de eyes of God. Right now we've our own special worship with Father Matthew on Saturday nights, but some of dese days Father Matthew wants us to be right dere with de rest on Sundays."

Luke merely nodded, but to himself this, more than anything else he had heard from or about the old priest, convinced him that Father Matthew must be insane. He had to be, thinking the rest of the country, especially back in the States, to say nothing of the world, would likely ever embrace this brand of religion.

Timothy went on to explain how he had first encountered Father Matthew in Centralia when he had come North on the Underground Railroad before the war, and how he had been with the old priest ever since, had in fact come West with him when he moved his small parish from Illinois to Stirrup Gap and from Stirrup Gap on to Eagle Cañon. The last hour or so of every day Timothy spent reading the Bible. When Luke finished eating, he rolled a cigarette, had a second cup of coffee with the hosteler, and then, after getting his saddlebags, was shown up to his small room at the back of the loft. Once there, it was just a matter of waiting, which he did by going out and sitting behind one of the two loft doors that was ajar, opening onto the main street. He patiently watched the town close down for the night.

Long before it was nearly midnight, Eagle Cañon was almost entirely dark. Timothy had told Luke a curfew had been imposed by the Avenging Angels. No one was allowed out or about after nightfall as long as Luke Barron and his gang were on the loose. There were no saloons or deadfalls, as there were in all the other mining camps Luke had ever seen, so there was no place for miners to go, even were they inclined to disobey the sheriff's order. It was now that he decided to wait no longer to set out on the errand he hoped to carry out while the town slept. After he had let himself down from the loft, by hanging onto the flooring and then dropping to the hard-packed earth in front of the stable, he drew deep lungfuls of the chill night air and found it a bracer to keep him awake. Today had been his eighth in the saddle, and he had originally planned to ride deeply into the cañon, unlace the blankets from his saddle, and allow himself the luxury of a night's uninterrupted sleep. But he had something more important than sleep on his mind now, and characteristically he set about doing it.

He moved through the shadows across the street, then alongside a hardware store, into the alley at its rear. He took the alley upstreet, past two more buildings and the construction site of the bank, until he came abruptly upon the rear of Eagle Cañon's jail. Earlier this afternoon he had become well acquainted with the front of the jail where Sheriff Sam Ingalls had his office. And from the street he'd looked along a passageway back toward the alley, his brief glance more searching than would have been apparent to the casual observer. Now, in the darkness, he picked out details he'd firmly sealed in his mind in that one fleeting glimpse.

Here, to the south of the jail, the bank's walls were already above the height of its single-story brick neighbor. Close by along the alley was a water barrel, an overturned mortar box, sacks of cement, and a huge stack of neatly piled bricks that must have cost the disciples a young fortune to haul in from the railhead at Stirrup Gap, fifteen miles away down on the flat. Above, at the corner nearest the jail, the long shadowy line of a strong derrick-boom angled up over the wall's edge. This boom was used to lift mortar and bricks to the scaffolding inside the rising new walls. Down from the boom hung a stout inch-and-a-half-thick rope with a hook at its end. Directly under the hook was a small stack of a hundred or more bricks already in its cradle of steel cables used for hoisting them to the masons, working above. The workmen had quit tonight, ready to hoist that load of bricks to the platform on the scaffolding.

The stranger's glance took this in casually, among other things, chief of which was a wooden stepladder that he sauntered over to pick up and carry to the rear wall of the jail, placing it directly at the edge of the building. Whatever Eagle Cañon's other temporary features, the jail had been built to last. It was as close to being break-proof as one could make it. The brick walls were thick, cut to fit closely and then cemented to make it virtually impregnable. Climbing the stepladder and pulling himself up and over the parapet, Luke saw that the roof was strong, probably reinforced by thick logs covered with boards, then several inches of dirt, and finally, he judged, tarpaper roofing. The chimneys, he had rightly guessed, were the only openings in the roof.

He let himself down once more to the top step of the ladder and then scrambled down to the ground. There were two windows in the rear wall with casement windows inside and bars outside, lodged firmly in the brick wall. The lower sash of the casement window nearest to where Luke had placed the stepladder he found was open about three inches. A coal-oil lamp in the front wall near the bullpen door gave off a dull light. Luke could barely make out the lumpy silhouette of a man, reclining on the bunk attached to the wall in the rearmost cell. Removing his .38 from the top of his right Justin, he tapped suddenly and gently through the bars over the glass of the lower sash of the open window. When he did it a second time, the silhouette on the bunk stirred.

"Ed?" he said in a whisper intended to carry into the room but not to be heard in the jail office. "Ed, is that you?"

The figure rose and moved toward the front of the cell. "Luke?"

Luke Barron said: "Big as life, Ed."

"Damned if I thought you'd even get here!" came Ed Tyler's low words from inside. Then, ruefully, Luke Barron's lieutenant added: "Looks now like you couldn't do me any good, anyway. They're going to hang me at sunup tomorrow."

"I know all about it. Maybe you won't be here at sunup."

"This ain't the time for jokin', Luke."

"I mean it! I'm goin' to bust you out."

"Yeah? How?"

Luke let out a long, worried sigh. This was going to be tougher than he'd thought at first. The cells were enclosed by bars as thick as the ones at this window. The walls couldn't be broken down. The roof was sturdy. He wished now that he had clubbed the jail guard, taken his keys, and let Ed Tyler walk out the unlocked door of his cell, as had been his plan at first before he had sat there in the livery stable, thinking about it. *No*, he told himself, *Ed has to get out of there without anyone knowing who got him out . . . if we're going to get the new start that the gold in this mining camp can give us.*

"Fat chance you got of gettin' me out," Ed whispered harshly. "This layout was built for keeps."

"The roof's dropping in on you in about a minute," Luke said on quick impulse. He had just seen the line of the timbers running crosswise to the long room of the bullpen, also the interior brick wall separating the jail from the office in front. "You just stand close to that cell door. Wrap a blanket around your head. When the roof's open, climb up the rope."

"What rope?"

"There'll be one," Luke answered.

"I can't use my arms or hands. Thet sheriff busted me up good."

"Then put the hook under your belt."

Without saying more, Luke took the stepladder and carried it back to its place at the rear of the new bank.

Now that he'd found a barely possible way of getting Ed Tyler out of jail, he was eager to be at it. He stepped up to the cable-slung pile of bricks, trying to lift it. It was a dead weight that he couldn't budge, and that satisfied him. He reached up for the hook dangling from the rope of the derrick-boom. Pulling it down to him, he breathed more freely when the absence of any creaking from above told him that the hoisting mechanism of the derrick was well oiled. He fastened the hook to the cable-sling of the pile of bricks, took a last look along the alley to make sure no one was about, then mounted the ladder to scale to the top of the wall.

The mortar-littered scaffolding ran ten feet high inside the four walls. In from the wall flanking the jail stood the sturdy vertical stem of the derrick, a cable from its top holding the swinging boom in place. On the platform of the derrick that was scaffold-high was the cable-drum and two sets of cogged wheels, both turned by long-handled cranks. One, the smallest, was for regulating the height of the boom. The other, geared to the drum, was for hoisting the load.

Luke gingerly turned the hoist-handle. The oiled mechanism worked smoothly, almost soundlessly. It was quiet enough not to be detected from the street out front, much less from inside the jail office.

He cranked the hoist until the heavy load of bricks swung into sight beyond the shadow of the rear wall. He brought the load higher, then reached up and swung the boom around until the load of bricks hung over the jail's roof. He was thankful that the beams where the cells separated made a series of slight bulges along the flat roof. Otherwise, he couldn't have been sure exactly where the enormous weight of the bricks was to fall.

By turning one crank, then the other, he finally had the suspended load of bricks where he wanted it. The long derrick-boom held it twenty feet above the roof. He leaped over the passageway onto the jail roof and looked directly upward, making a small adjustment in the boom's angle when he returned so as to be sure the bricks hung over the spot he judged

61

to be between two of the roof-joists as he remembered them from his glimpse into the interior.

Satisfied, he eased the drum-handle over a bare inch, tipped the ratchet that locked the gears, and let go the handle. Holding his breath, he caught the whir of the drum as it suddenly unwound. The brick load started falling slowly. Then it gathered speed and plummeted down toward the roof.

Chapter Six

The stacked bricks hit with the exploding impact of both barrels of an eight-gauge being fired at once. The flat surface of the roof gave way, the bricks going on through as though falling through cardboard. The sound of splintering timbers echoed up out of the opening, and the scaffolding on which Luke stood trembled as though the very earth were threatening to shake down these new walls. Out of the hole rose a cloud of dust. Luke saw the rope sway and suddenly tighten. He began turning the windlass, and slowly the rope began rising, the hook at the end attached around Ed's waist. Luke pulled the boom on around and once more released the drum catch to lower Ed into the alley.

The whole thing, from the moment of his releasing the ratchet to dropping Ed into the alley, had been accomplished in the space of half a dozen breaths. He jumped down off the wall, instead of using the ladder. Shouts were echoing from the street, and all at once he heard the slam of the sheriff's office door. He said urgently: "This way!" He turned up the alley at a run, Ed's quick boot tread pounding behind him.

A few doors above the jail Luke cut out at a right angle from the alley, climbing the uneven slope of the cañon wall toward the rim. Halfway to the rim he halted, breathing hard, and let Ed come up with him. Ed's square, homely face shaped a broad smile, dimly visible in the moonlight. He lifted a hand and ran it around his short-coupled neck. He drawled: "Thanks for keepin' this all in one piece!"

"Forget it!" Luke sat on a nearby low outcropping. He waited until his lungs weren't quite so crowded, thankful for his luck and the presence of this man who had been like a brother to him for almost ten years now. Then, seeing shadowy figures moving along the alley by the jail and the distant glow of a lantern on its roof, he said urgently: "There isn't much time. I've got to get back down there in case they start looking for me. So let's have it in a hurry. How come you wound up in that *jusgado?* And what happened to your arms?"

"My arms nearly got pulled outta their sockets by thet damn' psalm-singin' sheriff and his hardcase deputies, tryin' to prod information outta me 'bout where you and your gang are holed up." He rubbed the muscles over his right shoulder as he spoke, wincing as he did it. "You got the makin's, Luke? I ain't had a smoke in days. Them psalm-singers is ag'in' tobacco and whiskey an' a whole lot more."

"Dancin' and gamblin', too, I reckon," Luke said, smiling grimly as he handed over a sack of Bull Durham and papers.

"Would you roll it for me, Luke? I'm still kinda shaky."

"Sure."

"A couple of nights ago," Ed continued, as Luke rolled him a cigarette, "I saw 'em give old Yokum Bos the hot-seat they got rigged up in thet jail till they had him sobbin' like a baby, ready to confess anything just to make 'em stop." He took the cigarette Luke handed him and placed it in his mouth, then leaned forward to get a light from the match Luke struck. Inhaling deeply, he wagged his head and said: "God, that tastes good!"

"You wrote in your letter," Luke said, rolling himself a cigarette, "that you found this camp ripe pickings for us to make our final haul." He paused to light his own cigarette. "What went wrong?"

"I made friends with George Steele, old Bos's pardner. Thet's where I was holed up. They's a cave in the side of the cliff, hard to find, but ole George knew 'bout it, 'cause that's

64

where he has his sour mash still. I hid out there mostly. Thet damned sheriff picked me up when I come into town to eat at the Chinaman's. Guess he saw my face on an old dodger. I don't think Nan would 'a' give me away, even if she knew 'bout me being wanted, which she didn't. I met her up at George's claim a time or two, but I didn't like spongin' all my meals off'n George which is why I came in to see the Chinaman. George opines me thet hardcase doctor they got here is sweet on Nan. Cain't say. I've never seen 'em together. But George thinks a heap of thet girl. Named his claim after her . . . the Nan Steele. Don't surprise me none 'bout thet doctor nohow. All the hardcases runnin' this town are oversexed, if yuh ask me. Have you heard 'bout Father Matthew?"

"I've met him. He seems like a right smart gent . . . real educated."

"Well, he may be eddicated . . . wouldn't know nothin' 'bout thet . . . but old George told me thet back in Chicago or one of them Eastern cities Father Matthew got kicked out of the Church for goin's-on with his housekeeper, old Bos's wife. Bos, George says, forgave her and decided to head West, endin' up in Stirrup Gap, met Steele, and the two of 'em partnered in prospectin' up here on a little money George had set aside while he was workin' as a teamster. Thet was afore Nan come out here from back East where she was studyin' how to be a nurse or somethin' like that . . . now she helps thet local witch doctor. Anyway, like I said, Father Matthew got kicked out of the priesthood for carryin' on with his house-keeper. George says there was a big fuss 'bout it, but what do you reckon Father Matthew did? He ups and tells his whole congregation he's startin' his own church and headin' West. Them as wants can come along. He brings 'em, them thet's willin', to Stirrup Gap. When Bos and Steele struck it rich up here, the flock moved right after 'em, quick as you please, cuttin' out everybody else, and Ingalls and his hardcases are seein' it stays thet way."

Ed broke off to massage his other shoulder.

"You must've written me that letter before you went to jail, right? You told me how a wild bunch up here was framing all their night riding onto me, so why not surprise them and pull a job ourselves right under their noses, since we're being blamed for it anyway?"

"Thet's right. I got thet story on the way in, before I ever laid eyes on Eagle Cañon. It's all the talk down on the flat in Stirrup Gap. How Luke Barron's gang has this town and the diggin's by the tail. So I wrote yuh and sent the letter back with the driver of the stage I come in on. Then, when Ingalls found out I was one of your gang, thet give him ideas. He already had old Bos jailed. He made him confess to bein' in with you, an' they hanged him. Now Ingalls has Bos's claim, or will have it. These Avengin' Angels ain't no better than them who's playin' Luke Barron's gang. What finished me was thet dodger they put out after you broke me outta jail in Cripple Creek. Ingalls is a sheriff from down in Stirrup Gap, the county seat. Father Matthew, George told me, converted him somehow, so thet's how he got up here. It's paid off for him right smart. He got old Bos's claim, the richest in the diggin's . . . that is" — he grinned as he drew deeply from his cigarette — "if Luke Barron and his gang let him ship out any of the dust he's stolen!"

Luke fit Ed's story into the picture he had already formed. Until now, he had had little to go on except what Father Matthew had told him that afternoon. Ed's story added conviction to what he already suspected. Someone was obviously terrorizing the Eagle Cañon diggings under the name of Luke Barron. Father Matthew must have believed it was a hoax as much as Luke did. The way he had acted proved that much.

Well, they were about to learn a lesson from the real Luke Barron. He asked: "What'd you tell 'em when they were working you over in that jail?"

"Thet I'd quit you and your gang and was on my own now. Three nights ago, jest before I got bagged, a bunch of jaspers hit the diggin's ag'in and helped themselves to every ounce of gold they could lay onto. Two claim owners were shot down when they tried to argue. There was hell to pay. The flock's gone loco. Then, next day, the sheriff announced he'd arrested me. He had that reward dodger, which was all the evidence he needed for the miner's court today where Father Matthew, thet crazy doctor, and the sheriff preside as judge and jury. Ingalls told 'em thet I was Luke Barron's right bower and proved it with thet dodger. The trial took all of mebbe five minutes. They convicted me, and Father Matthew passed the sentence. I tell yuh, Luke, thet old boy's a damn' hypocrite! Look what he done to his old housekeeper's husband! Now, Ingalls has Bos's claim, an' Father Matthew mebbe can take up with Bos's wife ag'in . . . if she'll have him. Say, roll me another cigarette, will yuh?"

Both men were keeping their cigarettes shielded with their hands. Ed ground his cigarette out with a boot heel.

"Father Matthew believes like you and me," Luke said, as he extinguished his own cigarette and took out the makings again. "He hired me as his special deputy to find out about this Luke Barron and his gang."

"You! A deputy!" Suddenly Ed was laughing loudly.

"Quiet, or you'll have them up here after us," Luke cautioned. He handed Ed the rolled cigarette, lit it for him, and explained how he had come to get the job. He ended by saying: "So, we're one jump ahead of the sheriff and his bunch. But we'll have to move fast. I'll work along with Father Matthew. I took the back trail in, around the mesa, which is how I happened to see Bos, hangin' from that cottonwood."

"I wouldn't trust Father Matthew too far, if I was you, Luke," Ed said, inhaling tobacco smoke. "He's no regular priest, y'know."

"No, but he knows my real name. I told it to him, and he told me to go by the handle of Luke Ashford while I work for him. He let me keep my six-gun. I had the impression this afternoon that the old priest's playing his own game."

"What you want me to do now?"

"Can you trust this fellow, Steele?"

"If thet daughter of his ain't around, most pro'bly I can."

"I want you to stay out of sight up at his claim till I can slip out of Eagle Cañon with a horse for you. Here's some money." He reached into a pocket of his Levi's and pulled out three double eagles, handing them over to Ed. "Once I get a horse to you, then you head out and be careful not to get caught again. Ride down to Stirrup Gap. You hang around down there. Do you know any place special?"

"The Nugget saloon's the biggest layout they got. Gamblin' and drinkin' all night long."

"Good. Soon as I can get away, I'll meet you there. Then we can drift up toward Rattlesnake Mesa where they hanged that poor son-of-a-bitch. I camped out thataway last night, near a creek in the bottoms."

"Eagle Creek," Ed supplied, nodding. "Same one as comes outta this cañon. Thet's where it goes." He drew deeply again on his cigarette and then asked: "What'll I tell George? He sure'll be curious. I don't reckon he's got no use for Father Matthew and them other Bible thumpers, but mebbe it ain't thet way with his daughter. Now between thet doctor she works for and thet old priest, she's got more'n enough religion fer both of 'em."

"I might've met her in town earlier today. If so, you might

be right about her. But she doesn't matter. I've got to get back to the loft room in the livery stable where I'm staying tonight. If you mention me at all, call me Luke Ashford. That's the handle Father Matthew hung on me, like I said. Tell Steele and anyone else you meet you pulled out of the Barron gang years ago and have been trying to go straight, that you linked up with me, and we're on our way to Montana to start a ranch. That much is the God's truth, anyway. What none of 'em will know is how we're going to pay for that ranch. Tell Steele in particular that we've got to fight Ingalls and his bunch, that the Barron story is just a put-up job on the sheriff's part."

Ed Tyler's homely face took on a wide grin as he heard this calm statement. He was as unlike Luke Barron in physical appearance as any man could be, a head and a half shorter, thick-bodied, and as dark-haired as Luke was blond. But they had one thing in common, an ingrained recklessness bred of years on the dark trails, a quick-wittedness long trained in fighting trouble. Luke seemed to have no nerves, and, when he moved, it was with a studied, almost indolent ease that was deceptive and sure. Ed was different, quick-muscled, nervous, proud of a hair-trigger temper.

Just now Ed was relishing Luke's last statement, which was symbolic of the outlaw's readiness to do the impossible. Luke was probably right. It was as simple as that, as simple as most of the precarious living in their past years together. The companionship that had sprung up between them was of two unlike minds, each somehow grooved to work smoothly with the other. The two of them, originally prospectors in Colorado, had been outlawed by a claim-jumping syndicate and had had little choice but to live as outlaws. The gang had most recently been operating near Cripple Creek. It had become too hot for them there, especially after Ed had been captured. After springing Ed from jail, Luke had sent him packing north, told him to lay low, and attrition had broken up the gang. Ed had happened onto the Eagle Cañon strike and got in touch with Luke.

Ed was the inveterate gambler who had time and again been in hot water over his liking for marked cards. He had been born to the owlhoot trail. Luke had come to it as a matter of necessity and survival. For ten years they'd sided each other, in the Colorado mining camps where the law was lax and a man's life depended on his nerve and his quickness of hand to gun. It was no fault of Luke's that their activities had spread his name far and wide in blazing headlines. Now the country was growing up, and Luke wanted a different life. Ed had agreed. All he and Luke needed was a last stake to make good. Eagle Cañon could give them that. It was no fault of Luke Barron's that Sam Ingalls and others had chosen to use his well-known name to hide behind, but it was typical of the man that he knew how to turn the situation to his own advantage.

Ed shook, for the air was chilled although tonight there was no wind, then glanced out from the outcropping, and frowned, looking down onto the alley where a lantern was bobbing near the rear of the jail. He pulled back again. "Doc Logan, I heard, tried for some time to tell them believers down there that they'd have a typhoid epidemic here unless the town gets good water to drink. Anyone tell you about the doc's well?" He caught Luke's murmured assent and continued: "They have to buy thet water and thet witch doctor makes out like a bandit . . . pardon the expression!" Irony creased his grin.

"Let's be moving," Luke drawled, having leaned himself out from the outcropping and noticing that the lantern light was now moving from the alley behind the jail out onto the main street.

"Can yuh let me have them makin's?" Ed asked.

"Sure. Got more in my saddlebags." Luke handed Ed the

sack, papers, and a box of matches, before slipping a Colt he had carried in his other Justin into Ed's hand, who shoved it behind his belt on his right side. "I had this extra in my pack. Figured you'd need it. Just be careful and try not to shoot anyone."

"Sure not," Ed said. He was grinning again, but it was too dark where they were now standing for Luke to see his face.

The two parted then. Ed kept to the back cañon wall on his way upcañon toward George Steele's claim. Luke slipped again into the shadows of the buildings. All was silent and dark at the livery stable when Luke cautiously made his way back across the main street. The great doors in front were not locked, so he let himself in that way, climbed quietly the narrow stairs to the loft, and, after removing his gun, boots, and Stetson, wrapped himself in the blanket on the cot. He was about to drop off to sleep, it seemed, when they came.

Luke heard the hosteler being roused, and then a minute later three men tramped up the narrow stairs to the loft. The .38 Colt he had taken from his boot was hidden under his pillow, near to hand. Luke sat up on the cot. His hair was mussed, and his eyes were squinting into the soft glare of a coal-oil lantern, carried by the deputy who had been at the tent when he had entered town that morning. He came forward, followed by the others.

Luke said sharply: "Do you have to make all that noise?"

"Just checkin' up to see if'n you was here," the deputy with the lantern replied. "You been asleep?"

"No. Been countin' my toes here in the dark." Luke's right hand edged slightly toward the pillow, but otherwise he made no motion.

The deputy's glance caught that small movement. "Some-one busted a prisoner outta jail. We're huntin' him."

"Meaning you thought he was here, or that I busted him

71

out?" Luke asked. "Maybe I did. Maybe I came up them steps right ahead of you."

The deputy smiled meagerly, apparently having been made aware that he couldn't afford to lose his temper even under Luke's taunting words. "Hit the hay again, Ashford," he said harshly. "If you've been on your feet since Timothy says you came up here, it's been sleepwalkin'."

The speaker nodded to his fellow deputy, and the two of them filed back down the narrow stairs. Only Timothy remained, an indistinct silhouette now that the light from the lantern had been taken away. After a pause, having waited for the deputies to leave the livery stable, he spoke. His voice was soft, a very sad whisper in the stillness of the loft.

"Father Matthew tol' me something dis afternoon dat you oughta rightly know, Mistah Ashford. It was jest one sentence, an' he said it when he was leavin' me. 'Timothy,' he said, 'one of you will betray me.' I surely hope, Mistah Ashford, dat one won't be you."

Luke wanted to answer him, to reassure him, but couldn't, and then, because apparently Timothy could see as well in the dark as some men see in the light, he was gone.

Chapter Seven

Lee Hop's real name was Li-hop shih. He had found that no American could easily pronounce it, any more than he could readily pronounce most of the words of their language, so he had settled for the simpler form. He left the living quarters for his family behind the café about ten o'clock after a word of caution to his wife, Sung Yü, to tell no one where he had gone. Their young son, whom they called Li-chung shih and whom George Steele had dubbed Little Hop, was already asleep. Although Lee Hop and his wife had originally come to America from a farm they had shared near Canton by way of Hongkong so Lee could work on the Southern Pacific Railroad, sometime after Li-chung shih was born they had drifted north to Stirrup Gap where they had opened a café.

Father Matthew had met Lee Hop in Stirrup Gap and had asked the Chinaman to prepare his meals for him. It hadn't been too long before Father Matthew had invited Lee to attend religious instructions. Although not yet allowed openly to be a practicing believer, Lee Hop and his family had come to Eagle Cañon at Father Matthew's invitation and now had the only café allowed in the little mining camp. Both Lee Hop and Sung Yü had encountered Christian missionaries in China, of course, but none had been as singularly inspiring as was Father Matthew. Truly, here was a man who had been blessed by the divine light.

Notwithstanding this, Lee retained enough of his native Confucianism to know that a great man is conscious only of justice and the petty man only of self-interest. He was wise enough to know that self-interest in its purest form is never

73

just one man's desire to profit financially over others, but rather the exultation a man feels when he is able to force other men to conform to what he believes to be the proper way for them to behave in public and in private. Father Matthew lived an austere life devoted to contemplation and good works. The same could not be said of the sheriff and certainly not — in Lee Hop's opinion — of the devilish Dr. Logan. Lee Hop might take the half eagle a week the doctor paid him to serve him tea twice a day and his evening meal, but that had yet to persuade him the medical man should ever be trusted. What he had heard of the conversation between the sheriff and the doctor earlier that day was sufficient, in fact, to convince him that these men were not above betraying Father Matthew and what he hoped to achieve here in Eagle Cañon.

As soon as he had returned from serving the doctor his customarily late dinner at the tent hospital, Lee Hop had taken off on foot to find George Steele at his claim and warn him of what the doctor and the sheriff were planning. If, by chance, the prospector was not there, Lee hoped he would be able to locate Steele's distillery and hide it from discovery by the Avenging Angels when they showed up. Lee was well aware that strong drink had often led white men to make war on Chinamen and others they did not like, but not George Steele. Tiger tea, as George termed his brew in Lee's presence, only seemed to make the prospector mellow and convivial. Certainly Lee did not want to see his only true friend among the white men — with the exception of Father Matthew — killed through the connivance of the sheriff and the doctor.

The night was clear. An almost half moon and many stars shed their cold light down upon the narrow road that roughly followed Eagle Creek as it wove its way toward the cliff that encircled the cañon, sealing it off from the surrounding country. The air was cold. Lee Hop could feel it even through his three-quarter mandarin coat.

He passed fires burning outside camp tents along the creek and occasional shacks thrown up hastily on various claims. This was placer mining on the bedrock of the creek. The gold was sluiced with tin pans or rockers. It was evident that a fortune was being harvested from this strike, but very little of the gold along this twelve-mile stretch of the creek was any longer being sent out of Eagle Cañon because of the depredations of Luke Barron and his gang. Now miners were even being killed for their caches. The potential threat of the Barron gang was sufficient to make Lee cautious, if it could not totally discourage him from venturing out alone at night. However, even the claim owners would be inclined to look to the sheriff and the Avenging Angels for protection, and, therefore, on his present mission Lee Hop wished to avoid them. Twice he encountered riders along the road that he recognized, once two men heading upcañon from the direction of town, Bill Olds and Nels Larsen, and once a man on a mule, coming down-cañon — Fred Jeliff, possibly on his way to visit Gopher Parsons's claim since that was the direction in which Jeliff was going. Although Lee recognized these men, he still preferred not to be seen by them, either, and remained in hiding in the trees and brush along the road until they passed, and the way again was clear.

George Steele had nearly made up his mind to follow Nan's urging and leave Eagle Cañon while on his way out to help Neele Bos to give her husband a proper burial. Then what he had learned at the Bos cabin had been a shattering experience. Nan, from her training as a nurse, acknowledged the severe burns on Yokum Bos's body. If his dead partner had confessed being in league with the Barron gang, it could only have been as a result of the cruelest torture. Steele had never liked Sam

Ingalls and his hardcase deputies. He had distrusted Dr. Logan, but had kept his feelings to himself because Nan spoke so highly of the medical man. Now he had learned that Logan had apparently given his tacit approval to what Ingalls and his deputies had done in the jailhouse. The doctor was on the council of elders who had condemned Yokum Bos to death, although he had not been physically present at the execution.

Nan believed that Father Matthew could have had no knowledge of what was really going on in Eagle Cañon, but to George Steele's surprise Nan had not brought up to Neele what her father had hinted about the widow's previous relationship with the old priest back in Centralia. Ultimately, it perhaps did not really matter. Ignorant of what Ingalls had done or not, as far as George Steele was concerned, Father Matthew was the spiritual architect of the Temple of the Redeemed and, therefore, was as guilty as the sheriff for what had happened. Steele had himself accumulated nearly twenty thousand dollars in gold dust and hidden it on his claim, and Bos must have hidden as much or more at his claim. Yokum had stopped living on his claim once Eagle Cañon was taken over by the disciples of Father Matthew and had been staying with Neele ever since at this cabin near Rattlesnake Mesa. He had had to submit to a search coming or leaving the town, on his way to work his claim or to return to this cabin, so Steele was fairly certain Yokum had not tried to take out any more of his dust since the invasion by the disciples. Neele confirmed this. Yokum had told her it he had concealed it where Father Matthew and his followers would never find it.

Steele had argued with Nan against accompanying him on what he fully intended to be his last trip back to his claim in Eagle Cañon. She refused to remain behind. Yokum Bos was buried, and Neele, in her grief, was not as pressing to Nan as her need to inform Father Matthew of what was going on behind his back. Traveling at night in this district was bad enough, George Steele knew, even if he was armed, but it would be more dangerous were Nan to accompany him. He had every right to look out for her welfare, and he did not want her exposed to danger, from Luke Barron and his gang or anyone else.

George Steele was feeling keenly his failure as a father as the wagon at the junction turned into the road toward the camp, because Nan was sitting there beside him, right where she should not be, and would not be had he been strict enough with her in the past and properly taught her to listen to him. Louise, bless her soul, were she still alive, would, of course, have told George that Nan was only being as strong-willed as her father. Knowing that, George still wondered if Louise would now blame him for having given in by letting Nan come along. So far, their return trip had been uneventful, but, even after they came into camp, there was another eight miles or so still to go.

Ray Cune, one of Sheriff Ingalls's deputies, was at the weapons check point when they approached. He held a lantern in his hand, and there was a lit lantern on the front support of the guard tent. Steele halted the team as the deputy came over to them.

"Howdy, Steele . . . Miss Nan," Cune said, holding the lantern high so as to shed its illumination on them. "I don't know what you two are doin' out at this time of night. I won't turn you back, like I done with two prospectors who tried to get through earlier. There's been a jail break and that Barron man has escaped."

"Ed Tyler?" George Steele asked, his face without expression.

"Yep, that's the one," Cune confirmed, shining the lantern now over the wagon box which was empty except for the tools

77

Steele had taken with him. "You packin' a hogleg, George?"

"No," said Steele.

"Even if yer lyin', George, I'd let it pass tonight. Someone has snuck up here to the check point, probably durin' the jail break, and made off with all the weapons we had taken away. I'm short-handed with Sam and some of the other deputies out in the cañon, but even so I searched every building with another man still here. When Sam gets back, I figger he'll organize a posse and search the cañon good. That's probably where Tyler must be hidin'. Mebbe we'll be lucky an' nab him and his boss together. I opine Sam's orders will be to shoot Tyler on sight. The council condemned him to hang today, and he's cheatin' the rope. If yuh see him, put a bullet in him."

"How could he break out of that jail?" Nan asked, her voice colored slightly by a flush of excitement.

"Someone dropped a ton of bricks on the roof," Cune replied.

Nan laughed despite herself, and George smiled.

"Ain't funny, Miss Nan. It was thet Luke Barron, sure enough, an' the jail's been wrecked."

"Where'd anyone get that many bricks?" Steele wondered.

"From the new bank building. Some idjit left a whole raft of 'em right there, just waitin' to be dropped." Cune had completed his cursory inspection of the wagon. "Headin' up to your claim?"

"Yes," Steele said. "Nan's comin' along with me."

"O K, jest don't fergit what I told yuh, Steele. If yuh see thet jasper, plug him with the hogleg you ain't got."

If it was meant to be humorous, Ray Cune wasn't smiling. Steele joggled the reins, and the wagon began moving slowly up the street.

"What do you think it means, Dad?" Nan asked, as soon as they were out of earshot of the deputy.

"Don't know, Nan, and don't rightly care. What's plain is that Ingalls will have this cañon sealed tight as a drum, till Tyler is run down. That may make it a little hard to get my dust through town without some lawman findin' out about it. I don't trust Ingalls now any more than I'd trust Luke Barron. Maybe less."

"I may have been wrong," Nan sighed.

"About comin' back with me?"

"About either of us coming back. Seeing that deputy just now made me realize how hopeless it would be for Father Matthew, even if he wanted to do something about what happened to poor Yokum Bos."

"One thing's sure, Nan. I ain't turnin' in this wagon to Timothy. I'll leave my horse at the livery overnight. I want you to come out to the claim with me. With Cune and probably the townspeople on the warpath about Ed Tyler, I don't want you staying here for the night, not even in your room back of Summers's store."

In spite of George Steele's decision, the horse team wanted very much to stop at the livery, and George had to saw hard on the reins to keep them headed up the street out of camp. Nan said nothing. The trip back to Eagle Cañon had given her a lot of time in which to think, and she found that she was no less distrustful now than her father, even when it came to Dr. Logan and the rôle he might have had in Yokum Bos's death. Surely the medical man must have suspected something of what had been going on at the jail. How could Sheriff Ingalls possibly have kept everyone in the dark as to how he was able to extract a confession from Yokum Bos? Neele Bos had been adamant that her husband had known nothing about Luke Barron and his gang. In fact, he had told her he thought Sheriff Ingalls had been blaming Luke Barron, whom no one had ever seen, for something that was being done by others, perhaps

79

even by the Avenging Angels themselves.

It was very dark, the starshine a pale phosphorescence, with moonlight casting but a slight glow over the terrain. Trees stood almost menacingly with the hint of a breeze rustling their leaves. The wagon creaked as it moved, the bit chains jingling. George Steele had just taken another bite off the tobacco plug he carried in a shirt pocket when Nan heard the sound of running footfalls and then felt a lurch at the rear of the wagon. She twisted around to see what had caused it.

A dark figure was getting his balance while rising to his feet in the box. Nan let out an exclamation. Now George Steele also turned his head and was looking at the phantom form.

"Jest keep this wagon movin' along," the figure said. "You're both covered."

"Ed Tyler? That you?" Steele asked.

"Shore is. George? Whose that with yuh?"

"Do you know the sheriff has a posse out after you?" Nan asked sharply.

"Reckon he has, ma'am." Ed cautiously advanced along the wagon box to the rear of the front seat. "If it looks like we're gonna be stopped, I'll duck out and would ask both you and your father to say you ain't seen me."

"I want to know one thing first, Ed," Steele said, having turned his head again in the direction of the road. "Is it true you're in with the Luke Barron gang, or is that just a woolly that damned sheriff made up?"

"Don't worry yourself on that account, George," Tyler replied, now standing directly behind them. "I quit Luke Barron some time back. Thet sheriff jest happened to see me on an old reward dodger, and it gave him ideas. Iffen you want the God's truth, both of you, neither me nor Luke Barron have had anything to do with these robberies."

"If you broke with Luke Barron," Nan inquired in a clear

voice, "how could you possibly be so sure he's not involved?"

"Reckon you got me there, ma'am. I wouldn't swear on no Bible mebbe, but I know Luke Barron, and I ain't seen him anywhere 'bout these parts."

"What does he look like?" Nan asked. She was still twisted around in her seat, but her high-peaked Stetson effectively concealed her face from the fugitive.

"Well, ma'am, he's a mite taller than I am an' better lookin'. He's got blond. . . ." Ed stopped suddenly, remembering too late that Luke had mentioned meeting Nan Steele in town. He could only hope he hadn't given her enough of a description to figure out who Luke Ashford really was.

"Go on, Mister Tyler," Nan prodded. "Luke Barron has blond . . . hair?"

"Reckon he does, ma'am, but thet ain't all thet uncommon, y'know. Anyway, the important thing is, he ain't around here none, or I would 'a' recognized him fer sure."

"If Luke Barron isn't around here, who got you out of jail?" Nan persisted. "From what Deputy Cune told us in town, someone dropped a load of bricks and smashed in the jail roof."

"Thet's right, ma'am." Ed had shoved the six-gun back into the waistband of his Levi's and was rubbing his right shoulder, as much from nervousness under the girl's intense questioning as from the painful exertion he had experienced, lifting himself over the tailgate of the wagon. "But it wouldn't be right fer me to tell you who busted me outta thet jail. I'm a wanted man 'round here, even if I ain't guilty, an' I don't rightly want to get anybody else in trouble. Let's jest say, I got me a friend who helped."

George Steele was actually chuckling softly. Now he spit tobacco juice to the side of the wagon. "You see what she's like, Ed? You cain't pull a sandy on this young 'un. She's the same way, naggin' me about my drinkin' a mite up at the claim.

81

Hell, what's a body to do fer a little relaxation with them holy rollers runnin' the show in town?"

"Doctor Logan says alcohol and tobacco are no good for you, Dad," Nan replied in an austere tone.

"Don't fergit gamblin' an' dancin', ma'am," Tyler put in.

"If you ask me," George Steele remarked bitterly, "that so-called doctor can take over playin' God Almighty when Father Matthew tires of doin' it!"

"Dad, Father Matthew smokes," Nan said. "I've smelled tobacco smoke on his clothes."

"Do tell, child," George Steele said, and chucked again. "Nothin' that old priest'd do would surprise me none."

In the meantime Ed Tyler had pulled out the makings and was trying to sprinkle tobacco into a rice paper, not an easy thing to do in the relative darkness and with the wagon lurching along the uneven road.

"Hope you don't mind, ma'am, but this here is the first smoke I've had in some time," Ed commented wryly, as he lifted the rolled paper to his mouth to lick the edge.

"Actually I like the aroma of burning tobacco," Nan said, surprising the fugitive with her candor. "I was only repeating what Doctor Logan tells people repeatedly."

"Them as'll listen to him," George Steele said bluntly. "For my part, I've had enough of your doc and Father Matthew and 'specially that bastard of a sheriff."

"Dad, he's not *my* doctor, not any more . . . if he ever was."

"I won't argue with you, girl, not when you're talkin' sense," her father returned, and laid a hand gently on her right thigh and gave her a squeeze. "You might as well know, Ed, that we was out to Yok's place an' found that old Yok had been worked over a-plenty before he was hanged."

"You tellin' me?" Ed Tyler said, expelling smoke. "I was

right there in thet jail, watchin' thet sheriff half burn him to death on thet witch's chair he's got."

"You saw it happen?" Nan asked, her words strained. "From the burns we saw on his body, Yokum Bos was tortured horribly."

"Thet's 'bout the size of it, ma'am," Tyler assured her. "They heated up thet iron chair they got in thet jail, with old Bos clamped down on it. He passed out a couple of times. They'd bring him back, throwing some of thet's doctor's water on him, an' takin' him outta the chair fer a spell. He was sobbin' and would've confessed to bein' the devil himself by the time they was through with him."

"I simply cannot believe that Father Matthew knows about this," Nan insisted. "He's such a kind and gentle man."

George Steele spat with obvious disgust but remained silent.

"Mebbe the priest ain't in on it," Ed Tyler conceded, inhaling again deeply, "but thet doctor shore is. He come by an' checked the old feller when he passed out fer the last time."

"Doctor Logan?" Nan raised a hand to her mouth and drew in her breath.

"The same, ma'am. I saw it all from my cell . . . which is one reason, I figger, they had to hang me, Luke Barron or no Luke Barron. I'm sure all them sheep they got a-prayin' at the Temple, an' buyin' the good doctor's water, an' workin' these here claims would act the same as you done, seein' Bos's body yerself before hearin' 'bout it from me."

Sheriff Ingalls lived in a shack in the shadow of the cliff wall on which stood the water tower, about a block down from the Temple and the mercantile. The spigot was turned off at dusk. One of the Avenging Angels, usually either Tiny Hart or Pink Morgan, guarded the water spigot over night, generally in shifts. For this service Dr. Logan compensated them four dollars a day and free water for themselves and their livestock. Tonight the spigot would have to be left unattended. The sheriff wanted Tiny and Pink to join him and Mart Kemp in going out to Yokum Bos's claim where they would assist him in making a thorough search for Bos's cache of gold dust. Once that was concluded, the sheriff intended to ride over to George Steele's claim and arrest the old man for illegal possession of, and personal use of, sour mash whiskey. Ray Cune was to watch the weapons post on the road into town, and Arlie Michaels was to remain at the jail with the prisoner, Ed Tyler.

It was nearing dusk when Sheriff Ingalls and his three deputies rode out of town, heading up the cañon road. Bos's claim was almost at the very end of the cañon, upcreek even from George Steele's claim. It would take over an hour to get there. Ingalls had only been at the claim a time or two, prior to Bos's arrest for conspiracy with the Barron gang, but he knew the prospector had a canvas tent pitched there where he had lived before leaving Eagle Cañon. He had built that cabin near Rattlesnake Mesa, living there with his wife after the disciples of the Temple had arrived and claimed what remained of the Eagle Cañon diggings for its membership. If good fortune were in his favor, George Steele would have a supply of his sour mash stored in reserve. It was Sheriff Ingalls's intention to move this supply as well as the physical distillery to the tent on Bos's claim. He would have to assign one of his deputies to guard the tent, but it was all in a good cause. It had been some time since either he or his deputies had been able to wet to their whistles with good rot-gut. To do it involved a trip down to Stirrup Gap, and with the pressure of events in Eagle Cañon such side journeys were few and far between.

Ingalls, sided by Mart Kemp, rode slightly ahead of the two other deputies down the trail as it meandered along the course of Eagle Creek. The sun had dipped behind the cliff to their left, silhouetting the trees and bushes along the rim into sharply etched shadows, stirring only faintly in the slight breeze that usually seemed always to haunt this area.

If Sam Ingalls personally had any regret, it was that Dr. Logan, who was in so many ways such an excellent man, should waste his time venting his spleen against drinking, gambling, tobacco, and other minor pleasures when such emotion would be better spent in ridding the district of such undesirable human refuse as that Chinaman and his family or that nigger at the livery stable who was such a pet to Father Matthew. *What a sorry state of affairs,* Sheriff Ingalls concluded to himself, as his right hand crept to the inside pocket of his broadcloth coat, fetching out a virgin plug of Virginia cut sweetened with honey, and bit off a healthy chew. Of course, there was a way in which this whole situation could be turned around, and that would be if the law could find Timothy Kamu imbibing some of George Steele's contraband whiskey (a secret pleasure of which the sheriff already suspected him), or Lee Hop could be found smoking tobacco, or gambling. No one had yet been hanged for such offenses, but, if the terror being brought by the Luke Barron gang should continue unabated, anything might become possible.

Mart Kemp was in many ways Ingalls's most trusted deputy, a man who had been charged with rape in Stirrup Gap, and who Ingalls had managed to have released for what he claimed was lack of evidence after the move to Eagle Cañon. Kemp was a man whose belligerent features could not be enhanced by his uniform as an Avenging Angel. Ingalls knew his brutal nature and counted on it.

Riding behind them, Tiny Hart was a great hulk of a man, five or six inches above six feet, with a huge body that made him almost the equal of two men. He had a heavy mustache and beard and relatively small dark eyes for his enormous head.

Beside him rode the diminutive Pink Morgan, so named for his faded, red hair and pink complexion. Hart had been a bouncer at the Golden Nugget down in Stirrup Gap. Morgan had been a lookout for the gambling tables at the same saloon. After the move of the disciples to Eagle Cañon, Sheriff Ingalls had recruited both men to join his Avenging Angels. Both men felt they were on their way to making a true clean-up. Tiny Hart, although twilight was now descending, had seen the sheriff reach into his coat pocket for his tobacco plug. This was his signal that it was O K to bring out a twisted cigar from the supply he carried in his shirt pocket. He could only chew on it until they arrived safely at their destination, for fear that one of the miners might see him smoking and report it to Dr. Logan.

Pink smiled in Tiny's direction and licked his thin lips. He knew the sheriff's plan for tonight included a raid on George Steele's distillery, and he was only biding his time until they had seized the cache Steele undoubtedly had hidden on his claim. Should Steele be shot down while resisting arrest — a definite possibility from the way Sheriff Ingalls had talked earlier — there might even be time for a little game of chance before they would have to head back to town.

Chapter Eight

It was very late. Dr. Royal Logan had finished his supper much earlier, but for some reason Lee Hop had not come in an orderly fashion to clear away the dishes. He hoped the Chinaman would do so yet tonight, but if not he would have to lecture him about conscientiousness when he brought the medical man's morning tea. It was only another irritating example of the lassitude that was on the verge of becoming endemic in Eagle Cañon and probably stemmed from the same impulse to court vice that had permitted George Steele, so far, to escape punishment, a lassitude that certainly wasn't being helped by Father Matthew's persistent smoking in private.

There were now five patients in hospital. That the situation were not more severe Dr. Logan attributed to his monitoring of the water supply, and he hoped eventually to extend his protection of the faithful to include supervision over what they were allowed to eat and drink. Elias Benton, a Kentuckian who was both a recent arrival and a convert, was suffering from what appeared to the doctor to be scurvy with the attendant skin lesions, swollen gums and ankles, and general anemia. Cal Woods who had been one of the faithful since Stirrup Gap had what, in Dr. Logan's opinion, was typhus fever and not typhoid. The symptoms of the two conditions were similar, but typhus fever was contracted from lice, and Woods had definitely been infested with them when he came to the tent hospital, complaining of a persistent, debilitating fever. Millie Gerhard and her two children, Arthur, six, and Henrietta, four, had been devout members of the Temple since its founding, and with Walt Gerhard had taken the long trek all the way from Centralia. These three were now all stricken with milk sickness. Walt, alone, had not been affected, primarily because he did not drink milk. The Gerhards had brought two cows West and had bred them with a bull during the time spent in Stirrup Gap. They were, therefore, one of the wealthier families among the early disciples. But now these cows had evidently ingested tremetol, the toxic element derived from white snakeroot that the doctor, after a recent visit prompted by a sick call from Walt Gerhard, had found growing on the Gerhard claim. All three remained in serious condition.

The doctor did not like to leave the tent hospital unattended, but with Nancy Steele gone for the day and now the night there was nothing he could do about it. He felt it imperative that he have a decisive talk with the old priest, both about the harsh punishments soon to be imposed on infidels and those prone to vice and to persuade Father Matthew that, unless he wanted to face a similarly harsh tribunal, he must abandon his use of tobacco and see to it that Timothy Kamu abandoned his practice of imbibing spirits. Logan was well aware of what had been going on, and since he had carefully assembled his data and his targets, all sinners were to be given one last chance to reform before the blade fell. He did not doubt that the new power that had come to him through his alliance with Sheriff Ingalls would finally force the old priest to terms.

Following his knock, Father Matthew opened the door to his sanctuary at the rear of the Temple and bade the medical man to enter. Logan sniffed the air as he did so, and his face creased into a haughty frown.

"The stink of tobacco is like unto the stench of Satan, Matthew," he remarked with cold indignity.

"Our Lord, when he walked the earth, was not so intolerant of others," the old priest said gently. "It is good to see you,

Royal. Come. Sit with me here by the cross."

Father Matthew ushered the doctor to the same chair that Luke Ashford had occupied earlier that day.

"I am trying to be gracious about this, Matthew," Dr. Logan remarked, as he placed his Stetson on the left corner of the backrest of the chair. He was wearing black and white checked trousers that seemed, somehow, incongruous with the austere blackness of his suitcoat and vest. His shirt collar was very starched and so tight about his neck beneath his black four-in-hand it gave his face an ashen hue, as if he were getting insufficient air to breathe. He sat down stiffly.

"I know you are," the old priest assured the medical man as he sat down across from him. "It is sometimes difficult for us to understand that God simply has more imagination than any of His creatures. In this lower sphere we must exercise our free will to find the right path. Those things that you despise are not part of the ark of the covenant. You must remember also, Royal, that our Lord transformed wine through a miracle into His blood, nor did He object to wine being served at the marriage feast at Canaan, but in fact replenished the supply when it ran out."

"Sophistry, Matthew," the doctor rejoined. "I've now arrived at the point in my own thinking on these matters that I believe mere prohibition is not enough. In Eagle Cañon we have to go a step further on the path of righteousness."

"Please, Royal, I would beg of you that this meeting not be permitted to disintegrate to the usual stalemate we arrive at when we discuss the prohibitions you have imposed on the faithful. More serious matters are afoot."

"What, Matthew, can be more serious than redemption and eternal life in heaven?"

The old priest was determined to ignore a recurrence of this fruitless debate. "Were you aware that Gopher Parsons has called a meeting tonight among the Eagle Cañon miners?"

"Whatever for?" the doctor asked, somewhat surprised.

"I cannot be certain, Royal, but Timothy did pick up something concerning it. Apparently Gopher and some of the others wish to organize a vigilance committee so they can ship out safely the gold they have had to hoard because of the Luke Barron gang."

"That's nonsense! Sam Ingalls and his Avenging Angels are sure to get to the bottom of these robberies."

"Robberies, Royal, and now murder."

"Yes. I realize the threat is a grave one, but I have complete confidence in the sheriff when it comes to Luke Barron."

"Well, if my information is correct, your confidence is not shared by the faithful."

"Then I would suggest, Matthew, that you condemn any such action in your sermon this Sunday. Indeed, for some time now Sheriff Ingalls has prohibited all possession of firearms in Eagle Cañon as a means of preventing bloodshed. Perhaps the best solution would be a combination of these approaches. We can simply remind the faithful that it is part of Temple law that believers must accept surrender of their firearms as their means to redemption, and that vigilance committees are no less the work of the devil than alcohol, gambling, tobacco, and the rest. And that brings me to another reason for my visit tonight. When we broke with the Roman Church, you reintroduced the use of wine in Holy Communion, the way the Lutherans use it in celebration of the Lord's Supper. This, I feel, was a terrible mistake. How can we expect the faithful to abstain totally from alcohol when we include its use as part of a sacrament? It's a practice that must end at once. You could also make that part of your sermon on Sunday. I should advise you, Matthew, that Sam Ingalls and I are in agreement that more drastic measures may be needed to insure that the faithful are no longer exposed to alcohol in any form whatsoever."

"Oh?" Father Matthew asked, his high forehead furrowed with an almost anguished distress.

"Yes," Dr. Logan continued blandly. "It is not the province of human beings to mete out final judgment. That alone belongs to God. But we can and must mete out temporal punishment."

"Just what have you in mind, Royal?"

A frigid smile came to the doctor's constrained features. "It is, I believe, within our province to dispatch sinners at once to God's final judgment once their sin is known."

"Meaning?"

"I presume you know that the manufacture or sale of distilled spirits these days are prohibited in Her Majesty's Canadian Provinces."

"Yes, I have heard that."

"And it isn't working. Do you know why?"

"I am sure that you do."

Dr. Logan ignored the sarcasm in the old priest's tone. "Because American citizens are smuggling distilled spirits into the Provinces. Now, I am as certain as we are sitting here tonight that in time our government will similarly come to outlaw alcohol, gambling, tobacco, and the rest. After all, look at Eagle Cañon in comparison to any other American boom camp. The camp is closed down completely by nightfall. No saloons, no dance halls, no brothels, none of the impious diseases you can find as near by as Stirrup Gap. We have built ourselves a model community, Matthew. How long, though, before someone as close to us as Stirrup Gap starts making alcohol available to the faithful, as is happening today in the Canadian Provinces? The only feasible response for us is to put teeth into our Temple laws. If Her Majesty's Government were truly resolved to stop Americans from bootlegging into the Canadian Provinces, it would stop in a moment once a perpetrator understood that to be caught selling alcohol or drinking it was punishable by death. Now, I don't mean to invoke due process. Due process ought to have nothing to do with it. Possession alone should be what the lawyers term *prima facie* evidence of culpability. Anyone found in possession of alcohol, or tobacco, or dice, or cards should be summarily executed. How long do you think Americans would bootleg into the Provinces if they knew the penalty was immediate death?"

"I rather imagine," Father Matthew replied, "that there would still be some who would figure the risk worth the candle."

"For a while, maybe, but like battling any disease through amputation, or letting a plague run its course, there will eventually come a time when all the evil-doers have been removed. Then those who fear God would at last be free forever of these terrible scourges."

Dr. Logan fell silent, obviously inflated by the knowledge that he had made an insuperable defense for his case. Father Matthew's light blue eyes flashed, and his knuckles showed white where his hands gripped the polished wooden armrests of his chair. Yet, when he spoke, his voice was calm.

"And you believe this position of yours is consistent with the Hippocratic oath?" he asked.

"I do," Dr. Logan asserted positively. "The Hippocratic oath requires of the physician that he prescribe for the good of a patient, that he give no deadly drug, that he perform no abortions, cut no stones, leaving that work to the stonecutter, and that a physician always act only for the welfare of the patient."

"Yet," said Father Matthew, nodding his head, "the way you would have it, acting only for the welfare of one patient now requires of you that you must destroy other patients. I seem to recollect that part of the oath also admonishes the physician to keep himself from intentional ill-doing. You are blinding yourself to God's most precise commandment . . . *thou shalt not kill!*"

"Matthew, what is physical death compared to spiritual death and eternal damnation? Ultimately, by destroying the would-be destroyers, we will be saving lives. There can be no more sacred vow than that."

"It has been a long journey we have made, Royal," the old priest said, leaning back in his chair and finally relaxing his grip. "I am no less and no more a sinner than any man or any woman in our congregation. In Centralia my name was Ishmael. You came forward then, in what I presumed was my darkest hour, to show me a new path toward what for so long I had sought . . . *lux æterna* . . . the eternal light of divine wisdom. The experience for me was akin to what happened to Saint Paul on the road to Damascus . . . you helped me to perceive that light. But over these last days and hours I have been haunted by a terror greater than any I felt in Centralia. There, my sin was only my own. But now I am responsible for all those who have followed me, and no less for those who have joined our congregation since we have come West. And, therefore, should I . . . through my most grievous fault . . . even if with the best intentions . . . mislead others into folly and iniquity, my sin would be a thousand times compounded."

"Matthew . . . ," Dr. Logan interrupted.

"Please let me finish, Royal. I told you previously in this conversation that I am convinced that God has infinitely more imagination than we mere mortals. How could it be otherwise? We are given to understand so little. But there is one thing, as a sinner, that I do understand. And that is the nature of sin. At the bottom of it all, I suppose, is the contradiction between the Old Testament and the New."

"Contradiction?" Dr. Logan interrupted again. "There can be no contradiction in what is divine."

"The history of our Christian faith embodies that contradiction, Royal."

"And what contradiction, pray, is that?"

"Intolerance."

"My God, that is blasphemy."

"Then let me add that to my other sins, Royal. I wasn't sure when we heard Sam Ingalls's testimony in council about Yokum Bos that he was guilty of collusion with the Luke Barron gang."

"But Sam has the man's confession."

"You and I should know better, Royal. Even if Yokum Bos confessed he was Luke Barron himself, we should have mistrusted it. No one sinned more against that man than I did in Centralia . . . until the moment that I acquiesced in his execution. At that moment I betrayed him more even than when I had coveted his wife. I may still be walking in darkness now, but I shall not betray one more soul to this fiendishness."

"What fiendishness?" Dr. Logan asked, his features taking on an apoplectic hue perhaps enhanced by the tightness of his starched collar.

Father Matthew knew in his soul that finally he had reached the end of this trail he had been following for so long, where Royal Logan wielded so decisive an influence over what he did and said. There had once been a time when the doctor's support and encouragement had been his only succor. Now, as he saw the medical man's views coming to dominate every aspect of the Temple of the Redeemed, even condoning what surely any sane and rational person could only regard as murder, and all in the name of righteousness, he had come irretrievably to a crossroads, and it seemed that a break was inevitable.

Outside there came the sound of a loud crash.

"What was that?" Dr. Logan demanded, rising swiftly from his chair.

Lee Hop had been on his way back toward town, still afoot, dejected now and more than a little apprehensive over what he had seen at George Steele's cabin as well as what he had earlier heard transpire in the conversation between the doctor and the sheriff at the Eagle Cañon tent hospital, when he detected the slow approach of a wagon. Hiding behind a clump of bushes along miners' trail, he had waited in silence until the wagon was nearly past. It was the sound of Nan Steele's voice, and then that of George Steele himself, that prompted him to run out into the road and trail the wagon as swiftly as his flat-bottomed shoes could carry him.

"Geolge Steele!" he called while running. "Geolge Steele, stop!"

"That sounds like Lee Hop," George Steele said, pulling on the reins and looking toward the back trail at the same time.

"It is thet Chinaman from the café in town," Ed Tyler clarified, as Lee Hop came up alongside the wagon bed, moving in the direction of the driver's seat.

"I'll be whelped if it ain't!" Steele remarked, still tugging on the reins even though the team, which had been going at a very slow walk, had already stopped.

"You cannot go home, Geolge," Lee Hop said, placing a hand on the sideboard, his voice audible if somewhat breathy.

"Why in tarnation not?" Steele demanded, peering down hard at the diminutive figure whose face was visible only dimly in the moonlight and starshine.

"The sheliff and some of his men ally come," Lee replied. "Doctol Logan sent them to kill you. They haven't found whiskee masheen yet, but they found whiskee. I saw them

95

dlingking and know what they say."

"That can't be true, Lee," Nan protested, leaning in his direction. "Why would Royal want my father killed?"

"Because he dlinks and makee othler peeple dlink. Doctol man say Geolge is eevil man, Missy Nan. I no lie. I listen to talk between doctol man and sheliff. That's why I come to waln Geolge. I walk allyway from town, missy."

Ed Tyler laughed in spite of himself, louder perhaps than was prudent. "You say, Lee, the sheriff and his men are getting drunk on George's whiskey, an' thet's why they want to kill 'im? 'cause he lets 'em get drunk?"

"Doctol man don' know they gletting dlunk," Lee Hop returned. If he was surprised to find Ed Tyler in the wagon with the George Steele and his daughter, it was not betrayed by any inflection in his voice. "He pro'bly wannee them killed, too, if he see them."

"Dad, I can't believe this," Nan said urgently to her father.

"I believe it," Ed Tyler affirmed. "Thet doctor was as much a part of gettin' a phony confession out of Yokum Bos as thet sidewinder of a sheriff was."

"They both in it t'glether, Missy Nan," Lee Hop insisted.

"You say they ain't found my still yet, Lee?" Steele asked.

"No. Onlee whiskee. They dlink and dlink."

"I know where you got thet still hid, George," Ed Tyler said. "They ain't gonna find it at night like this. You can lay to thet."

"They want gold, Geolge, you gold and Yokum gold. They search for gold. That's what they wannee. They say they no findee Yokum gold. They think you havee. They say they makee you tell about gold before they kill you. Allee I know. Then I makee back for town."

"I reckon yer right, Lee," George Steele said. "Now, Ed, you give this feller a hand up into the wagon. We cain't be

96

a-palaverin' out here all night without someone gettin' wise. I'll turn this rig around, an' we'll head over to Gopher Parsons's claim. I know for a fact he don't want no part of them devils callin' themselves the opposite."

Nan Steele remained silent as Ed Tyler leaned over and gave Lee Hop his hand. The Chinese used a spoke in the right front wheel for footing to help himself up and over the sideboard. Then George began turning the team in the middle of the road.

Nan was actually more anxious than she had been before. It wasn't merely a matter of Dr. Logan's being in collusion with Sheriff Ingalls. What Lee Hop had told them only corroborated what Ed Tyler had been saying. No, the truly terrifying thing in all of this was the way in which the latest turn of events totally undermined and made senseless their return to Eagle Cañon. Where could her father hide that he would not eventually be found by the Avenging Angels? While it was personally humiliating to her to learn how wrong she had been in her esteem for Royal Logan, she had already decided — as gently, to be sure, as she could — to decline his proposal of marriage. But, now, even that decision was fraught with potential danger. According to Lee Hop, Royal Logan was as intent on her father's death as Sheriff Ingalls, if for an entirely different reason. That Ingalls and his men were bound by greed did not really surprise Nan in the least. Lust for gold was the one thing that made the ruthless murder of Yokum Bos comprehensible. Pity the poor miners who now had to contend not only with whatever gang was masquerading under the ægis of Luke Barron, but even with those who were supposedly sworn to protect the miners from such brigandage and were themselves no less bent on the same objective.

Ed Tyler was filling in Lee Hop about what had happened in the Eagle Cañon jail and about his escape — the two of them sitting now across from each other in the wagon bed immediately behind the driver's seat — with George occasionally adding a comment to Tyler's narrative.

"Dad," Nan said suddenly, "give me one good reason why we shouldn't head this wagon straight back through town and go down to Stirrup Gap? We won't find a better chance to get past the guards they have there than we have tonight, with the sheriff and so many of his men out at our place."

Ed paused in mid-sentence when he heard Nan speak.

"I guess there's no easy answer to that, Nan," her father said in his slow-reasoning way, " 'cept all the dust I got hid, and part of Yok's, too, is up at my claim, an' I'm not ready yet to give up without some kind of fight."

"You may never live to see that dust, Dad. Not if what Lee says is true. What chance did Yokum Bos have?"

"Pardon me, ma'am," Ed Tyler broke in, "but I'm willin' to side your pa. My friend, Luke . . . Ashford . . . in town feels thet same way, I'm sure. If your pa can get some of these miners together, I figger thet sheriff an' his gang will have a fight on their hands they can't lick."

"Ed's right, Nan," George Steele said. "Runnin' away won't bring old Yok back, an' I got other friends here I don't want to see killed fer their gold."

"If you was to be able to handle this rig, ma'am," Ed continued, "you could take Lee Hop here back to town with you, while your pa and I could stay with Gopher Parsons and work from there. Luke is stayin' at the livery stable while he's in town. You could get a message to him 'bout what's goin' on. You could also keep an eye on thet doctor an' know what moves he an' the sheriff plan next. It would be a tol'able big help to us all if you was to keep your ear to the ground."

"You can hardly expect me to continue working with Doctor Logan, knowing what I now know about him?" Nan flashed, turning sideways in her seat to look directly at Ed Tyler.

"Beggin' yer pardon, ma'am," Tyler said, looking up at her silhouette directly above him, "but thet doc ain't got no idea what yuh know an' what yuh don't know. You cain't go mixin' up sideoats grama with burro grass. I figger the rannihans most against whiskey an' the like are like thet murderin' sheriff an' his men. They want to stop others from doin' it so they ain't tempted themselves. Then, when they come upon it an' they figger no one's lookin', they jump in with both feet. Even a man ordinarily not inclined to drink hisself will find himself buildin' up a mighty thirst the moment yuh tell him he cain't have it. Thet's the way we're made is all."

"Listen up, girl," Nan's father interjected. "Ed's talkin' sense."

"He may be talking sense to you, Dad, but I'm not going anywhere near someone who wants to kill my father."

"I'll wager you ain't got a better scheme to save old George's hide than the one I'm proposin', ma'am," Ed persisted. "Jest what I been hearin' here tonight is almost enough to give all of us a fair notion as to who's playin' at Luke Barron in Eagle Cañon."

"But it couldn't be Sheriff Ingalls," Nan said, not sounding very convincing even to herself.

"Why not? Who's got old Yokum's claim? Ingalls. Who's at your pa's place now, lookin' to make him tell where his gold's hid? Same jasper."

"And you believe Royal Logan is in it with him?" Nan asked.

"Nope. I reckon the doc is playin' his own game. Some folks is crazy mean like thet sheriff of yourn. Some's jest plain crazy. Thet fits the doc. But even Logan ain't no complete lunatic. He's got most of the folks in Eagle Cañon off John Barleycorn mebbe, but he's sellin' 'em water, ain't he? How's thet make him any different in his way than if ole George here was to open up a saloon and sell his brew across a bar to them as is willin' to pay fer it?"

"Doctor Logan knows people get sick and die from drinking the wrong kind of water," Nan argued. "He also says people have been known to die from drinking too much whiskey. I've heard him say, if we can stamp out alcohol and tobacco in this generation, it will save all the children of the future."

"I don't doubt Logan thinks thet way, Nan," George Steele cut in, "but who elected him as God Almighty in these parts?"

"Doctol Logan," Lee Hop supplied.

"Yon celestial's got thet right, ma'am," Ed Tyler pressed his case. "I'm not much of a hand when it comes to religion, but I seem to remember my ma tellin' me as how it was jest such a fight a long ways back thet . . . as she told it . . . made fer heaven an' hell to begin with."

Gopher Parsons may have been in his sixties or early seventies. It was impossible to tell. In the somewhat distant past he had been a mountain man, later a wagon train guide and scout, who had long possessed only contempt for the boomers with their lust and greed for gold and who ran helter-skelter from one strike to the next. He had been married for a time to a Crow woman. He had a number of children, scattered in the West, but he had been alone in Stirrup Gap when word reached him through George Steele of the rich strike at Eagle Cañon. It was at this moment that his lifelong contempt vanished in a flash of gold fever, and he was off to Eagle Creek.

"I'm an old man, an' I've lived a long time," he had once told Nan Steele when visiting at her father's claim. "I've seen all the Injun varmints in the Rocky Mountains . . . have fought 'em . . . lived with 'em. The Crows is one brave nation . . . the bravest of all the Injuns. They fi't like white men. They don't kill yuh in the dark like the Blackfoot varmints, takin' yer scalp and runnin' the way a sidewider does. I cain't see so well now as I did forty years back, but I can still hit the game I want. I'd be even a better shot iffen it weren't for this infernal humor in my eyes I caught three years ago bringing emigrators over the daysart."

Parsons, for political reasons, had joined the Temple of the Redeemed, but he was rarely at Father Matthew's services. When Nan had urged him to consult Dr. Logan about the problem he said he was having with his eyesight, he had demurred. "I jist don't cotton none to thet jasper," he had told her. "He'd probably tell me to stop drinkin' yer daddy's brew, or not to want to wanna dance with a pretty girl sech as yerself. 'Sides, I been to a doctor in Denver City. He said I burned my eyes good in the daysart an' t'weren't nothin' I cain do 'bout it, 'cept stay away from daysarts."

Now he held a kerosene lantern above his head and was studying the figure on the seat to whom George had handed the reins before clambering down.

"Who's that purty boy yuh got with yuh, George?" Parsons asked, peering hard in the glow cast by the lamplight.

"That's no boy, Gopher," Steele told him. "That's my girl, Nan."

"Well, sir, she shore ain't dressed like no female I ever seen, an' I've seen the elephant an' heerd him roar."

"It's really just me, Mister Parsons," Nan said, the shadows concealing the blush that had come to her cheeks.

"Iffen it's really you, Miss Nancy, how come yer in disguise?" Parsons persisted.

"We've been out to see Neele Bos," Nan replied before her father could speak. "Dad will tell you all about it."

"I recognize yuh, now, Miss Nancy," Parsons assured her. "Say, George, what're yuh doin' with thet Chinaman in tow, and whose thet owlhoot there in back?"

Ed Tyler jumped down from the wagon bed and introduced himself to the old miner.

"Heerd tell they was gonna hang you tomorry," Parsons said suspiciously. "Yer s'posed to be in with that Luke Barron gang."

"There ain't no Luke Barron gang, Gopher," George Steele put in. "Thet's what Ed Tyler an' I've come over here to tell you. The Barron gang broke up some time back and hasn't been operating anywhere since."

"Well, now, George, it's kinda funny yuh should say thet," Parsons commented, holding his lantern closer to Ed Tyler so he could better see the fugitive. "Thet's jest the idee the boys an' I had at the vigilante meeting we was holdin' here earlier. We come to reckon the murderin' varmints is a mite closer to home than this here Luke Barron."

"Lee," Nan broke in, "why don't you climb up front and sit with me?"

"Sure thing, missy," Lee Hop responded, and agilely climbed up and perched himself beside her on the driver's seat.

"Now, jest hold on here a dang minute, Miss Nancy," Parsons said, raising the lantern again in her direction. "What makes yuh think yuh cain handle thet wagon by yer lonesome, 'specially late at night like this?"

"We can't go back to my claim, Gopher," George Steele explained. "Lee Hop's been there, and Sheriff Ingalls and his deputies have taken it over, waitin' for me to come back. Thet's why we come here. I figger we can hide out here for a spell. Ed's willin' to side us, and I got no reason not to trust him, seein' as what's been done to old Yok."

"George," Parsons protested, "I'm tellin' yuh thet no girl cain drive no wagon in the dark, despite Miss Nancy bein' dressed in them togs. T'ain't right nohow."

"Lee'll be with me," Nan said.

"Ha! I'll augur thet Chinaman ain't never fired a gun."

"Gopher, be reasonable," George Steele replied. "I can't go into town. Ed can't go."

"Then let Miss Nancy stay here, at least till it's light," Parsons argued. "If yer so all-fired shore thet sheriff is out to get yuh, how do yuh know what he'll do with Miss Nancy should he catch her?"

"I'll be all right, Mister Parsons," Nan assured him. "If I leave now, I can get this wagon back to the livery stable before morning. I'm sure Timothy will cover for Dad and me. If anybody asks me, I'll just say I don't know where Dad is, that he headed back to his claim."

Gopher Parsons shook his head broadly. "George, iffen she was my gal, I'd take that 'un across my knee, britches an' all. Then she wouldn't be in no shape to sit a wagon seat, much less give me any backtalk."

Steele decided to ignore the old miner. He reached up and patted Nan's right thigh. "Jest be careful, girl."

"Thanks, Dad," Nan said softly. "So long Mister Parsons . . . Mister Tyler." She signaled for the team to move and began to turn the wagon back toward the main trail.

"She knows how to handle a team, Gopher," George Steele said. "Taught her myself when she was some younger than she is now."

"I'm gettin' too old, I reckon," Parsons sighed, bringing the lantern back to his side. "Young folks these days do jest as they damned please, no matter what yer tell 'em. My own daughter's the same way, an' she's half Crow, an' yuh'd think'd know better."

"Was it thet different when you was a young 'un?" Ed Tyler asked the old miner.

"Cain't swear as to thet, son. I run away from home when I was eleven."

Years of vigilance had made Luke, of necessity, a light sleeper. It seemed to him that he had just dropped off to sleep when, once more, he became aware of a tread on the narrow staircase leading to his room at the rear of the loft of the livery stable where he had left the door ajar. From the sounds, it appeared to be more than one man.

"You-all awake, Mistah Ashford," Timothy Kamu whispered loudly from the top of the stairs.

"Reckon I am now, Timothy. What is it? That deputy back to search this room again?"

"No, suh. You've done got a caller here. You-all dressed?"

"I'm not wearin' my boots, if that's what you mean. How about some light?"

"No, suh. Dis here meetin' is best done in de dark."

"O K, come ahead."

Luke threw back the blankets and placed his stocking feet on the cold boards of the loft floor. His hand had crept under his pillow and had laid hold of the .38 Colt. The light was virtually non-existent, but Luke could make out another darker shadow coming forward with the hosteler.

"I'm not armed, Mister Ashford," a voice said softly, a contralto that sounded somehow familiar.

"Come ahead, then," Luke said, releasing his hand from the Colt. "Can I light a match, Timothy, so I can see who's come callin'?"

"Best not, least till we're inside your room an' de door's shut."

Luke waited silently while Timothy, apparently holding the hand of the smaller figure, entered the room. He paused to close the door to the loft.

"Now?" Luke asked.

"Now, suh," Timothy replied. "Dey's a candle nailed to

the wall at the head of yore bunk."

Luke took a match from his shirt pocket, struck it, and, by holding it aloft over the bunk, found the candlestick Timothy had indicated. Turning, he recognized the girl wearing the Stetson, man's waist overalls, and plain cotton shirt he had met on the main street of Eagle Cañon when he had first ridden into town.

"I remember you," Luke said. "I thought I recognized your voice."

"You only heard it once," she said.

"Got an ear for voices."

"Dey's a chair ovah dere, Miss Nan," Timothy said, gesturing with an arm. "Lee Hop's waitin' downstahrs. Ah'll be down dere, if you-all need me."

"Thanks, Timothy," Nan said, walking the brief distance to the chair. "You might as well make yourself comfortable on that bunk, mister. I've a story to tell, but not a whole lot of time in which to tell it."

"Anything you say, miss." Luke sat down on the bunk and reached to his pockets for the makings. "Mind if I smoke?"

"It's as dangerous in this town as wearing a gun, but, if you want to, go ahead. My name's Nancy Steele. Your friend, Ed Tyler, tells me your name is Luke Ashford."

Luke nodded as he rolled a cigarette. Nan took off her Stetson and shook out her long, light blonde hair. "That's the only trouble with these hats . . . what they do to your hair."

"Reckon so, Miss Steele. I meant to ask you when I saw you in the street below . . . why the man's get-up? . . . an' how come you to see Ed? You know, he escaped jail tonight?"

"So I've heard." Then, for the first time, the girl laughed, and her face filled with the same sparkle Luke had earlier seen in her eyes. "You can call me Nan. Everybody else does."

"Nan, it is. An' my name's Luke. Now, how did you come to see Ed?"

Nan rose from the rather spindly chair, placed her Stetson on the seat, and looked directly at Luke as he lit his cigarette. There was a lot to tell this stranger and, as she had said, not a whole lot of time in which to tell it. She started at the beginning, with the visit she and her father had paid to the Bos cabin, and then what had transpired when Ed had jumped their wagon on the way to the Nan Steele mine, and finally what Lee Hop had told them about what the sheriff and his men were doing.

"Had Sheriff Ingalls and most of the Avenging Angels been in Eagle Cañon tonight, it might not have been so easy for Ed Tyler to break out of jail," she concluded. "They tortured him, you know?"

"Yes . . . Nan . . . I know," Luke said, dropping his cigarette to the floor and grinding it out with a boot heel. "Since you've been so open with me, I might as well be the same with you. I'm afraid I know who broke Ed out of jail earlier tonight."

"I just thought you might," Nan said, and smiled. "Did the sheriff take away your gun."

"As a matter of fact," Luke said, also smiling and lifting the pillow on the bunk, "he didn't. It's right here."

"Did you know that someone tonight removed all the guns from the check point before you get into Eagle Cañon?"

"Do you have any idea who did it?" Luke asked.

"No," Nan admitted, "but had I stayed a bit longer at Gopher Parsons's claim, I believe I would have learned the answer."

"I hope you're right, Nan. I'm afraid, from what you've told me, that those men are going to need all the guns they can get their hands on."

"You can find out for yourself in the morning when you

ride out to Gopher Parsons's claim. Dad and Ed are both there."

"How much of all this does Timothy know?"

"Probably a whole lot more now that he's talked to Lee Hop than he did before."

"Do you reckon Father Matthew can be trusted, Nan?"

"I don't know. Under ordinary circumstances I doubt that I would trust you or Ed Tyler, but at this point there doesn't seem to be any alternative. I'm staying in town. I have a room at the back of the mercantile and work as a nurse with Doctor Logan. I'll see both him and Father Matthew in the morning. I may know a whole lot more then."

"I don't have to tell you how dangerous these men are . . . ?" Luke asked, rising.

"Doctor Logan has asked me to marry him."

"Do you plan to turn him down?"

"No . . . ," Nan said slowly, "certainly not right away. I may have been naïve, Luke, but I'm not a fool."

"Surely not," Luke agreed. "For what it's worth, Nan, you can count on me and Ed to help all we can."

"I had best be going now," she said, and walked to the chair where she picked up the high-crowned Stetson once again and put it on her head, tucking her light blonde hair beneath the brim.

Luke asked softly: "If we get out of this, might you be willing to come to a dance with me down to Stirrup Gap?"

Nan paused and gazed at him circumspectly in the flickering candlelight. "When we get out of this, Luke Ashford, I want any dancing we do to be done right here . . . in Eagle Cañon."

It was then that they heard the sound of a horse's hoofs out front, as a rider headed out of town up the cañon trail down which Nan had earlier come.

Chapter Nine

Since he had returned to his sanctuary at the back of the Temple following the confusion and excitement in the wake of Ed Tyler's escape from the Eagle Cañon jailhouse, Father Matthew had devoted himself to meditation and prayer. He had read and re-read Chapter Twenty-Eight of the Book of Job. "But where shall wisdom be found? and where is the place of understanding?" It was God who had answered, who had said: "Behold, the fear of the Lord, that is wisdom; and to depart from evil is understanding." It had never in his life struck him so profoundly as it had earlier this evening that, rather than having departed from evil, he had been embracing it.

Father Matthew had believed that he had lived long enough to have learned that most important lesson — when Satan grinned at him, to grin back. He had even come to believe that this was the highest, the most exalted state of elation, of jollity a human being could achieve. It had seemed that everything else that people regarded as joy was only a foreshadowing, an intimation of this, the finest art that brings the greatest pleasure. Yet, this time, when Satan had grinned at him, he had not grinned back. Indeed, he had demurred. He had backed away. He had sought to persuade by reason and moral argument.

For the last hour he had been kneeling before the great wooden crucifix, impervious to the coldness of the pine-board and the coldness in the room — for at this elevation it became cold at night even after the hottest days. His soul was besieged by torment. When he had first come to Eagle Cañon, it had been his custom, as the Temple was being built, to wander at night, wending his way arduously to the summit of the cliff on which Dr. Logan had located the artesian well that supplied his water tank. It hadn't made any sense, pure water being so high up above Eagle Creek now clouded and polluted by the incessant placer mining, but it had been there, and Royal Logan had located the spring. There on the rim with the stars spread icily across the deep blue of the evening sky where there would often be a strong wind, but sometimes, too, just a gentle breeze, Father Matthew had believed that he had at last found the road embodying the happiness of all true wanderers.

All day and into the night in those days, far more than now, so many wayfarers had come on horses, on mules, even on donkeys, by stagecoach from Stirrup Gap, by wagon, by cart as had Lee Hop and his family, by any means they could find, wayfarers who had found a direction in life. Would it not have been strange, indeed, that when so many had found a direction that he should not have found one? But he had. The lamplight from the growing township, the noise, the smell of woodsmoke on the wind and frying food had pleased him. The air of Eagle Cañon and the wind from Rattlesnake Mesa beyond, wafting down from mountains and across Eagle Creek, had laid itself boldly against his face.

"Behold, the fear of the Lord, that is wisdom; and to depart from evil is understanding." He knew now, in his anguish, that he had lost the finest art. He was no longer able to grin back at the devil. The dark son of God had not really tricked him. Father Matthew had had his eyes open — wide, innocent eyes they had once been, and so lacking in wisdom — and he knew now that, precisely when he should have grinned back, he had flinched. He had, because of his belief in the power of reason, only resorted to sophistry. When the devil grins at you, it is wrong, even sinful, to presume that you can argue or convince by logical demonstration or moral debate. After all, that was only to challenge Satan by proposing to engage in a game he himself had invented and for which he had long ago created all the rules.

Eli, Eli, lama sabachthani! The Hebrew words resounded through Father Matthew's soul, for this first time with true understanding. Even the son of God could become so estranged to the Lord, through physical suffering and spiritual affliction, that he believed He was forsaken, that the Lord had become lost to Him. It was that way now for Father Matthew. All of his conscious life he had sought the Lord and now, in this darkest of nights, he felt the Lord was lost to him. "My God, my God, why hast thou forsaken me?" he whispered in prayer, his cheeks wet with tears.

It was at this somewhat inopportune moment that there came a soft knock on the back door. Father Matthew's first inclination was to ignore the knock. But then it came again, and he couldn't. Struggling to his feet, his cassock showing the imprints of where he had knelt, he had a good idea who it was but felt it was too late at night to call out. He wiped his eyes with a white handkerchief he carried in his sleeve, replaced it, then lifted the latch and threw open the heavy wooden door.

"Timothy," he said, seeing the man only vaguely in the faint glow of candlelight from within the room, "is there more trouble?"

"Ah'm afraid dere is, Father."

"Come on in, then, and tell me about it. I was at prayer."

"Ah'm truly sorry to disturb you-all, Father," Timothy said as the priest closed the door behind him, "but Miss Nan is ovah at de stable talkin' to that gent you hired to look aftah things. Ah've done learned from Lee Hop who was with Miss Nan an' her daddy tonight dat dere was somethin' wrong with the body of Yokum Bos. Accordin' to Lee Hop, Miss Nan and her daddy done both saw it, and dere weren't no mistake. Dat

110

man was burned all ovah beefore he died. He was tortured, Father."

The old priest stood before the door, the stable man facing him. His face had turned pale involuntarily, although in view of what he had heard earlier from Dr. Logan, he wasn't totally surprised. "Sheriff Ingalls?"

"Dat's what Lee Hop says, Father. He also says dat he overheard de doctor and de sheriff talkin', and dat dey plan to kill George Steele . . . when dey find him. De sheriff an' his Avengin' Angels is out lookin' for him now, which is why dey wasn't 'round earlier when dat Luke Barron man broke outta de jail. Miss Nan jest got back with de wagon a short time befo' Ray Cune comes ovah from de jail to get his horse to ride out to George Steele's claim. A few minutes sooner an' he would 'a' seen her for shore. Dat girl is mighty lucky. Ray done said dat he's leavin' only Arlie Michaels to watch de road. Traffic is quiet tonight, as it has been for de last few nights. Mostly dose dat come now show up durin' de day an' gets turned back when dey finds all de claims is done claimed."

"Where is Nan Steele now?" Father Matthew asked, visibly upset with what he had just heard.

"She's ovah at de livery stable, seein' dat man you done hired today. She had a message for him from her father and Gopher Parsons, accordin' to Lee Hop. Also dat escaped convict Ray Cune and Arlie Michaels was lookin' for earlier is out to the Parsons claim."

"In view of the travesty of justice committed against Yokum Bos, we can be grateful that this other man escaped, I suppose," Father Matthew said, assuring himself as much as Timothy. "Do you think Nan Steele is in danger?"

"From de sheriff, mebbe, but Ah don't think from de doctor. Ah've heard dat he's in love with her."

"I've heard the same thing. I understand Doctor Logan has

111

even proposed marriage to her." The old priest's face remained ashen with the distress he was feeling. He went over to his favorite chair in the shadow of the great wooden crucifix. "Don't leave me, Timothy. Please, take a seat. I have to think this through."

"But, Father, shouldn't Ah get back to de livery to see what's goin' on between Miss Nan an' dat stranger? She's alone with him, you know." The black man was nervously holding his hat in his hands and was glancing toward the door, although otherwise he had not moved.

"Timothy, please," the old priest said gently, "can you not watch even one hour with me?"

"Shorely, Father, if dat's what you-all want." He walked cautiously over to the chair opposite Father Matthew and sat down, still holding onto his hat.

"Is there more? Have you heard anything else? What does Lee Hop think?"

"Lee done said he's taking his family from Eagle Cañon as soon as he can . . . tomorrow, mebbe. With only Arlie Michaels on guard at de check point, he might decide to do it tonight yet."

"On foot?"

"He's afraid for his life, Father. So must we all be."

Father Matthew became abstracted, and Timothy sat in patient silence. He had not known what to expect, but he had seen the old priest similarly preoccupied in the past, and on those occasions the mere assurance of his physical presence had been sufficient. It was his love and honor for the holy man that now held him to the chair, even though the urgent prompting was inside him that Lee Hop was right, and it might well be the time to leave Eagle Cañon.

The priest's mind was not on Nan Steele, Luke Ashford, or Ray Cune's ride out to the Nan Steele Mine. It was no longer even on Dr. Royal Logan. He was besieged by a terror far greater than any of human origin could be. So much of his spiritual life had been concerned with his contemplation of the Holy Ghost. When the occasion demanded, as it sometimes did in his dealings with the members of his congregation, he could plead with Christ for His divine intercession on behalf of another human soul, or even on behalf of his own, but now his terror was of the wrath of God. The lightning drama of those last days envisioned in The Apocalypse, the merciless sufferings of Job notwithstanding that God, through His omniscience, should have known beforehand that His disciple would remain true to his faith, the inexorability of the Deluge — this was now the face of God before which Father Matthew stood transfixed.

When he had first heard from Timothy about what had really happened to Yokum Bos in the privacy of the jail, his inclination had been to go at once to Neele Bos. But what could he say to her after all of this time, and what would be her feelings toward the man who had participated — however misguided he may have been — in the destruction of her husband? Earlier he had had a presentiment of betrayal, and he had voiced it to Timothy. Now he understood the full extent of that betrayal. When he had engaged Luke Ashford, he had still felt himself in control of events. Now he knew that he had lost all control, that he had become as helpless as Lee Hop, or Nan Steele, or her father in the course of future events. He had claimed so many times that God had more imagination than any of His creatures. How confident he had been in that belief! Now, to his horror and his shame, he was experiencing the greater imagination of God, and, truly, he did not know what to do or where to turn.

To his chagrin the old priest remembered how he had once counseled Neele Bos that there was a reason beyond the commandment that one must never bear false witness. It was his conviction that the lies you tell are likely somehow to become the truth. Nemesis might, indeed, be a manifestation of God that the ancient Greeks and Romans had mistakenly regarded a deity in itself. What in practice this had always meant for Father Matthew was that he had to be very careful in the kinds of lies he would tell. He recalled how, once in Centralia, he had begged off an invitation to the home of a parishioner because he had wanted to spend the afternoon reading Tertullian's ADVERSUS JUDAEOS. He had claimed that he had had a swelling in the toes of his right foot that made movement painful. The next day he had wakened with precisely such a pain, so great, in fact, that he had had difficulty putting on his right shoe. He had consulted Dr. Logan who had diagnosed his malady as paroxysmal arthritis and inflammation of the great right toe and joints. He had not believed that was possible, since no one in his family had ever before suffered from gout. Dr. Logan had prescribed a rigid change in diet, and for days he had had to keep his foot bound in cotton. Father Matthew's own prescription had been a week-long fast, and, in that time, the condition had been alleviated. The only possible kind of lie open to him was the kind he had once told Neele: that he had been celibate because the opportunity to express passion in a physical way had never presented itself to him.

Now, as he wondered what lie he had told here in Eagle Cañon, he knew at once what it had been. He had never really believed Yokum Bos was guilty of being in a conspiracy with the Luke Barron gang. He could trace the entire chain of events from his hypocritical acquiescence in that judgment to his recent hiring of a man whom he knew to be Luke Barron himself to work on his behalf. Had he been willing to admit it to himself — and he had not been — he could easily have guessed whom the dark son of God had chosen as his agent

114

in Eagle Cañon, and that Yokum Bos had had nothing what-soever to do with the murders and robberies. Father Matthew had consented to tell a lie, and that lie had in a bizarre way become the truth. The very act he had committed to help protect the community had now placed not only the whole community but himself as well in the gravest jeopardy.

"Timothy!" the old priest said so suddenly that the black man nearly jumped off the chair. "If your eye offend thee, pluck it out! If your right hand offend thee, cut it off!"

"Yes, Father."

"Go thee from this day forward and sin no more!"

"Yes, Father."

"Find Nan Steele. Bring her to me."

"Yes, Father, Ah shore will," the liveryman said, going toward the back door.

"I must see Neele Bos tonight. I want Nan Steele to ac-company me."

Luke and Nan remained outside his room in the loft until they were certain that the rider they had heard had been alone. As Nan cautiously descended the narrow staircase, a solitary coal-oil lamp lit in the stable below provided sufficient light for her to find her way. She did not want Luke to follow her, and told him so. Timothy was not around. Knowing the hosteler, she was certain he had learned what he needed to know from Lee Hop and had probably gone to see Father Matthew. Nan had no idea who the lone rider had been but suspected it was probably one of the Avenging Angels going out of town to find the sheriff. She called twice in a loud whisper for Timothy. When he did not respond, she turned and looked toward Luke who was standing on the third step from the top, not exactly following her, but also not staying put as she had asked him to do.

"I'll be all right," she assured him.

"Probably so," Luke agreed, keeping his voice low. "But I'll feel a whole lot safer once I saddle my horse and spend what's left of this night out of town somewhere."

She nodded and let herself out through the smaller door located in the left-hand double door to the livery stable. Both of these big doors were now closed.

Luke went back to his room, pulled on his boots, buckled on his holster and gun, put on his hat, blew out the small candle stub, and made his way down the narrow staircase. Once he had the black horse saddled, he led the gelding to the double doors, carefully opened the one on the right-hand side, and guided the horse out into the street. He closed the door and mounted, riding slowly out of town in the same direction the lone rider had taken.

Later he made camp alongside Eagle Creek, hobbling his horse in among some cottonwood trees. He figured he would be safe here, at least until it got light, and by that time he expected to be on his way again. Being a light sleeper, he was roused about an hour later when he heard the sound of men, riding in a group, toward Eagle Cañon. There was no way he could be certain as to their identity, but he felt sure this would be Sheriff Ingalls and his deputies. He congratulated himself on his decision to leave town when he had and dropped off again to sleep.

It was very dark in the alley that ran behind the town buildings between the livery stable and Frank Summers's Eagle Cañon Mercantile and the west cañon wall even with some starshine and dim moonlight. Nan had to proceed cautiously, frequently reaching out with her left hand to guide her along the rear walls of buildings and tents. As she drew closer to the mercantile, she could see yellow lamplight vaguely coming from the one rear window of the room where Father Matthew lived at the back of the Temple. She had not seen Timothy Kamu at the stable and supposed he had probably gone to see Father Matthew. Depending on how much Timothy had learned from Lee Hop, it might not even be necessary for her to tell the old priest what had happened to Yokum Bos.

Father Matthew could be dictatorial, as Nan well knew, but she was convinced in her soul that he was essentially a good man. She recalled how he had once spoken eloquently on the perfect justice and mercy of God. The religious man believed that human beings had been created after the divine image and likeness, and but for Original Sin would be far more enlightened now than they were. Nan did not possess her father's belief in his own nearness to the Lord, but she hoped some day this might be also true for her. What had occurred this night, since their return from the Bos cabin, was sufficient evidence for Nan that her father spoke the truth. The Lord had to be watching out for him, or how else should he have escaped so narrowly the trap the sheriff had set for him?

The back door to the mercantile was not locked at night. Until the robberies had begun at the claims, blamed on the Luke Barron gang, those who lived and worked in Eagle Cañon had felt a total security. Even now, Nan suspected, the only place in the little town that was kept locked at night was the jail. That thought brought a smile to her face — because that lock had proved incapable of keeping Ed Tyler behind bars.

Nan's groping hand found the latch to the back door, and, as quietly as she could, she opened the door. A small coal-oil lamp was burning in the storeroom. On the left-hand side of the storeroom, as Nan entered, was the small bedroom she occupied when staying in town. On the right-hand side was the bigger bedroom shared by the storekeeper and his wife. Closing the rear door behind her, Nan turned toward the door to her small bedroom. It would be a relief tonight to get out of these Levi's and in the morning back into a civilized dress. She was certain of how closely Luke's eyes had followed her after their meeting of the previous morning, and she had noticed again tonight how carefully he had been looking at her. She felt both flattered and embarrassed.

Once she was safely in the privacy of the small bedroom, she lit the lamp that stood on a trunk at the base of the narrow bed, took off her half coat and hung it on a hook behind the door, placing the Stetson over it. Then she sat down for a moment on the bed to think about all the changes that a single day had brought. The terrible revelation at the Bos cabin, her tears on the way there over the dilemma she felt confronted by Royal Logan's proposal of marriage, and the certitude she had experienced when she had confided to Luke that she now had no intention whatsoever of marrying the physician. She gave an involuntary shudder when she reflected on how naïve she had been in her trust and admiration for the doctor. Even now, in reflection, she could not say she had ever been attracted to him physically, the way she was — in a manner that nonetheless also puzzled her — to Luke. What was the matter with her? If Royal Logan's marriage proposal was finally absurd, why should she feel this warmth come to her cheeks, gentle as a puff of air? Even though the small bedroom was cold — maybe she should light the compact potbelly stove in the corner — why should she see Luke's face now so clearly in the deepness of her soul?

She lifted up one leg and began working at removing the Justin boot she was wearing. No more dressing like a boy — not ever again — not from this day forward! It was at this moment that she heard the rear outside door to the storeroom through which she had earlier come scrape against the puncheon floor. Someone was entering. Nan could hear the soft padding of the footfalls as the person approached the door to her room. There was a light tapping.

"Miss Nan . . . you-all awake? It's me, Timothy. Father Matthew done sent me to fetch you-all." His voice was a husky whisper behind the wooden door panels.

"It's . . . it's very late and very dark, Timothy," Nan said softly. "Can't it wait until morning?"

"Ah'm afraid not Miss Nan. I tol' Father Matthew what happened to poor old Yokum Bos, an' he's done got it in his head dat he must go see Missus Neele."

Nan pulled the boot back on, rose from the narrow bed, and walked softly to the bedroom door. She drew it open enough to see the black man, standing there in shadow created by the dim lamplight. She could not make out his face or any expression except the urgency that was conveyed by his posture.

"We can't go out there tonight, Timothy. It's dark and possibly dangerous."

"Ah've hitched up Father Matthew's buggy, an' it's waitin' in front of de Temple. You should make it out dere befo' dawn."

"But why me?"

"Father Matthew has his reasons, Miss Nan, Ah'm shore." His voice remained wispy and soft in the gloom. "For one thing Ah don't think he'd dare go out dere to see her alone all by hisself."

In view of what her father had implied on their earlier trip to the Bos cabin, Nan knew that something had happened in the past between Neele Bos and the old priest, although she was not certain yet exactly what. Royal Logan had also once made a cryptic comment to the effect that once in Centralia the old priest had not grinned at the devil — whatever that had meant — and that somehow this had led to the move to the West.

119

Nan had been too wrought up, while sitting on the bed, to feel much like sleeping, although she had known she must get to bed soon. Now the sense of excitement that had been with her so much during the day and night returned.

"Let me get my things," she said, keeping her voice in a hushed whisper.

Timothy stood outside her door silently as Nan once again put on the Stetson and then slipped into her half coat. The thought occurred to her that she could change into a dress, but she had already dressed this way for one trip to the Bos cabin, and now it appeared she would be making another trip to the same place. She hoped the Summerses wouldn't be aroused by all this commotion.

Father Matthew's buggy had sidelamps, and these had been lit by Timothy before he had parked it in front of the Temple. Father Matthew was coming out one of the double doors leading to the assembly room of the Temple, as Nan stepped alongside the near side of the buggy. The priest wore a great black cloak over his black cassock, fastened at the neck so as to conceal the fact that he no longer wore a Roman collar. On his head was a flat-crowned hat with a broad brim that sloped downward in the front and back. In his right hand he carried a leather-covered Bible and the leather wallet in which he carried Holy Communion, a scapular, and the ointments for the Last Rites.

The old priest could not help but glance disapprovingly at Nan's boyish attire, but he said nothing. It would, no doubt, have been inappropriate under the circumstances, since she was foregoing sleep and making a considerable personal sacrifice to accompany him on this journey.

"Thank you, Nan," he said gently, "and may God bless you for what you are doing this night."

"That's all right, Father. The ride will give us a chance to talk, and I believe we should. Do you wish me to take the reins?"

"Most certainly," he answered and smiled, nodding his head before climbing aboard.

"Dere's a full canteen of de doctor's water under de seat, Father," Timothy said.

"That was, indeed, most thoughtful of you," Father Matthew said, "but, Timothy, the water does not belong to Doctor Logan but to the Temple and, therefore, to all of us."

"He done gets paid for it," the stable man said stubbornly as he helped the priest up the step and onto the front floorboard. "Ah'll get de hitching weight, Miss Nan, after Ah gives you a hand up."

Father Matthew had made himself comfortable on the passenger side of the double front seat. The buggy had a collapsible black canvas cover that was pulled up to shield the backs and heads of the occupants. Nan mounted after the priest, with Timothy providing her a hand up the step. The girl took the reins to the single horse from where they were wound around the metal casing, holding the buggy whip, while Timothy went forward, scooped up the hitching weight, and placed it along with the connecting rope behind Nan's boots on the driver's side.

"If anyone inquires, Timothy," the priest said, his lower face, not shadowed by the broad brim of his hat, appearing yellow like withered parchment in the lamplight's reflection, "just say that I had to make a pastoral visit, that Nan Steele is assisting me, and that you do not know when I will be back."

"I beg your pardon, Father," Nan interjected, "but I don't know if I can afford to be away from Eagle Cañon very long. The sheriff and his Avenging Angels intend to kill my father, and Royal Logan supports them in this. My father is in hiding now, but I do not know how long he will be safe, and I don't want to leave him very long. I came back to town mostly to talk to you and see if I could dissuade Royal from backing the sheriff in what amounts to murder of an innocent man."

"Child," Father Matthew said in a most kindly tone, "I was merely giving Timothy his instructions . . . what he was to tell anyone who might be curious. Of course, we'll be back by late tomorrow morning."

The old priest was trying his best to be persuasive and allay Nan's apprehensions, but he would not wish to swear on the Bible he held on his lap that he was speaking the truth. Most fervently he hoped, were this a lie, that it would surely become the truth.

Nan flicked the reins for the horse to move, saying good bye to Timothy who now stood in shadowy isolation in front of the Temple. Father Matthew kept his glance forward, expecting them to be stopped at the check point. To his surprise, although Arlie Michaels was now visible in the light from the lantern suspended outside the tent behind the empty gun rack, he did not signal for them to stop but merely waved an arm, *somewhat abjectly*, the priest thought.

"It's a good thing we have these buggy lamps, Father," Nan remarked. "I don't think I'd be sure of finding the cut-off to Rattlesnake Mesa without them to light the sides of the road." She paused for a moment before continuing. "How much did Timothy tell you of what's been going on in Eagle Cañon and about who tortured Yokum Bos, who knew about it and apparently approved of it, and now this pursuit of my father, which is surely an attempt to jump his claim."

"Nan, please, tell me all that you know, all that you've heard, and then I can better put it together and tell you what I believe is behind it, and what we must do about it."

When Nan had finished her narration, they were approaching the cut-off, and she deftly turned the horse into the road leading toward Rattlesnake Mesa.

"Nan," the old priest said after a pause, "earlier I told Timothy that I was certain that I had been betrayed. I can see now that I had not phrased that altogether accurately. It is not so much that I have been betrayed, but that the Word of God has been betrayed . . . and, I fear, I have played no small rôle in that betrayal myself. I know this won't seem at once a proper response to what you have told me, but on a pastoral visit to Lee Hop, his wife, and child, I recited a prayer for Lee to teach his son, Li-chung shih, to say at bedtime. It goes . . . now I lay me down to sleep and pray the Lord my soul to keep. If I should die before I wake, I pray the Lord my soul to take."

"I know that prayer, Father," Nan confessed, looking over at the priest who was huddled in shadow. "I . . . I stopped saying it every night after I went East to study nursing. But, sometimes, I still say it. I would . . . I believe I would have said it tonight. I am so afraid and confused over what I should do."

"I know, Nan, the prayer seems childish, and so perhaps it should be put away with childish things. But, if you examine it carefully, what a wondrous act of faith it really is. When we say that prayer, we believe that the Lord guards our soul while we sleep and, should we die, we pray that He will take our soul to be with Him forever, as His only son saved the good thief who died on the cross next to Him. It is only that as we grow older . . . as we become more aware of how much we have sinned . . . that we fear, if we should die, the Lord will no longer be able to take our souls. As children we are so innocent. We do not realize yet that there are always consequences for the things that we do. Later, once we do realize it, we have lost our innocence. It is such a realization that has prompted me to make this journey tonight. I shall never forget your kindness to an old man, Nan, one who has been arrogant

123

enough to try to teach to you, who are so good and kind, the way of truth."

"Please don't say such things about yourself, Father," Nan interrupted, "or about me."

"In the seminary," the old priest continued, waving aside what she had said with a hand that was almost invisible in the enveloping darkness, "it was our masters who taught us . . . *veritas vos liberabit* . . . the truth shall set you free. At my age and through my experience I am not certain that it is so. Had you asked me yesterday if I still believed it, I might have reluctantly agreed, but no longer. I have wandered in error, Nan. I have wandered and did not know that I was lost. Once before I had wandered and been led astray, but this time I was so certain I had found the true path. I have been a spiritual guide to others and guided them onto the same path. Royal Logan had a rôle to play in all this, I will not deny it, but I daren't blame him for what I have done. It was verily of my own choosing. I . . . I have become so tired of late."

"Father," Nan said, "that isn't true. I don't know of anyone who has your energy. Look at all that you do in just a single day."

"But, dear Nan, my house has been built on sand." Father Matthew sighed and then sat forward slightly. "I have been a fool," he continued, sighing again, "but I am not so great a fool as to judge my fellow man . . . not any more. I know that Timothy Kamu drinks spirits. I know that he gets them from your father. I thought that in time Royal would come to realize that what is best is moderation in all things, but I learned in a talk with him earlier this night that he will never come to that realization. He would rather put your father to death for distilling spirits, and Timothy, I suppose, for drinking them, than to believe that the Lord alone decides who is to die and when, and that the Lord alone can judge any man's . . . or any woman's . . . life. Years ago . . . before we ever came to Stirrup Gap . . . I did Neele Bos a wrong. Now I have compounded it by allowing myself to be a party to her innocent husband's execution."

"Father," Nan implored, "you couldn't possibly have known. Dad and I only found out what had been done to Yokum Bos when we went out to help with his burial."

"Child," Father Matthew replied sternly, "you do not really understand. If Sam Ingalls and his men succeed in murdering your father . . . if, as I surely believe, the real Luke Barron is innocent of the charges brought against him . . . if one more innocent life is claimed in the name of the Temple of the Redeemed, to say nothing of the innocent lives already lost in its name, all of these are sins in which I am culpable. *Mea culpa, mea culpa, mea maxima culpa* . . . through my most grievous fault, Nan. I may try to set things aright now, but even if I succeed, that cannot excuse me entirely from what already has happened. Again and again I am brought back to that word . . . innocent. Oh, it is a heavy mantle of guilt I wear, and it is one of my own making. I wish I myself could say that child's prayer even you said you were going to invoke tonight when you prayed. I wish I could say it and believe it. But I have noticed of late, when I have kneeled near the great crucifix in my sanctuary in the Temple or walked out under the stars of a night to contemplate, that I seem somehow distant from myself, as if my life were nearing its end."

"Surely, Father, you have many more years yet to live," Nan insisted.

"Once I would have welcomed that assurance, dear girl, but I do not believe it is so. I have spent so much of my time here actually evading life. I thought once it was wrong for members of the clergy to remain single. I came to agree with Saint Paul that it is better to fornicate than to burn . . . after all, to desire a woman in your soul is the same as to commit the physical act itself, and the consequences, I fear, are no less severe. Seeing you in Levi's tonight met, at first, with my disapproval, because I realized that other men would see more of your exquisite form than is modest. . . ."

"Father, I regret wearing these jeans," Nan said. "Gopher Parsons was also put out by it, and I suppose others have been. I bought them at Frank Summers's mercantile because I knew Dad and I would be going out to help bury Mister Bos. It seemed like a good idea at the time."

"But don't you see, Nan, that is precisely right? Why should you be blamed for dressing as you please, just because of what others might think? It is all part of this terrible conspiracy that Royal Logan's thinking has conjured among the faithful . . . and, I must now admit, those who have apparently no faith at all other than in selfishness and greed. It is your right to dress as you feel prudent. It is Timothy's right to drink spirits, if it so pleases him. It is, indeed, your father's right to distill the spirits he and others wish to drink. And . . . it is no other man's right to deny anyone those rights. That is what's wrong with Royal's proscriptions against alcohol, tobacco, gambling, even dancing. He is terrified himself of temptation. There is no other explanation for it. He fears that, if others are allowed to do it, he will want to do it. So he arrogates to himself the right to decide what is allowable and what is prohibited for everyone. Thou shalt not place false gods before me . . . was not said merely about graven images. It can be said of a distorted set of principles as well."

Father Matthew leaned back against the seat of the buggy. He looked overhead and saw that the moon was setting, although the heavens still seemed brilliant with starshine. The rhythmic *clip-clop* of the horse, drawing the buggy, beat a tattoo that could have been mesmerizing were he to have surrendered to its syncopation. They were climbing out of the trees now and ahead, ghostly and forbidding in the shadows, was the barren clearing with the hanging tree standing starkly at its center. A wind had been rising as they journeyed, a cleansing, rude wind that tugged at Father Matthew's hat and cape, and touched Nan's Stetson so that she bowed her head slightly forward.

"I would like to smoke my pipe for a time, Nan," Father Matthew said.

"Does Royal know you smoke?" Nan asked, a playful humor accenting her voice.

"I'm afraid he does," the old priest confessed. "And he also knows that I occasionally drink wine outside of Holy Communion."

Nan's smile could barely be seen in the darkness, save for the flickering illumination from the sidelamps. "If you wish my permission, Father," she said, "you surely have it."

"Thank you, Nan, but there is one thing I want you to know before I light my pipe . . . a bit of a trick in this wind that's come up. I had started to say it before, but I got sidetracked. It is the real reason I asked you to be kind enough to accompany me on this journey. Indeed, had it not been the case, I would have been perfectly happy to have had Timothy go with me, or would have gone alone. I do not know just how Neele will respond, seeing me again after all these years. Once, long ago . . . oh, it doesn't really seem all that long ago to me . . . well, it is difficult for me to put it into words, but. . . ."

"You don't need to, Father. Dad hinted at something of the kind when we drove out together today to the Bos place."

"Yes," sighed the priest, "I should have known Yokum might have said something about it to your father. After all, they were partners . . . made the strike in Eagle Cañon together. . . ."

"Saint Paul . . . ?" Nan put in.

"Yes, Saint Paul. Then you understand how difficult it will be for me to offer solace . . . ?"

"She may not accept it, Father, . . . or you."

"Believe me, Nan," he said so softly his words were scarcely carried on the wind, "I know it. Perhaps in even this I shall fail."

Chapter Ten

Neele Bos had found it difficult to sleep. Her life here in this cabin, as well as the small barn nearby that her husband had had built with day labor he had hired in Stirrup Gap after striking it rich in Eagle Cañon, had been a lonely one even when Yokum was alive. He had been gone so much of the time, working his claim. She knew that he had been hiding the gold dust he had accumulated after the followers of the Temple of the Redeemed had come to occupy Eagle Cañon. There had been robberies, and he did not trust the promise of the Temple's hierarchy, Royal Logan, Sheriff Sam Ingalls, and Father Matthew, that the Eagle Cañon bank, still being constructed, would offer anyone security for deposits of gold dust. He had been outraged — and outspoken about it — when Father Matthew and his followers had stampeded to the Eagle Cañon diggings after he and George Steele had made their strikes and filed on their claims at the Land Office in Stirrup Gap. Yokum had denounced Father Matthew back in Centralia, once he had learned of what had been going on between Neele and the old priest, and subsequently had had no further use for any kind of organized religion but especially one that imposed celibacy on its clergy without at the same time castrating the priests, turning them into physical as well as spiritual eunuchs.

Yokum could not really have been blamed for his contempt toward the Roman Catholic clergy when he was alive, or Father Matthew in particular even in his present guise as the spiritual leader of a new religious sect that had supposedly come to the frontier to find freedom to worship, nor did Neele blame him now in memory. She had been grateful to him when, once she had told him the sordid truth of her two-year affair with Father Matthew, he had forgiven her, refused even to consider divorce, and proposed as a solution to the emotional awkwardness of the situation that they head West and seek their fortune in a new land. Yokum Bos had been a simple man, so involved with his work, first as a carpenter and then as the owner of a building construction company, that he had had little time for the amenities of married life. If he had been unfaithful to Neele, his infidelity had been confined to his obsession with his work which had required long hours, and about which he thought constantly even when he was not physically at his office or a new construction site. He promised Neele that this would also change. He had been willing to abandon his business, take what money they had saved, and start life over in a new profession or occupation in the West. He had thought of farming or ranching, only to rule those out once they had come to the frontier, at least as far as Stirrup Gap. Once there, he had returned to the trade he knew best — carpentry — and it was while living there that he had fallen in with George Steele. Steele's wife had only recently died and at the time his only daughter was away in Kansas, studying nursing. Steele wanted to quit his job as a teamster and exchange it for prospecting. He had learned much about geology on his own and talking with assayers on his freight routes. He was getting older, and, if he was going to make something of his life, he was convinced he had better get to it.

Yokum had felt the same way. Once away from Centralia and the business he had built up, he had never pursued carpentry work with the same enthusiasm and energy he once had had. It had become simply a means of earning a living, as he had confessed on more than one occasion to Neele, and he now wanted something more from life. Prospecting for gold, with its potential of tremendous wealth, held a promise for him as nothing else ever had, and George Steele's talk and hopes for himself had only further fired Yokum's ambition. Even in Stirrup Gap, George Steele was known to have a small home distillery — he was, as he openly admitted, a man who loved to drink. It came as no surprise to Neele when Yokum told her that George had a distillery out on his mining claim, even though he had enough gold dust to buy any kind of liquor he might have wanted. It was as much a part of George Steele's character as carpentry had once been part of Yokum Bos's.

Neele was not in the least afraid to be living alone in the shadow of Rattlesnake Mesa. Being lonely was not the same thing as fear of being alone by yourself, even though she had heard riders in the night and suspected they might well be members of the terrible Luke Barron gang that had been murdering miners and stealing their gold. In her heart she knew Yokum had been totally innocent of any connection with that wild bunch of cut-throats, that he would never willingly associate with such men, and that he was totally without any motive to resort to murder and robbery when he had taken more gold out of Eagle Creek than he himself could safely transport to the bank in Stirrup Gap. In some twisted, demented way Yokum's execution must have been wholly the doing of Father Matthew, and it was obvious to her, as it had been to George Steele and his daughter, once they saw the body, that any confession Yokum had made could only have come about as a result of the most fiendish torture.

When Neele had been a young girl, come of age on her parents' farm outside Centralia, the idea of death or failure had been intolerable to her. Indeed, she could not even bear the possibility of ridicule. She had had an unswerving faith in the will of God, and firmly believed it was utterly impossible that anything should venture to go against her in life. It was only as she aged, from a young bride into a middle-aged one, that she had slowly come to believe that inevitably everything would turn out badly for her. God had turned his brightness away from her, and had left her in a fading gloom. At first it had been only to occupy herself and the many hours with nothing to do that, having found herself incapable of bearing children and lonely in Yokum's long absences, and because of money difficulties he was having, that she had applied for the position of housekeeper at Father Matthew's small rectory adjacent to the Church of the Sacred Heart on the outskirts of Centralia where he was the parish priest. She knew Father Matthew, of course, from his sermons at Sunday Masses and from various church activities in which she had become engaged, and even Yokum knew him, although he attended church much less of the time than his wife did. It had seemed like a very good idea.

Convinced by then that failure was in the nature of things for her, Neele had come not to mind one way or the other what became of her, and so she had assumed her duties as the priest's housekeeper. In retrospect, as Neele considered the past, she must have been suffering from some derangement of the soul. Although she had begun the housekeeping job with a perfect indifference to what might become of her, she found herself very soon joining to this resignation as a hard-won advantage of middle age the privilege of youth, the arrogant and unwarranted optimism that allowed her once again to believe that nothing could go wrong in her life. Falling under Father Matthew's intoxicating spell, hearing of his lifelong devotion to the Holy Ghost and his intention of someday writing a tract of how it is through the Holy Ghost that God becomes human in each one of us, it is doubtful that Neele Bos believed she might ever die. What she experienced in her soul, during those hours when she and Father Matthew were first alone, had been too great and too moving to be merely

132

love — which she had so long ago felt for Yokum and for which reason she had married him. No, it had to be something else, on an altogether different, a higher plain, a wholly new existence. He had not, it seemed, crept up on her. There had been no preamble. It was just that one moment they had kissed, and it had been so impassioned for both of them, that it became more and had led to more, until at last they joined physically and — she had believed — spiritually. When she would look those days at herself in a glass, she no longer saw the lines of weariness, of a skin that had been lived in so long as to leave behind imprints, but rather the unabashed ecstasy of a girl of sixteen who finds herself in love for the first and, most assuredly, the last time.

Her countenance had altered as she had undergone this magnificent revolution of the soul and, at a time in life when other women with money sought refuge in rouge and belladonna, her rapture produced in her an augmented youthful coloring and a scintillating, almost bewitching flashing in her eyes. She had become, in fact, closer to being a beautiful woman than she had ever been a pretty girl. Other women had whispered that she looked like nothing so much as a witch, but in the throes of her second girlhood her appearance had assumed all the magic of a fairy godmother in a children's tale. It was to Mary Magdalene of the Gospel to whom she prayed, and not the Holy Ghost, consecrating in her heart this fallen woman with the beatitude of a saint. Just as Father Matthew, upon occasion, would muse how, some day, he hoped to retire to a desolate isle in the New World as Patmos had been in the Old, and there, as Saint John the Divine, to surrender himself entirely, in mind and in body, to a contemplation of the Holy Ghost and the life to come, so she had dreamed of a divine sisterhood with Mary Magdalene. If Father Matthew were to retire to a desert isle, so she would camp upon the shifting sands of some vast wasteland, with no more human company than a skull and a shrine to the woman who in life had known both the sweetness of sin and the blessing of forgiveness as she had knelt before the Lord.

It had been Dr. Royal Logan, ultimately, who had destroyed this spiritual and physical rebirth for her. She had believed that no anguish of conscience would ever destroy the peace she had found, nor danger darken the quiet joy of fulfillment with the ghastly specter of fear. But Dr. Royal Logan had — this odd man with his quirky beliefs that the Church must instruct the faithful that they were righteously to separate themselves from those who drank or used tobacco or gambled or danced just as white people avoided those of inferior races, allowing them to be equal but insisting that they must be separate. Father Matthew had been amused at first with all of this, convinced that the Church of Rome would never elect such ridiculous whimsies to be laws of the Church, if not actually adding them to the Commandments of God. After all, twice a year the Church of the Sacred Heart sponsored bazaars at which there was gambling, to raise money, of course, and four times a year there were community dances. It was unlikely that, no matter how generous he might be with his own money, the doctor could single-handedly replace these sources of revenue from his own funds. Besides, while the congregation did not object to the presence of Timothy Kamu, then a hosteler at a nearby stable, or two other black church members, provided they remained in the back of the church and sat apart, it was unthinkable that Christian men and women would pull away in disgust from those who used alcohol and tobacco as if they were the same kind of social pariah as a member of an inferior race. Father Matthew, it must be said, believed that all men and women, regardless of race or personal habits, were equal before the eyes of God, and even had urged Timothy Kamu to move to the front pews in church. Timothy had been too timid to do so, but he, if any man, belonged in the front of the church because, as Father Matthew said, he was the only truly decent person he had ever known. At the Church of the Sacred Heart the old priest had finally been able to persuade Timothy to learn the Latin responsories and to become an altar boy, but that, apparently, had all ended when Father Matthew had organized his own church and come West. Yokum Bos had heard that Sheriff Ingalls and others objected to Timothy or Chinese people, like Lee Hop and his family, from participating at all in the services with white people.

It had been Father Matthew's strange fascination with how a lie, once spoken, would become truth that had led to his telling Dr. Logan of his relationship with Neele. She was not quite certain to this day exactly how it had occurred, but something having to do with Father Matthew's contracting the gout had prompted him to confess to the medical man that he had been committing adultery with Neele Bos. Just how the archbishop in Chicago had come to hear about it, Neele was uncertain, but, again, she felt sure that Dr. Logan had had a rôle in it. There was no question that Dr. Logan had forced an end to the relationship. In indignation, as senior warden of the Holy Name Society, he had fired Neele and had threatened, if she did not leave peacefully and at once, to expose the whole sordid business to her husband.

Never had Neele been so torn in her life as she had been then, not until now, when she was utterly bereft, when the love she had once felt for Father Matthew had been replaced by the most deep-seated hatred. He had murdered Yokum Bos, as surely as if he had held the hang rope from which his limp body had dangled on that windswept plain. Perhaps Dr. Logan was to be hated as much, because he was the demon behind Father Matthew's Temple of the Redeemed, and he had sat in judgment over Yokum Bos, as had Father Matthew, but the hatred she felt for the medical man was more impersonal since he had never meant anything to her except an intrusive presence in her life, in Centralia, and now in Eagle Cañon.

Neele Bos had preserved an almost elfin lightness of the spirit from those days, and a leanness of body, and she had never lost her remarkable skill as a dancer, although she had had no opportunity to dance since leaving Stirrup Gap. If she possessed a little cloven hoof at all, it was concealed by the folds of her gingham house dress and the woolen shawl she wore as she moved cautiously in the dim lamplight from the rocking chair before the little sheet-iron stove to the front door of the cabin. She had heard a wagon of some sort drawing up in the dreadful, oppressive solitude that surrounded the cabin on a night like this, even when the wind was blowing. There was a knock on the wooden panels of the door, and Nan Steele's voice. Not having any longer a fear of anything in heaven or on earth, Neele had not placed the bar across the front door, and so she could throw it open onto the night. There, as if he were the Prince of Darkness himself, in a dark cape, his white hair having been blown by the passage of his transit into an aureole about his high forehead, stood Father Matthew alongside Nan Steele. Neele could see him in the glimmer of the light, emanating from the coal-oil lamp on the kitchen table. She did not think at all. Her response was automatic and instinctive, as she raised what might have been a little cloven hoof, masked as it was by shadow, but it took the shape of a Colt House Pistol with a clover-shaped cylinder. The hammer was clicked all the way back, and, holding it now with both hands, pointing it directly at Father Matthew, who seemed so tender and sorrowful, with his right hand extended in supplication, she fired. Gunflame spouted in a brief flash from the mouth of the barrel, and the stench of gunsmoke rose in the air. The leaden missile, so suddenly and perhaps unexpectedly dispatched, struck the old priest in the chest, thrusting him backwards into Nan Steele, who was knocked from her feet by the impact of his falling body. He did not even moan as he fell, and perhaps the anguish in his face, so dimly visible, was not caused alone by the terrible impact of the bullet.

Chapter Eleven

George Steele did not house his sour mash distillery in his shack, which was near Eagle Creek, but rather in a hidden cave at the back of his claim in the east side of the cañon wall that Ed Tyler had discovered. It had taken the sheriff and his deputies about fifteen minutes to search Steele's shack rather thoroughly. If Steele had hidden his gold somewhere in that shack, it hadn't been in any obvious place. What the men did find were two jugs of sour mash. Sheriff Ingalls suspected there was a lot more of George Steele's home brew to be had than this, but, like where Steele had hidden his gold dust, it wasn't readily to be found, and the darkness worked against an extensive search beyond the shack. Two jugs, however, even though one was only about half full, should prove sufficient for the needs of the hour.

Pink Morgan had brought a deck of greasy cards that he produced when he was seated at the kitchen table, and the hulking Tiny Hart, firing up a twisted cigar, had joined him for a game of two-handed stud poker. Mart Kemp pulled a small barrel marked **Sugar** from a corner and seated himself on this alongside Sheriff Ingalls who occupied the rocking chair near the front door of the shack. Ingalls had the full jug with him, and he poured liberally into the two tin cups Kemp had brought from the makeshift cupboard near the sheet-metal stove. The night had turned very cool, and Mart, before joining the sheriff, had kindled a fire in the stove that soon took the chill off the room.

"You know, Mart," Sam Ingalls said expansively, "this is the best damned sour mash whiskey I think I've ever tasted.

Steele is a fool. He doesn't need no gold, not with talent like this. I been thinkin' on it. Once we ketch him, I don't figger we'll hang him, no matter what Doc Logan says. With what we'll be takin' out of Yokum Bos's claim and with our share of what Buck Rollins and the boys can steal from the other miners, I reckon there'll be enough fer me to set old George up in the whiskey business. If we can expand his operation, it won't be long before we could be sellin' barrels of this sour mash, starting down in Stirrup Gap and then other places. And sour mash whiskey ain't like the gold thet'll play out eventually in these here diggin's. It's old George's know-how that'll keep this stuff comin' and comin'. Hell, we'll all get rich a second time over."

Mart Kemp took a healthy swig from his tin cup, savored the whiskey for a moment, and then swallowed. "You're right about this stuff. It shore does go down easy. I hope there's gonna be enough in that jug till we can nab Steele and make him show us where he keeps his cache."

"Say, Mart," the sheriff frowned, ". . . an' this goes for you, Pink and Tiny, too . . . we're stoppin' here for a snort or two, an' then we're headin' back to town. There's a hangin' we gotta attend tomorrow."

"Don't you worry none 'bout me, Sam," Tiny Hart assured the sheriff, studying through a cloud of cigar smoke his cards face up on the table, "I can hold my liquor."

"In that case," said the sheriff, "maybe I'll leave you here to watch Steele's claim. Even though he ain't jailed yet, I regard it has jumped in my name." He laughed and leaned over to pick up the earthware jug to pour himself another drink. "What's more, I figger the miners are plannin' on sending out an ore shipment. If they ain't, I still intend to follow up the hangin' of that Tyler feller by organizin' a gold shipment down to Stirrup Gap with the Avenging Angels along as guards. I intend to send out what we've been able to get out of Bos's claim so far at the same time."

"Will Buck and the boys be hittin' that shipment?" Mart asked.

"Hell, no," insisted Sam Ingalls, "not with my gold goin' down. The way I figger it, Buck and the boys can hit a couple of the biggest claims . . . probably Gopher Parsons's and Fred Jeliffe's . . . before the shipment goes out while they're gettin' their gold from where they got it hid, and the other, smaller claims can just get theirs through that one time. There's got to be somethin' to keep these fool miners workin' their heads off. Lettin' some of them get their gold through will keep the others workin' hard." He laughed again.

Mart Kemp asked seriously: "Don't you figure Father Matthew's gonna catch on eventually, or 'specially Doc Logan, if we don't knab George Steele an' make an example of him the way we did Yokum Bos?"

"I'll tell you the truth, Mart," the sheriff replied, taking a sip of whiskey, "the way I see it, the doc's gonna make a move against Father Matthew. You know that old priest smokes on the sly. His nigger stableman drinks, an' Father Matthew just looks the other way. Fact is, I think Father Matthew nips at his church wine now an' then."

"Just how do you see Doc Logan kickin' Father Matthew out?" Kemp asked in puzzled astonishment. "Not that I really care who's runnin' the show there, as long as it keeps the flock quiet and ready to get sheared, but they follow Father Matthew, don't they, an' not the doctor?"

"There's one thing you can't see, Mart, that I can, 'cause I'm a bit closer to the doc," the sheriff replied. "Logan's off his nut 'bout drinkin' and the rest of it. But he's got one thing goin' for him that the old priest ain't. All Father Matthew can promise his flock is happiness in the next world. Now, I've

140

been thinkin' on this some, an' I reckon if Doc Logan can promise 'em a better life in the here an' now, they'll show the old priest the door an' take right nacheral to the doc. The way I see it, we win either way. If they stick with the old priest an' look for a better life than this'n after death, that'll just have to be enough for 'em. If they opine a better life while they're still kickin', an' take the doc as their leader, that'll still have to be enough fer 'em. I ain't got a stake in either one of 'em. My aim is simple. I want the gold. The miners can have whichever they want . . . either one of 'em, or both . . . for all I care. When we've cleaned out these diggin's, there ain't a one of us that won't be settin' pretty for the future. We may have to hang a few more miners for bein' in with Luke Barron before we're done, but done we will be some time. That's when we pull our freight an' leave the redeemed to shift for themselves with their Temple and their camp."

Mart Kemp had to smile at that. He pulled the makings from a pocket in his jacket.

"Pass 'em over to me when you're done," Sheriff Ingalls said, reaching down again for the jug. "The only trouble with drinkin' is that you can't chew at the same time."

It was growing light over the eastern cliff of the great boxed cañon when Luke rose. He washed in the creek, boiled some of the water at a small, smokeless fire he built, and made coffee that he got from his pack. He also chewed some beef jerky. By the time the sun became visible over the cañon rim, he was on his way.

His emotions were mixed. It was obvious Nan Steele had been sincere in coming to him with her petition for help, and the more he thought about it, the more evident it appeared that Ed Tyler had committed them to getting involved in the miners' struggle against the sheriff and his men. Just how Ed thought this would get them the stake they wanted, he hadn't the least notion, and he was rather irritated with his friend. On the other hand, he found himself quite against his will attracted to Nan Steele. In fact, try as he might, he couldn't drive her from his mind. He had never met anyone like her. She was a nurse, but somehow certainly wasn't dressed for the rôle. Not that he had had any previous experiences with nurses and hospitals, except once in Texas in a town where he had brought a wounded man to a country doctor and the physician's wife had acted as his nurse in assisting him. He knew that during the War Between the States men had been nurses. But, surely, Nan couldn't dress like that when she was assisting Dr. Logan. This thought changed the direction of his musing, and he came to believe now that he had heard enough about the doctor and the sheriff to understand how Ed might have come to want to side the claim owners.

Luke was keeping to the west side of the cañon and Eagle Creek, figuring that he could ask about Gopher Parsons's claim from the first miners he met. To his surprise, since there was no newspaper in Eagle Cañon and presumably little communication outside of town, from the very beginning of the diggings he found not only men up and at work, but his run-in with Sam Ingalls was already known to them. The first miner who laid eyes on him, grubbing in the sand along the creek bottom with pan, straightened, looked at him sharply, then called cordially: "Mornin', stranger! We was hopin' you'd be up this way. Heard all about what you did while I was at Gopher Parsons's claim last night."

"About what?" Luke queried, reining the black to a stand.

"You buckin' that blamed ornery sheriff yestiddy. Say, how come you're packin' an iron? Thought everybody knowed they wasn't allowed." As had happened yesterday, when he had stopped Nan Steele in town, this man's eyes had gone to Luke's gun and remained fastened on it. Then he laughed, as if he had some knowledge he wasn't divulging.

"Father Matthew told me I didn't have to hide it, except in town," Luke answered.

The claim owner slapped his knee and guffawed even more boisterously. He hailed his closest neighbor, fifty yards up the draw, and presently the two men gathered around and were talking eagerly to Luke. What had Father Matthew said yesterday after the kick in the belly he'd given Sam Ingalls? Had Ingalls tried to arrest him? Why was Father Matthew letting him openly carry a gun? Had he heard about the jail break in town? Did he believe Luke Barron and his gang were operating in the district?

Luke debated his answers carefully. He told the two miners that Father Matthew had told him he could keep his gun, providing he didn't cause trouble. He wasn't looking to tangle again with Sam Ingalls, and he didn't know anything about the jail break, except what he had learned when his room at the livery stable had been searched the previous night by a couple of deputies.

"Sounds to me like Father Matthew is finally coming to his senses 'bout that sheriff?" the second claim owner commented enthusiastically. Then he asked eagerly: "What do you aim to do now?"

"I'm looking for Gopher Parsons's claim," Luke answered truthfully. "I reckon I'll know a whole lot more about what comes next after I've seen him."

Laughter greeted this answer. Then, mysteriously, the men agreed that it would be a good thing for him to call on Gopher Parsons. He was told Parsons called his claim the Little Crow and was upcreek on the same side. They were certain Parsons could tell him what measures they were taking to protect their gold dust and their lives against Luke Barron and his gang as well as anybody else who might be of a mind to rob them. "I never did believe that hogwash about Yokum Bos!" the miner he had first encountered insisted. The other agreed with him.

Lifting his hand as he left them, Luke went on soberly, considering the testimony of these men who had, until now, worked and eaten and slept while haunted by a fear for their lives and the scant ounces of yellow dust they were taking from the placers. These men were obviously an assortment of all breeds, some honest, probably some who weren't. He now doubted that the Temple of the Redeemed meant very much to them, other than providing their claims with a legitimacy, and perhaps the conviction that some sort of religious belief was better than nothing. Neither of the men he had met had come with Father Matthew, Dr. Logan, and the others from Illinois. He supposed there would be some who had, and he suspected they would probably be the ones with the better claims. Whatever the case, it was obvious that these miners had been drawn together by two common denominators: first, the quest for gold, and now second, the fear of losing it. They were apt to reach out eagerly for the help of a man who could show them a way out from under the threat of the past weeks. They seemed to think that Gopher Parsons was that man.

Riding on up the cañon, he saw evidence of the enormous amount of work these men had put in to make their claims workable. Water was evidently at a premium. To conserve it, common sluices had been built along the two sides of the creek, flanking the diggings. The bed of the cañon was torn up into hundreds of holes, piles of pay dirt, and, higher beyond the sluices, discarded tailings that had been worked for gold. Crude shacks or tent dwellings were unevenly spaced on either side of Eagle Creek, closer in to the walls. The farther Luke rode, the more activity he saw on the claims. A number of them, those paying the best, were fenced strongly with barbed wire. As they became bigger, they were worked by more men. He passed what he believed to be Gopher Parsons's claim but did not stop. He was curious to find out what was at the farthest point. The Nan Steele had a sign proclaiming it but appeared otherwise abandoned. Beyond that, enclosed by a strong six-wire fence was an even bigger claim. Here he could see a giant ore wagon being loaded, probably for the trip down to Stirrup Gap. At a narrow gate in this fence was a boldly lettered sign.

Keep out!
No Trespassers
Sam Ingalls, Owner

Here, then, was the first and richest claim, the mother lode, Yokum Bos's mine, that the sheriff had appropriated after the man had been hanged for conspiracy and murder. Luke kept his horse out of sight while he dismounted and crept closer to the fence. He could see three men working the sand along the creek bottom with a sluice box and another loading the wagon. He had now followed Eagle Creek back to its source, where it burst above ground at the base at the back wall of the cañon that was in the shape of a giant ellipse, bounded by equally high cliffs on both sides. At its widest point the cañon below was at least a mile across, but the sides here at the rear gradually narrowed to slightly more than a mile. Up here, opposite where the sluicing started, was a pool formed by a small dam on the headwaters of Eagle Creek over which the water still flowed. Ingalls's workers definitely seemed to have no regard for wasting water, spilling it from the sluice box and a rocker with a carelessness that was certainly symbolic of the iron grip the sheriff's authority and that of the others on the council of elders held over this boom camp. All of

Ingalls's workmen were armed, Luke saw, whereas below he hadn't spotted a single weapon on any miner.

He made his way back to his horse and rode again downcreek. He passed George Steele's shack and saw that it was somewhat different from the majority of those he had seen below, even though it was built of the same materials: raw lumber, lath, and tarpaper. Its outline was the same as the others, low, squat, and flat-roofed. But it stood on a low knoll beside the narrow stream, and flowers grew at either side of its doorway. A tall cedar, the first of many that grew along the cañon above this point, shaded it coolly from the sun's brilliant glare. In the two windows that faced downcañon were curtains. These and the garden were visible evidence of a woman's hand that had been lacking in many of the shabby and litter-filled yards around the shacks downcañon. This dwelling had more the look of a home. It made him think again of Nan as he had last seen her.

Returning downcreek to the claim Luke believed to belong to Gopher Parsons, he made no effort to conceal his presence. As Luke rode up to a canvas tent, he saw the front flap was open. A man stepped out of it. He was well beyond middle age and wore a close-clipped gray beard that didn't quite hide the sharp angles of a hawkish face. His frame, stooped slightly at the shoulders, was spare. A long acquaintance with the sun had blackened his face, and at the corners of the eye-sockets were webbed lines that further marked him for what he was, a grizzled old wanderer who had spent many seasons staring into the bright glare of the desert's hot sands. To Luke's surprise he was smoking a hand-carved, short-stemmed pipe.

"Gopher Parsons?" Luke queried, as he reined in a few feet from the door.

"That's me," Parsons answered briefly. His lack of an invitation for Luke to dismount made plain the look in his squinted eyes that was faintly hostile. Gopher Parsons was a suspicious man.

Luke took the most direct way that occurred to him of wiping out the old prospector's wariness. "George Steele and Ed Tyler here?"

Parsons's look sharpened, turning even more wary. "Who's askin'?"

"Nan Steele told me last night she had left them here before she drove the wagon to town."

Suddenly Parsons's manner changed. He even smiled meagerly as he drawled: "You must be him. Luke Ashford. The one Ed mentioned would be comin'. Yore a mite previous, but light down?" He turned and called: "It's all right, George. You can come out. And bring a dipper of water with you. I'll wager we got a thirsty man out here."

Inside the tent Luke heard the ring of a dipper against a tin pail. As he swung aground, he asked: "Where's Ed?"

Parsons jerked his head toward the abrupt slope of the near cañon wall. "Up there somewheres. Said he wouldn't run us the risk of stayin' around the tent. So we give him a blanket, some grub, and a jug of water last night. He's due back down here right after dark."

As the old-timer finished speaking, a figure moved out from inside the tent behind him. George Steele wasn't nearly as old as Parsons, but he was rough-hewn, appeared capable, and had a smile on his face as he brought over the dipper of water and handed it to Luke.

"That there's from Logan's spring," he said. "Gopher bought two small barrels of it day before yesterday."

"An' thet's the last I intend to buy off thet snake charmer," Parsons announced.

Luke drank deeply from the dipper, then handed it back to George Steele.

"Got somethin' a bit stronger'n thet up to my claim, if the sheriff an' his men didn't drink it all when they was up there last night a-lookin' for me. Ed Tyler says he hopes to check out my claim later today to see if it's been jumped. I figure the sheriff's jumped it by now, same as he did old Yok's."

Luke was aware that whatever Ed had told these two had accomplished its purpose. Steele was showing range courtesy in not being overly curious. He was also obviously accepting Luke as his friend.

"How come you rode up here in broad daylight?" Parsons queried.

Luke told them of the errand Father Matthew had sent him on and, while he talked, a sober expression gathered on the faces of both of the prospectors. When he had finished, Steele said worriedly: "There ain't a lot a man can be certain of these days. Take even Ed Tyler. When I asked him why you and him was slingin' in with us, he said you had your own reasons, that he and you wanted to even things with the law. I reckon I can be satisfied with that, so long as you're helpin' us. But what'll the others say when it comes to trustin' you?"

"I don't know who is worse," Parsons put in, "that damned sheriff and his Avenging Angels or Luke Barron and his killers. I believe that sawbones is cheatin' us with his water business, but cheating is one thing. Murderin' men to get their gold is another. Luke Barron is by far the greater evil, and, I've heard, he and his gang did the same thing in the Colorado mine fields for years before the honest element drove them out. Now it's happenin' here, too."

"Parsons," drawled Luke, "you seem to know a heap about this Barron *hombre*."

"Ought to," he answered sharply. "Ed told us he used to ride with Barron in the old days, before he decided to go straight and struck out on his own. It were an acceedent thet

Sheriff Ingalls tied him to Barron's gang, based on an old reward dodger. A man who still rode with Barron wouldn't've done what Ed did when he put his life on the line, comin' back into the cañon instead of lightin' out for parts unknown once he was sprung outta jail."

"I reckon not," Luke admitted. And to himself, strangely enough, he also had to admit that he was concerned at what these men might think of him. He decided he could tell half the truth, and so he said: "Maybe Ed also told you that the Barron gang split up some time back, and that Barron left Colorado to return to Texas. I reckon it can't be Barron on the loose up here, no matter what Ingalls and his deputies have been saying. As for me, I've known Ed from when we were kids together. When I heard he was in trouble up here, I came up to get him out of it. One thing led to another, and here we are. It was Ed who proposed we stay on and help put down this Luke Barron scare. Guess he wants to clear his old pardner's name."

Gopher Parsons's forehead was knotted in intense concentration. "I don't know about clearing Luke Barron's name," he said. "Men have been killed, and no one can ship out any gold. We've all managed to eke out a heap of gold from our claims, but what cain we do with it, an' if we hang onto it, we'll probably get murdered. Organizin' as vigilantes is our last hope fer gettin' our gold out, an' savin' our hides."

Steele had been listening, chewing tobacco. "Don't take this wrong, stranger," he interrupted. "We appreciate what Ed's doin' for us, and what he says you and him intend to do to help the camp, but why does it matter to you? I understand how it must be in Ed's case. He wants to put the past behind him. But you?"

"Ed's pretty close-mouthed," Luke lied casually. "You never know what's going on inside that head of his. But about this

149

other, this gold that's to be shipped out. It. . . ."

"It ain't goin' to be shipped out now!" Steele said. "Not so long as Ingalls knows about it."

"I've got an idea it should be shipped and the sooner the better," Luke told them. "Only not the way Ingalls may think. Send down word that it's to go by wagon. But instead of filling the money chests with dust, fill them with sand. Load the wagon to the axles with guards. Then. . . ."

"But we ain't allowed to show any guns!" Steele protested. "A lot of 'em were collected back last night, but we still got to keep 'em hidden from Ingalls and his deputies. So we ain't likely to go sportin' 'em in front of them, gold shipment or no gold shipment. We were countin', instead, on sneaking out a special shipment down the road at night."

"All right. Keep your guns hidden. Have the men who're to act as guards go down the trail tomorrow, before the wagon leaves, taking plenty of guns with them, but concealed. Then, after they leave, load your wagon with those chestfuls of sand and pile on some unarmed guards and pass through the camp. Your unarmed guards can meet up with the others down the road and pick up their guns."

"If the gold ain't in the wagon, what's the use of runnin' that kind of a sandy?" Parsons wanted to know.

"To decoy the bunch that's after the gold, Luke Barron or whoever." Luke paused to glance meaningfully at both men. "They'll stop the wagon somewhere along the trail to Stirrup Gap. Your guards can high-tail and leave the wagon, taking to the brush." He paused a moment, remembering something he had noticed riding in. "There's a side road forks from the main trail right below town, isn't there?"

Steele nodded, puzzled over what Luke was driving at. "Leads down around Rattlesnake Mesa. It's rough and washed out, but a man can get through. Yokum Bos and his wife have a cabin up that way. The trail hits out beyond the mesa. It also runs toward Stirrup Gap eventually, but it's a long way 'round."

"Then send a man in a light rig on down ahead of the wagon," Luke resumed. "Send him alone. Load the rig with whatever you want, maybe furniture, like he was a man headed out for good. Pack the gold in with the load. Have your man take the trail around Rattlesnake Mesa to be sure nothing goes wrong. Before anyone knows what's happened, your gold's in the Stirrup Gap bank."

Steele's eyes sparkled with ready admiration. He hit an open palm with a clenched fist. "It could work! Slick as saddlesoap, if it does, eh, Gopher?"

"I . . . I hope no one'll be hurt," Parsons said in a low voice. Looking at Luke with a strange light in his eyes, he said abruptly: "I opine yo're the one to take the gold out!"

"I am?"

He nodded. "In case anything goes wrong, you'll know what to do. It'll be like . . . like your breaking in the roof of the jail last night to get Ed Tyler out. No one would have thought of that. But you did."

"Who said I did?" Luke asked in astonishment.

"Never mind thet, now. You don't know how bad things are here. There isn't a man working a claim who'll trust his neighbor these days fer very long. If one of us was named to drive thet gold down the mesa road, someone would shore object, 'cause no two can agree on nary a thing. Last night's meetin' proved thet. Everyone is in favor of havin' vigilantes, but they're a-scared as can be of Ingalls and his gang, all the same. Some also believe in that Temple high priest, Father Matthew, and fear defyin' God if it means defyin' Ingalls."

"Why would they trust me?" Luke couldn't help smiling at the thought.

"They'll trust yuh," Parsons assured Luke gravely. "I know. You have thet look about yuh. They know what yuh did yesterday to Sam Ingalls, and Father Matthew's trustin' yuh will put yuh in right with 'em as believes in the Temple."

Steele put in: "Gopher's right, Luke. You're the man to do it."

"What excuse can I have for driving a rig out of town?"

George Steele's mind had been at work these past moments while Parsons was urging Luke to help them. Now he had a ready answer to Luke's question. As far as Steele was concerned, Nan, more than anyone else, was the one person in the whole world in which he would, and could, place his absolute trust. "You talked with Nan last night," he said now. "Thet's how come you say you're here. Well, I'll stay in hidin' here, along with Ed Tyler. You go back to town, get Nan to get the wagon from the livery, go up to my claim, and load up most of the stuff from our shack into it. No one's goin' to object to Nan's headin' outta town with my stuff, and you're jest along to lend her a hand. You can get that gold from us miners and get it to Stirrup Gap with the stuff from our place. Leave Nan in Stirrup Gap. Soon as I can, I'll slip out and meet up with her. I know thet girl wants out, anyway."

"And leave your claim here for Ingalls to steal it like he did Yokum Bos's?" Parsons asked in disgust.

Steele stubbornly shook his head. "We were the first men in here, Yokum and me, with two pack burros. I'll be glad to leave alive, and not the way Yokum went. If Luke can get my dust through with Nan, I'll have my little pile. I'm as greedy as the next man, but my life ain't worth a plug nickel now with thet doctor on the warpath. To be honest, I've had a bellyful of Logan, Ingalls, Father Matthew, and the rest of them. I'll be happy jest to get shut of here."

Luke could see worry in Gopher Parsons's old eyes, and

real anger behind that. But for the interruption that came at this moment — the whistle that sounded from a patch of scrub cedar close by up the cañon's slope, he didn't know what else might have been said. At the sound of that call all three turned to look above. There, waving down to them, exposed from any concealment, was Ed Tyler.

Steele gave a quick glance around. He said sharply: "Stay here, Gopher! Give us a call if anyone comes up the trail."

He led the way up the slope, Luke following. Ed Tyler's dark, homely face took on a broad grin as Luke made his way up to him. He said: "You've got gall, Luke, strayin' up here at this time of day."

They talked a minute or so, Steele and Luke posting Ed on recent developments and the plan for taking the gold out. Ed had worked with Luke so long he was able to take in the situation quickly and play right along. He even had something to add.

"George, you know you were tellin' me only last night thet you're convinced this wild bunch maybe is forted up some place on Rattlesnake Mesa? Well, if Luke here can help me get past the guard, I reckon I'll take me a little *pasear* in the direction of Rattlesnake Mesa. Mebbe I can locate where thet gang's holed up. I did some scouting from the top of the ridge here, an' I'm sure I can scale the back wall and get back here without bein' seen."

"It'll be good work, Ed, if you can pull it off," Luke said.

"Sure," Ed agreed, "an' if I strike pay dirt, we can take a few rifles up there and let 'em taste some lead?"

Luke considered this. At first he was against the idea. But on second thought, to raid the outlaws' camp, if they had one there, might help create a distraction while he and Ed were getting away with the gold. Nan, of course, would present a problem, but not an insurmountable one, and he might be able

153

to get through with the gold himself without interference. No doubt this was the way Ed was seeing it.

Luke said: "All right, Ed, if you find their hide-out, I'm sure Gopher Parsons and George here can get some men to side you."

"Just what I was thinkin' about shippin' thet gold out," Steele said. "No one's to know you're takin' it down the mesa road, Luke. No one but the four or five men we pick as guards for the wagon and the miners whose gold we'll send through, and ourselves."

"To cut down those numbers even more," Luke said, "pick the guards from those who will be sending out their gold."

"Yeah, before this gang pulls another raid," Ed put in. "Gents, this thing's shapin' up right nice." He held out a hand toward Steele. "Can I borrow thet tobacco pouch of yours, George? I used up what makin's Luke gave me last night, but I got a few papers left."

Steele took a pipe pouch out of his shirt pocket and passed it across. "It's right fine cavendish," he said, "only don't let thet damned doctor know I'm packin' it." He grinned. Luke and Ed smiled back at him.

Not long before Ray Cune had arrived at George Steele's shack along Eagle Creek, Sheriff Ingalls and his deputies had decided to call a night of it. There was a small bedroom off the combination kitchen and sitting room that was obviously Nan Steele's when she stayed there to be with her father. Ingalls had chosen Nan's bed, narrow but with an iron bedstead, to sleep off an over-indulgence in the contents of the jug he and Mart Kemp had shared. Kemp claimed George's Steele's cot near the sheet-metal stove — after all, he had started the fire and kept it stoked — while Tiny Hart and Pink Morgan had brought in their bedrolls and positioned themselves on the floor on either side of the kitchen table.

Pink Morgan, despite having drunk his fill from the half-full jug that he and Tiny had shared, was a light sleeper, and he had heard the approach of Ray Cune's horse and was ready to meet him at the door with a drawn Colt after the deputy dismounted, tied his horse, and walked to the single step that served as a stoop before the entrance. Old cowhides were tacked up over the front windows, covered by oiled paper on the inside, and in the dark Cune had overshot the mark at first and found himself halfway to the former Yokum Bos claim before he had reined up, turned back, and finally with only starshine to assist him — the moon had nearly set — had found the shack looming in the surrounding darkness. He might have missed it even then had not one of the horses, hobbled in back of the shack, whickered to his pony.

"Hello, the house," Ray called before even knocking.

Having recognized his voice, Pink opened the door, wondering what could possibly have brought Cune all this distance from town, where he was supposed to be keeping an eye on the check point. Sheriff Ingalls was aroused and proved completely out of sorts when he heard the news of the escape. By this time both Pink Morgan and Tiny Hart were also awake.

Rather than to try going back to sleep, the sheriff ordered his men to saddle up, with the exception of Mart Kemp who was to be left behind on the off-chance that George Steele might return to the shack. Even more than the escape, the theft of the guns at the check point outside Eagle Cañon worried Sheriff Ingalls. In all probability this meant that, henceforth, the miners would be armed, making the job of robbing them all the more dangerous.

Ingalls's intention was to return to town, sided by the Avenging Angels with him at the Nan Steele mining claim. What little there was left of the sour mash they had been

155

drinking was left behind for safekeeping with Mart Kemp, but not before Ray Cune took a slug as a protection against the night's chill.

Once Sam Ingalls and his men arrived back in Eagle Cañon, the sheriff gave out orders to Arlie Michaels, to be supported by Tiny Hart and Pink Morgan, that everyone was to be turned back at the entrance to the camp on the Stirrup Gap road except freighters with supplies intended for the local merchants or the workmen on the construction of the new bank building, since they would now also be needed to repair what had happened to the jail, and that no miner or his family was to leave the district without being thoroughly searched for firearms. The sheriff was invoking martial law — notwithstanding that he had actually no legal authority to do so — because Ed Tyler was a fugitive at large, and his liberty presumably placed the lives of everyone in jeopardy. Having attended to all these matters and with dawn perhaps only an hour away, Sam Ingalls had retired to the small shack he maintained. Arlie Michaels had informed him that he had passed Father Matthew and Nan Steele on their way out of Eagle Cañon well after midnight, but he had had no idea whether Timothy had told the truth that they were heading out to the Bos cabin near Rattlesnake Mesa. Ingalls had been puzzled by this news, had not known what to make of it, but also didn't see any potential threat coming from such a visit to the martial law he had imposed.

It had been Ingalls's intention to look up Dr. Royal Logan the first thing in the morning and ask if the medical man had any idea why Father Matthew would want to visit Neele Bos in the dead of night, but the nascent effects of the sour mash he had consumed earlier were still with him to an extent, and he overslept, so that it was Dr. Logan who came first to the sheriff's door. Ingalls, when finally aroused by the doctor's repeated knocking at his door, crammed a piece of jerky into his mouth in case the sour mash had left any residue on his breath that might be detected by the Puritan son-of-a-bitch — as he referred to Logan in the privacy of his own thoughts.

"Good to see you, Doc," Ingalls said with a heartiness he scarcely felt, as he opened the door and bid the medical man to enter. He had pulled on his pants over his longjohns, but his suspenders were still dragging at his sides. "I'm afraid I slept a little later than I wanted to this morning."

"I suppose, Sam," the medical man said, entering, neatly dressed in a dark suit with a starched collar, "you know that Ed Tyler was broken out of jail last night?"

"Yeah, I know all about it," the sheriff admitted, closing the door. "Why don't you sit down at the table there, Doc, while I put on some coffee?"

"I didn't come to visit, Sam," the doctor said, somewhat coldly, as he stood stiffly just in the room. "I came to learn what happened to my nurse and Father Matthew. They're both gone. You should also know that Lee Hop told me, when he brought me my morning tea, he is planning to move back to Stirrup Gap with his family, perhaps as early as this afternoon."

"Good riddance, I say," Ingalls commented. "You know I got no use for that Chinaman, or any others with slant-eyes. They're human vermin, that's what they are."

"Be that as it may, Sam, I didn't come here, either, to hear you hold forth on the superiority of the white race. What makes us . . . any of us . . . superior is the success with which we avoid indulgence in vice. The truly redeemed among us shies away from those who drink or smoke or gamble or engage in decadence like dancing. As far as I know, Lee Hop and his family have never done any of those things."

"Aw, Doc, he probably smokes opium on the sly," put in the sheriff, who was becoming argumentative at the same time as concerned lest the doctor might suspect what he or his deputies had been doing at George Steele's shack. "All those Chinks do, you know."

"I know nothing of the kind, Sam. But, frankly, this is getting us nowhere. I don't suppose you captured George Steele, at least Tiny Hart . . . who looks in terribly bad shape . . . told me so at the Eagle Cañon check point. If I didn't know better, Sam, I'd swear that man had been drinking."

"Can't be, Doc. We found nary a drop out at Steele's shack. Comes to it, we didn't find no still, either, but I reckon there is one, only well hid. We'll find it, Doc, an' we'll find Steele himself before very long."

"I told you yesterday, and I'll tell you again now, Sam, I want George Steele found, and I want him hanged. The only way for prohibition to work is to catch the reprobates and smite them from the face of the earth. I told Father Matthew the same thing earlier last evening, before he disappeared. Wine is no longer to be used even with Holy Communion."

"Listen, Doc, Father Matthew ain't disappeared," Ingalls said, moving away from the medical man, back into the room toward the stove and the coffee pot on it.

"Where is he, then? And where is Nan Steele? You must know I've asked Nan to become my wife. I plan to marry her in a Temple ceremony."

"Don't fret yerself about those two, Doc. As I heard it, they left town together late last night."

"Left town?" the doctor asked, confusion, even apprehension now in his voice.

"Yeah, but there's nothin' to get head up over." The sheriff was lifting the coffee pot and pointed now to the barrel he had of the doctor's water. "Let me put some fresh grounds in here, an' we'll have a cup of coffee together."

"I've already had my morning tea, thank you," the doctor

said. "Now, just what do you mean Father Matthew and Nan left town together late last light?"

"Don't know too much more about it, Doc, but what Arlie Michaels told me when I got back here to camp from Steele's place. He said Nan Steele and the old priest rode out of town well after midnight in a buggy."

"Did Michaels say where they were going?"

"As a matter of fact, Doc, he did. I was figgerin' on lookin' you up this mornin' to ask you about it. According to Michaels, Timothy said they was headin' out to Neele Bos's place, but that don't hardly make no sense, not after Father Matthew was among them as sentenced old Yokum to be hanged."

"My God, man, are you sure?"

"That's what Michaels told me."

"I've got to stop them," Dr. Logan said, turning quickly toward the door.

"Reckon it's a little late to do that, Doc. They're shorely out to the Bos place by a considerable spell. . . ." He stopped speaking because the doctor had torn the door open and was now hurrying on his way.

Chapter Twelve

It was past noon when Luke Ashford rode into Eagle Cañon, his Colt tucked in the top of his right boot, his shell belt and holster in a saddlebag. He was tense, in part because of the an imposing challenge of just how he was going to manage to get a saddle horse for Ed Tyler out of camp and past the check point. George Steele was no less a fugitive than Ed was, but his situation was not quite so pressing. On the other hand, in order to obtain Nan Steele's co-operation in the ruse to get the miners' gold shipment out of Eagle Cañon, Luke had to make George Steele's liberty an essential part of the plan.

What had been rankling Luke increasingly since he had ridden into Eagle Cañon was a deep-seated opposition to what was going on here. This irritation was now going beyond any consideration about his own enrichment once he and Ed succeeded in making off with the gold shipment. Sheriff Ingalls was no cipher. The man was motivated by simple greed. Yet, it disturbed Luke in a fundamental way that what depredations had so far occurred had been so unjustly blamed on Luke Barron and his gang. What a devilish joke. There wasn't even a Luke Barron gang any more!

The powerful windmill and the water tower near it, containing Dr. Logan's water supply, were visible on the cliffside before Luke even entered the outskirts of the camp's main street. They were for him symbols of something more powerful and more terrible than any lust for gold. Royal Logan depended for his power on human fear. He had somehow been able to convince everyone that they needed this water in order to avoid illness or worse. In its way it was just another link in the design

160

that everyone in Eagle Cañon had embraced, whether they believed in the tenets of the Temple of the Redeemed or not, that somehow they all benefited from the prohibitions that had been imposed through the medical man's own successful grasp for power over their lives. Intolerance is what fired the mechanism of Dr. Logan's control over their lives. He had twisted the natural human inclination of clannishness with its attendant hatred and distrust for outsiders into a systematic abridgment of personal freedom — and the most incredible aspect of the whole tyrannical scheme was that no one seemed aware of the consequences or, if they were aware, able to do anything to combat the system of choices the doctor had imposed on them.

This whole business was forcing Luke to do a lot more thinking than he had been accustomed to do in the past, and the basic reason that he was doing it, he knew, was that a desperate anger within him toward Dr. Logan no less than toward Sheriff Ingalls and his men was literally tearing him away from what appeared such an easy way to start his life over on a new basis. What did it matter that Ingalls should have tortured and then hanged a man to get his gold claim for himself? What did it matter that, if he were caught, George Steele would be hanged because he distilled and dispensed home-brewed sour mash whiskey? Did it even matter that two men had been killed, and probably others would be as well, and their murders blamed on Luke Barron? None of this should matter, and the most infernal thing about it was that, somehow, they all did matter. The more he thought about them, the more outraged Luke found himself becoming, almost, if not quite, to the point where he might be willing to sacrifice his own immediate prospects for enrichment to break the strangle hold that had been imposed on these poor fools in Eagle Cañon.

Luke knew how dangerous this kind of thinking could be. If he followed the thrust of his inner rebellion at both the physical and subtle mental tyranny he had seen since coming here, he could very well end up losing not only the gold shipment but his own life in the bargain. It was into this crazy, divisive mêlée of his own thoughts that there came, as a vision, the image of Nan Steele. She was standing there again, near the door to his small sleeping room in the livery stable, the high-crowned Stetson on her head, her light blonde hair tucked beneath its brim. He was asking her softly — "If we get out of this, might you be willing to come to a dance with me down to Stirrup Gap?" — and she was pausing, while gazing at him circumspectly in the flickering candlelight, before saying — "When we get out of this, Luke Ashford, I want any dancing we do to be done right here . . . in Eagle Cañon."

He would have thought that a woman, and especially one dressed like a boy with the airs of a range man despite having been educated in the East, could never affect him the way she had, yet he couldn't get that image of her out of his soul. It threatened all that he planned, all that he had been, all that he might become, and there she was, her trust and belief in him, however tentative, somehow more important to him right now — to his essential being — than any other prospect before him. He could not have said why this was so, but it was, just as a sudden fury at the ridiculous injustice of it all suffused him as he saw dimly ahead the men and women gathered into a line, waiting to buy their daily ration of Dr. Logan's water.

The double doors of the livery stable were open when Luke rode up and dismounted at the entrance. Taking the black gelding's reins, he walked the horse along the center runway between the stalls, the combined odors of ammonia, horse manure, and fodder strong even though the sliding back door was also open, allowing the air to circulate. The black hosteler was in a nearby stall on the left, rubbing down a horse.

"Howdy, Timothy," Luke said, halting before the stall.

"Sheriff Ingalls or his deputies looking for me?"

"Don't reckon dey is," Timothy said, pausing in his work and smiling. "Dere's plenty to keep 'em busy dis day. No one from outside is allowed in de camp any more. Sheriff's orders. No one 'cept de stage, which only comes once a week anyway, an' freight wagons for de stores an' such."

"Why? Is the sheriff worried about that escaped prisoner getting out of Eagle Cañon?"

"Dat's what he says, an' I hope dat's de reason. If it ain't, mebbe Lee Hop's got de right idea. He wants to pull out dis aftahnoon."

"Is this being done with Father Matthew's approval?" Luke wondered, reaching unconsciously to his shirt pocket for his makings before he caught himself.

"If'n y'all wants to smoke, it's O K, I'd guess, since de doctor's gone. Went headin' lickety-split outta town soon's he heard dat Father Matthew and Miss Nan done gone out to de Bos place."

"When did they leave?" Luke asked, dropping the gelding's reins and preparing to roll a cigarette.

"Las' night, not long aftah Miss Nan was talkin' to you upstairs."

"Is there anything wrong that the doctor headed out of town, too?"

"Ah reckon he has his reasons, Mistah Ashford. It weren't muh place to ask."

"Do you have any idea when Miss Nan will be getting back?"

"No, suh, Ah shorely don't. Since she was drivin' de buggy for Father Matthew, Ah expect she'll be back when he is."

"Mind if I leave my horse here for a spell? I want to have a word with the sheriff."

"Put him in an empty stall. Ah'll rub him down and grain

163

him soon's Ah get de chance."

"Thanks, Timothy. Let me know what I owe you."

The Negro nodded and smiled but said no more.

Luke stalled the black gelding, removing the saddle, saddle blanket, and bridle reins, concerned now with what impact Nan's unexpected absence from Eagle Cañon might have on the plan he had worked out with Gopher Parsons and George Steele.

Nan Steele, picking herself up from where she had stumbled when shoved backward by the impact of Father Matthew, had rushed forward. She was numb with shock and terror over what had happened, but her instincts were focused not so much on her emotion as on what possible medical assistance she could now be to the old priest.

Neele Bos, after she had fired the fateful bullet from the Colt House Pistol, dropped the gun, horror-stricken at what she had done, and then stumbled forward, collapsing over the fallen man.

"I am sorry, so . . . so sorry, Matthew," Neele Bos sobbed, lifting the old priest's head. "I didn't mean to kill you!"

"You have done a terrible thing, Neele," Nan said sternly, kneeling beside Father Matthew across from the grieving woman. "Just let me see how much damage has been done."

Father Matthew's hands now were clutching his chest just slightly below the heart. Nan pried the hands apart to see the small, gaping wound from which blood was slowly pulsing.

"We have to get him inside, Neele," Nan said. "We have to stop the bleeding, if we can. We don't want him to die."

Father Matthew was still conscious. He turned his eyes toward Nan, looking up at her. "I'm afraid it's too late for anything else, dear Nan." His voice was strained through pain, almost a whisper.

It was exceedingly hard to get the priest's body up off the ground, into the Bos cabin, and onto the only bed. This was not because Father Matthew was so heavy. He seemed, in fact, to Nan Steele to be a surprisingly light burden, as if the fullness of his soul had now somehow come to manifest itself through a surprising degree of weightlessness, combined with the ascetic thinness of his physical frame. The difficulty was with Neele Bos who was nearly hysterical with grief. Yet, somehow, together they managed it.

"Put some water on to boil, Neele," Nan ordered, "but first bring me something I can use as a compress." While she spoke, Nan was reaching forward and examining the area of the wound behind the cloth of the priest's cassock. "I also need a knife. Oh, never mind, I'll get that myself."

Nan hurried across the narrow bedroom and into the kitchen-sitting room as Neele was rummaging in an old chest of drawers at the foot of the bed. Finding a knife, Nan also paused to carry the lamp from the kitchen table into the small bedroom, putting it down on an old trunk set near the head of the bed. Neele was there now with an old shirt that had belonged to her husband. Nan took it as Neele rushed at once into the kitchen to see to the boiling water.

Slitting the priest's cassock near the wound, Nan could see that it was indeed serious, and felt very much at a loss over what to do. If the bullet was still in his body, that would present a problem. But a worse problem was the bleeding that she was uncertain she could stop, as she cut a sleeve from the old shirt and used that to stanch the flow.

Father Matthew's eyes fluttered open, and he looked gently at Nan.

"Please, Nan, ask Neele to come here."

"Father, she's getting some hot water," Nan explained. "I have to stop this bleeding somehow."

"It is too late . . . I fear," he said, his voice still a low whisper. "I beg you. Call her."

"Neele," Nan said in a louder voice, but without rising, "Father Matthew wants you."

"Yes, Matthew," Neele said, coming in the doorway, her craggy face wreathed by tears.

"Come here, Neele . . . please," the old priest gasped softly, under a great strain to speak.

Nan cut off another sleeve, rolling it up to replace the compress that was already blood-soaked.

"Matthew, I am so sorry . . . I didn't know what I was doing," Neele said brokenly as she leaned over him in front of where Nan was sitting on the bed.

"I came here tonight, Neele . . . ," the old priest said, so softly that he could be heard only with difficulty, "because . . . there was one thing . . . one thing especially . . . I wanted to tell you. Now it may be all . . . that I can say."

"Yes, Matthew . . . ?" Neele asked, bending farther over and reaching out to touch him mutely, gently, fearful of hurting him any more.

The old priest's eyes had grown dark, perhaps an illusion caused by the dim, flickering lamplight. He spoke now even more softly, his voice a wisp, a gossamer strand amid the quiet breathing in that room.

"One needs . . . Neele . . . in this lower sphere . . . to love so . . . many things . . . in order . . . to know . . . after all . . . what one . . . loves . . . most."

It must have cost the old priest all the energy he had to say that. His eyes were open, but he said no more. There was only an involuntary gasp, and then nothing.

Neele stood in silence. Nan, tears now rolling down her own cheeks, clutched helplessly at the compress. The flow of the blood had stopped.

Chapter Thirteen

Sam Ingalls certainly made no secret of the contempt he felt toward Lee Hop, Sung Yü, and their child. In this, several of the members of the Temple of the Redeemed at least tacitly agreed with him, not yet having transferred, as Dr. Logan wished, those same feelings toward those who broke the prohibitions he had put in place. Some frontier communities had even passed laws forbidding people of Chinese extraction to engage in mining of any kind. Such laws, like the Greaser Act in California which had applied to Mexicans still living on what had once been Mexican territory, were felt necessary to prevent these foreigners from robbing hard-working white men of what was rightfully theirs. However, when it came to Lee Hop and Sung Yü, the sheriff was only too ready to concede that they posed no threat to his mining interests in Eagle Cañon or to those of the other claim owners. Ingalls had had some time to think over the consequences of what Dr. Logan had told him, early this morning, Lee Hop was planning, and he decided the time had come for him to intervene.

The estimate the contractor from Stirrup Gap gave him on repairing the damage to the jail — and thus interrupting work on the bank building — was at least two days, possibly three, and this was true only if arrangements could be made to house the workmen overnight in Eagle Cañon. The sheriff, as one of the council of elders, had taken it upon himself to arrange with Frank Summers at the mercantile to outfit the work crew with tents, blankets, and other requirements to accommodate the workmen on a temporary basis. To see that they were properly fed, Lee Hop would have to be called into service. Since the

Chinaman could not possibly serve this crew were he to pull up stakes and move back to Stirrup Gap, Ingalls had gone to Lee Hop's café in an effort to persuade the man to stay. He offered Lee Hop protection against all harm from members of the Luke Barron gang and found, after negotiating with the shrewd café owner, that he must also agree to a payment of fifty dollars in gold before Lee Hop would even consider the proposal.

They had just concluded their agreement — in fact, the sheriff had just counted out two double eagles and an eagle and laid them on the counter — when Luke Ashford strolled in to have lunch. He was dusty from his ride and badly in need of a shave. He took a stool at the counter.

Lee Hop, having picked up the money and placed it in a pocket of his pajama coat, walked over behind the counter and asked the stranger what he could get for him. Luke was studying the menu written with chalk on a board behind the counter.

"You really serve eggs here?" Luke asked.

"Yes," the Chinaman replied. "We have our own chickees in a coop in back."

"O K, then. Eggs, bacon, a biscuit, and coffee," Luke ordered.

Lee Hop nodded and walked back to the kitchen where Sung Yū helped him with the cooking. At the same time, Hank DeForest, the contractor who also acted as superintendent for the work crew, had called lunch, and the workers were entering the café, shifting three of the four square tables so they could eat together. Sheriff Ingalls, who had been staring truculantly at Luke Ashford, approached him now, as Lee Hop came out of the kitchen and headed toward the workers to get their orders.

"I see you ain't healed today," the sheriff remarked, pausing next to where Luke was sitting. "Keep it that way, an' mebbe

168

you won't have any more trouble with the law around here."

"Actually, Sheriff, I'm glad to see you," Luke said, smiling, and pushing his Stetson back on his head. "I was planning on looking you up right soon."

"That so? How come?"

Luke gestured for the sheriff to join him at the counter. The workers were giving their orders to Lee Hop and talking among themselves, making quite a din. Two more customers in the meantime entered, making for the counter.

"Father Matthew appointed me a special deputy yesterday," Luke said to the sheriff after he parked himself on the vacant stool next to him.

"I know that," the sheriff said gruffly.

"I had a meeting with some of the miners this morning out at Gopher Parsons's claim," Luke continued, dropping his voice. "A secret gold shipment is being planned. I'd like to discuss the details with you."

Sam Ingalls was obviously startled. "Say nuthin' more," he warned. He looked toward the end of the counter and nodded to one of the two men who had just sat down there. "Meet me over at the livery stable soon's you finish eatin', an' we'll have a good talk."

"Right you are, Sheriff," Luke said, smiling again.

The sheriff stood up, squeezed Luke's shoulder, his face still somewhat expressionless, and made for the door of the café. Frank Summers and his sister, Rebecca, were entering as he was leaving, and he paused briefly to exchange greetings, glancing warmly at the tables were the workmen were sitting, obviously pleased at the way things were going.

Luke considered himself fortunate, having got his order in early, since by the time he was served, the place was so crowded that some people were standing just outside the entrance. One of the newcomers was Ray Cune, the deputy who had an order to place for himself and also was to order meals to go for Tiny Hart and Pink Morgan who were unable to leave the check point. This morning Cune was in charge of dispensing the doctor's water and had had to lock the spigot during his lunch period. He didn't really know Luke Ashford, despite their run-in at the check point and their encounter last night, but he may have been talking to the sheriff, since he pushed his way forward to claim Luke's place at the counter and winked at him as Luke passed on his way to the door.

There was a horse corral behind the small wagon yard alongside the livery stable, and Luke found Sheriff Ingalls, sitting on the top rung of the horse corral, indulging himself in a chaw of tobacco, more or less out of sight of Temple members who would certainly have disapproved.

Ingalls, espying Luke, motioned for him to come over. "We'll be able to talk privately out here," he said, as Luke walked up to where he was sitting at the back of the corral. "Even Father Matthew's nigger is havin' lunch."

Luke climbed up the rungs and sat next to the sheriff. He shook his head, no, when the sheriff held out his square plug of tobacco with a corner already bitten off.

"When's the next stage due in?" Luke asked.

"There's one run a week, usually," Ingalls replied, placing the plug back in a vest pocket. "Next one's due the day after tomorrow. Mostly we got to turn back drummers and boomers, but there's mail and other things that come through. Why?"

Luke told the lawman that the miners would be getting ready a gold shipment, hoping to send it out on the next stage with several of them acting as guards. The sheriff thought the plan probably a good one, especially if it was kept secret even from the other miners whose gold wouldn't be involved.

Although she wasn't back as yet that he could see, Luke then decided to confide in the sheriff how he had agreed to

170

help Nan Steele move out of Eagle Cañon, but he never got to it. The livery stable blocked a view of the main street until the old priest's buggy had passed the building and appeared in front of the small wagon yard. It was for this reason that neither Sheriff Ingalls nor Luke Ashford saw Dr. Logan until the buggy came into view.

Seeing the medical man, and knowing he didn't have time to spit out his wad of tobacco without being observed, the sheriff to his obvious embarrassment was forced to swallow it. Luke kept a straight face. This action could only win the sheriff's silent gratitude.

"Sam!" the doctor called from the buggy. "Come here."

An older woman was sitting next to the physician in the buggy, her head bent forward, her face partially hidden by the shawl she was wearing. The sheriff turned around and dropped from the corral rail, as did Luke, who joined him in hurrying over to the buggy. As they cleared the corral, Pink Morgan came running up main street, evidently having followed the buggy here from the check point.

"Who you got there, Doc?" Ingalls asked, his throat perhaps still a little thick, having been constricted by swallowing his chewing tobacco.

"Neele Bos," the physician said abruptly. "She is to be tried for murder."

"Murder?" the sheriff repeated. "Who'd she murder?"

"Doc says she killed Father Matthew," Pink Morgan huffed, as he joined them next to the buggy.

"Shot him, Sam," the doctor said. "Shot and killed Father Matthew."

Luke looked confusedly at the woman, sitting beside the physician. The shawl about her head reminded him of the vision he had had when, riding toward Eagle Cañon, he had seen someone, cutting down the hanged body of Yokum Bos.

"You can't be serious, Doc," Ingalls said awkwardly. "Father Matthew can't be dead."

"He most certainly is, Sam," the doctor said. "I've left Nan with the body out at the Bos cabin. I didn't want to do it, but I had no other reasonable choice. Nan's a trained nurse. She saw it happen. This witch shot and killed Father Matthew."

"But . . . but . . . for God's sake . . . why?" the sheriff stammered.

Pink Morgan had his Colt out now and was covering the prisoner.

"What'll happen to the Temple of the Redeemed?" the sheriff asked, unable to recover very quickly from the shock of what he had just heard.

"The Temple will go on," the doctor assured him.

"But how can it?" the sheriff blurted. "I mean . . . without Father Matthew?"

"Now, Sam, you're thinking just like Satan who has possessed this woman," the medical man stated with authority. "The true faith in which we all believe cannot be destroyed, even if we have lost our prophet."

"But . . . ?" the sheriff began, still befuddled.

"I want this woman jailed, Sam," the doctor directed. "I want her tried before the council of elders and executed before the entire membership."

"Sure, Doc, sure . . . anything you say," the sheriff agreed. "We'll build a scaffold right down in the middle of the street . . . you just say the word."

"No!" thundered the physician. "This woman . . . Neele Bos . . . is to be dealt with the same way men have always dealt with the brides of Satan. She's to be burned at the stake."

If Luke had expected any reaction from the prisoner, upon hearing the doctor's decree, he was disappointed. Her head had dropped even more, effectively hiding her face from the fury in the doctor's voice and from the glances of those standing around the buggy. When he looked toward the street, Luke could see men coming over now from Lee Hop's and from other places of business.

"Will someone go tell Timothy what's happened?" the doctor asked, his gaze falling on Luke Ashford. "I will want him to hitch up a wagon to go out and bring Father Matthew's body back to town for a Christian burial."

"Yes, sir," Luke said, somehow feeling the need to respond to what he had heard would best be served by his doing something.

Pulling away from the group gathering around the buggy, Luke made his way quickly toward the back of the livery stable. The large sliding door was still open. As he stepped into the stable, Timothy was already coming out of the door that led to his living quarters, no doubt having heard something of the commotion outside.

"Doctor Logan is outside with Yokum Bos's widow," Luke told the hosteler in a level voice as he came over toward him. "He claims she shot Father Matthew out at her place. The doctor wants you to get a wagon harnessed and go out there. I'll ride along with you. Miss Nan is at the Bos place with the body."

As he heard Luke's words, Timothy stopped moving. A deep anguish flickered in his eyes, visible even through the gloom inside the stable. "He's dead, then?"

"Yes, Timothy, that's what the doctor says. Probably the woman held against him what had happened to her husband."

"More dan dat, I fear, Mistah Ashford," the Negro said quietly. "Father Matthew knew de end was near. Ah done tol' you dat only yesterday afternoon he said he'd be betrayed. Now it's happened." He shook his head sadly, his hands held helplessly at his sides. "Ah knew it, Mistah Ashford. Ah knew it when he was so het up on goin' out dere las' night. Ah figgered no good could come of it. But so soon . . . ? Is de doctor shore?"

"Seems he is."

"O K, den you get your horse saddled. Ah'll look to harnessin' de wagon."

"I'd better get a horse for Miss Nan, too," Luke said, and turned to where his black was stalled.

Timothy went toward the wall where the wagon and buggy harnesses were hung.

It had taken Ed Tyler the better part of three hours to climb the cañon wall behind Gopher Parsons's claim, make his way across the top, work his way down and along the outer cañon wall, and finally through the heavily wooded area between where he had descended and the road leading to Rattlesnake Mesa. He had no idea how Luke would accomplish it, but he was certain that by some means his partner would get him a horse. If he had ever despaired in Luke Barron, the dramatic fashion in which Luke had brought off his escape from the Eagle Cañon jail had more than dispelled it. His faith in Luke's ability to achieve the impossible would never be shaken.

What preoccupied Ed, as he made his way furtively among the trees, the forest's floor covered with a heavy accumulation of fallen leaves from past seasons and underbrush, was how easily everything was playing out just as he had hoped it would. The miners could always pan more gold from Eagle Creek, and maybe in time their vigilante methods could overcome the threat presented by whatever group was operating in the district, posing as the Luke Barron gang. By then, however, he and Luke would be long gone with a sufficient fortune to give them the right kind of start in cattle ranching. His recent brush with death in Eagle Cañon, more than any other single event

174

in his shady and dishonest past, had convinced Ed that, truly, this had to be their last job. Even in a place as crazy as Eagle Cañon, the threat of apprehension and death by hanging had become far more ominous than it had ever appeared to be before. One by one he had seen the gang whittled down to where just he and Luke were left. There was absolutely no sense in pushing their luck any further. No sense at all.

Looking up at the sky above and through the lofty fringe of the limbs of the trees, Ed placed the time as early afternoon. Several yards before him was the Rattlesnake Mesa road. It was quiet with no traffic. There shouldn't be. The busy thoroughfare was the road to Stirrup Gap. He dropped behind the bole of a large tree, resting on his boot heels, and decided to have one of the two smokes he had rolled himself from George Steele's supply of cavendish before he had set out on this journey. He had also packed three sulphur matches. There was a light breeze, but he was shielded from it here somewhat by the tree, and he cupped his hands around the match after he had scratched it alive with a thumbnail.

He had smoked the cigarette down to a nub, paced around a bit, and then reclined again, resting his back and head against the bole of the same tree, daydreaming of ranch life farther West in Montana, when he first detected the creaking of a wagon and the jingle of harness. Keeping himself concealed behind the tree, Ed saw shortly that Timothy, the black hosteler at the livery stable, was on the wagon seat, driving the wagon. Then, riding behind it, he saw Luke, leading a second, saddled horse, a piebald, tied by a halter rope to his saddle horn. Luke had done it! Of course, he had. There wasn't anything Luke couldn't bring off, once he put his mind to it.

Ed waited until Timothy on the wagon seat passed, before he ducked out, waving silently to get Luke's attention. Luke saw him almost at once. He nodded covertly and then, clandestinely, undid the halter rope.

Luke slowed his own horse only slightly, dropping a little farther behind the wagon before flinging aside the halter rope. Ed caught it at almost the moment it hit the ground, got a tight grip on it, and pulled the horse back into the trees. The Negro's mind seemed elsewhere. He kept looking straight ahead, while Luke's horse continued in a plodding gait behind the wagon.

Ed had the horse in among the trees, both Luke and the wagon having vanished around a curve in the road, when he heard the approach of another rider. He reached up and held shut the nostrils of the piebald, not wishing the horse to give away their location by whickering to the oncoming horse. It was Ray Cune. If anything, he was riding even slower than Luke had been, following Timothy Kamu in the wagon.

On the instant, Ed decided he would follow after Cune. If the deputy was up to no good, Luke might need Ed as a backup. If he was about other business, Ed very much wanted to know where he was going and for what purpose. Once Cune and his mount disappeared around the curve up the trail, Ed stealthily led the piebald from the forest into the road, pausing to listen if anyone else was coming up or down the trail. Satisfying himself that Ray Cune was alone, Ed hopped into the saddle and gently nudged the piebald into a gentle walk, following the deputy.

Buck Rollins was a man of medium height with gigantic shoulders that threatened to burst from the blue cotton shirt he wore. His heavy features were somewhat shielded by his rusty beard. He sported a rattlesnake hatband on his high-crowned Stetson. There was one camp chair, set outside the sod and wood lean-to they had built with some effort, and Rollins was sitting in it. There was good grass here, and their

176

four horses, unsaddled now, were allowed to roam freely in this pasture.

Two entrances led to this hide-out atop Rattlesnake Mesa. On the eastern side there was a wriggly arroyo that meandered up from the forest that was the way they came and went, but there was also a steep trail up the sheer western side of the mesa. They had not yet had occasion to use this trail, but it was there, if the need ever arose for a quick getaway. The tough part was having to keep a guard posted at all hours. Shorty Taylor — Buck could barely make him out from where he was sitting — was watching the eastern arroyo entrance. Behind him, at a greater distance from camp, Matt Geis was serving as lookout on the back trail up the steeper side. Jack Hardy, who acted as camp cook for the gang, was in the lean-to, taking a snooze.

Since the sun was beginning its decline in the west, Buck Rollins would have to rouse Hardy soon to get supper ready. That was the really bad part of this set-up. He and Hardy would eat supper, and then the two of them would have to go out to relieve the others so they could come in to eat. Rollins would take over the watch above the arroyo, and Jack Hardy would relieve Matt Geis.

At first they hadn't been so vigilant. Shorty Taylor had gone into the Eagle Cañon camp to deliver to Sam Ingalls his share from the raid on several of the miners' claims. Somehow or other Yokum Bos had either followed Shorty as he rode away from the sheriff's shack in camp, or possibly had picked up his trail while heading for the cabin where he lived about two miles to the south of Rattlesnake Mesa. At any rate, Bos had seen Shorty riding up the arroyo on the west side of the mesa and had gone to town to report the matter to Sheriff Ingalls. But for that fatal error on Bos's part the knowledge he had gained of their hide-out could have turned out badly for the gang.

The sheriff had turned the tables on Bos and arrested him for conspiracy with the Luke Barron gang, the outfit Ingalls was publicly blaming for the robberies.

Of course, there shouldn't have been any shooting this last time any more than there had been the first time they had raided the stage to Stirrup Gap and stolen a huge gold shipment. After all, the miners had been disarmed by Sheriff Ingalls and his so-called Avenging Angels. What this had meant in theory was that the miners had traded their firearms for protection under the law, but what it had really meant in practice was that they were totally at the mercy of armed robbers, since now — and Buck certainly had to include the sheriff and his deputies in this group — only the outlaws were armed. Shorty Taylor had claimed the first killing was purely an accident. He had thought that the miner had had a hide-out gun. He and Jack Hardy had been together, pulling that job. Matt Geis had been no less trigger happy, when he and Rollins had been confronting another of the miners at his claim, but in this case the man had had a Bowie knife and had been in the act of hurling it at Geis when he had shot him.

It brought a smile to Buck Rollins's rather thick lips as he thought about the aftermath to those gun plays. Ingalls had figured on getting both of the claims for himself, as he later intended to do with the Bos claim, but Father Matthew, the head of the holy rollers, had interceded. One of the claims, that adjacent to Bill Olds's claim, had been given to Olds by the old priest, and Nels Larsen, who had been a member of the Temple of the Redeemed all the way back to the days in Illinois, was given the other claim to work because the murdered man had been his brother-in-law, and Larsen's sister and family had remained in Centralia. Now that her husband had struck it rich, she was supposed to come out with the kids, but it hadn't happened before he was cut down.

As fine as this set-up was for Buck Rollins and the others, he was aware that it was, at least potentially, even more lucrative for Sam Ingalls who planned, Rollins was certain, to take over most of the better-paying claims in time. Before that happened, Buck Rollins intended to move out. In fact, he intended to pull only a few more jobs before calling it quits. There was no telling how long it would take those miners to decide that going around unarmed was only playing into the hands of the thieves — Luke Barron's gang or Buck Rollins's gang — and that would be when matters could become dangerous. Rollins was familiar with miners' courts and the swift justice they handed out. It was only a matter of how long these easy pickings would last before something of that kind was put in place, and by then he intended to be long gone. Let Sam Ingalls and his deputies deal with a miners' court. Buck Rollins wanted no part of it.

The wild card in this deal was the holy rollers. Ingalls might have placated them for a while by hanging Bos as one of the Luke Barron gang, but they were too severe in their convictions to allow the sheriff to continue whittling down their numbers by this means only to take over their claims legally. Hell, Ingalls and his deputies couldn't drink, smoke, or gamble in front of those holy rollers as it was. The only reason the blockade on Eagle Cañon was working at all was because the holy rollers wanted it that way. Bos had been an outsider, and so his death may not have hit very close to home, but let Ingalls start accusing some of the faithful of being in with the Luke Barron gang, and the holy rollers were sure to get suspicious and maybe even take the law into their own hands. Buck Rollins didn't want to be anywhere around when that time came. He had heard how tough the Mormons had made it on outlaws in their conclaves in Utah, and the same thing had happened where other religious sects had taken over a district and claimed it for their own. The holy rollers in Eagle Cañon weren't trying to go against federal law and practice polygamy, or anything like that. Being against alcohol, tobacco, and other pleasures might be eccentric, but they weren't sufficient to offend other groups the way the Mormons had through polygamy.

Shorty Taylor was waving his right arm in which he held his .44 Henry rifle. Rollins could see the westering sunlight glint briefly from the brass sideplate. That signal meant a rider was coming up the arroyo entrance but that there was nothing to be feared. Buck had brought out his Bull Durham sack, rolled a cigarette, had lighted it, and had even partially smoked it down, while the rider, whom he recognized as Ray Cune even at that distance, was sitting his horse and talking to Shorty. Now Buck saw Shorty swing up behind Cune's saddle, and the horse carried both men at a trot toward the lean-to camp.

Nan Steele had felt the Bos cabin palpably cloaked in silence during her lonely vigil with the corpse of Father Matthew, reposing on the bed. The light had seemed to shine but dimly into the one window of that narrow bedroom, and no less dimly into the two windows in the combination kitchen and living room. One window there faced to the east, and one faced north, with Rattlesnake Mesa looming in the distance. It was when she had taken a chair from the kitchen area, had placed it at the foot of the bed, and had sat there that she had first become aware that, notwithstanding the dim light, the old priest's body gave off no shadow. There was nothing dark or sad in his nearness, and the brighter shafts of care, regret, ambition, or fear — so inseparable from all human beings — seemed somehow to have been permanently banished from that room.

Death had left his eyes open, but Nan had been able to close them early on, so it had come to seem that he was, indeed, merely asleep. As she had sat there, she had thought back to his words to her, as the previous night the buggy had come into the clearing. The Bos cabin had been barely visible, for the moon had set behind the mesa, and Father Matthew's voice had been soft, a murmuring like the wind that had rustled among the leaves of the looming trees on their way out from the camp. He had finished smoking his pipe, had knocked out the spent ashes, and had placed it in an inside pocket beneath the folds of his cape.

"I had been trying for so long to understand God," the old priest had said. "It was, I am certain, through the intercession of the Holy Ghost that finally I came to know Him, however incompletely. To love God truly, you must love change, Nan, for change is essential to all that exists in creation. Change is fundamental to the universe. How should it be otherwise, for God who exists for all eternity would long ago have grown bored with it. Beyond this, to know God is to know that He loves nothing more than to laugh. How else are we to understand the greatest of all miracles . . . when God chose to become man? It brought about a collision when He became man. Even to this day that miracle is rejected by so many more than the few who are able to believe in it. The fulfillment of that life, when God became man, was crowned with unbearable pain and the most profound suffering.

"It is totally incomprehensible unless we are able to see in it a cosmic sense of humor, a divine joke, if you will. There was only one inexpressibly poignant moment in the whole passion of the Lord, and that was when He cried out, when He, too, despaired, when on the cross He asked God why He had become lost to Him. At that moment all laughter had to cease, because for the first time God had become aware enough of Himself as a man to know what it means to exist without God."

Father Matthew had then fallen silent, nor had he really spoken again, until he had uttered what were his final words to Neele Bos. Perhaps that was why, in the terrible silence of that narrow bedroom, in that isolated and deserted cabin, the corpse of the old priest cast no shadow. Nan in her perplexity wondered if Father Matthew had, indeed, perhaps at some time in the past bartered his shadow to the devil and so now was without it, but then she saw in reality what had happened to it. He had taken it with him into eternity. It was as if she heard again his voice in that silence, telling her as from a great distance in a tone that was transparent but yet exceedingly clear, that his shadow now belonged with his soul, and his soul was forever gone.

Nan had then moved the chair back into the kitchen. She had added wood to the fire in the stove, but the two rooms remained quite cool, notwithstanding. A shudder passed through her as she looked idly around, something reminding her now that Neele and Yokum Bos owned two horses, obviously draft animals, but they could be pressed into service. There was a wagon in the lean-to next to the cabin. It had been in this wagon that Neele Bos had brought back the dead body of her husband after Sheriff Ingalls and his deputies had hanged Yokum Bos. Or there was the horse the medical man had ridden out to the Bos cabin. Why must she wait here alone in this cabin for Dr. Logan to send someone back from town?

Any comfort she may have drawn from the silence that engulfed the cabin was suddenly shattered as she remembered, in terror, how the doctor had responded when he had come out from Eagle Cañon. She had never seen such barely suppressed fury, yet a fury so cold that it had seemed he was possessed by some evil spirit. She had been frightened of him to her very depths. She had insisted to Dr. Logan that Father Matthew's death had been an accident, that he had come on

182

a mission of mercy, and Neele, perhaps fearful, perhaps, as she claimed, blaming the old priest for Yokum Bos's death, had fired the small gun while not in her right mind. Surely she hadn't really intended to kill the old priest. There had been once — his dying words to Neele proved it — a love between them. Love can, sometimes, bring about more cruelty than outright hatred.

Dr. Logan had heard her, but he hadn't listened, and Neele Bos had done nothing and said nothing. She had accompanied the doctor silently to the buggy. Nan knew now what the woman must have been feeling. Was it so different from those words spoken from the cross so long ago, those words that Father Matthew believed had come at the moment when God was most aware of what it meant to be human?

She probably would have hitched up the wagon in the lean-to herself and tried to transport Father Matthew's body back to town without waiting longer for any help had she not seen, even though obscurely through the eastern window, a wagon come into the clearing, with Timothy Kamu on the driver's seat, and riding alongside, his hat pulled down to keep the slanting sun from his eyes, the figure of the man who called himself Luke Ashford.

Chapter Fourteen

Although he was a member in good standing, even one of the counsel of elders, in the Temple of the Redeemed, Sam Ingalls did not regard himself personally as a God-fearing man. In fact, sometimes he wasn't certain that he believed at all in God, and quite definitely he had taken the tenets of Father Matthew's sect with a shrug of the shoulders. Stirrup Gap was the county seat and, technically, that should have been where he maintained his office. He actually had a office there, only he was seldom in it. He had moved to Eagle Cañon when Father Matthew led the great exodus out of Stirrup Gap, and he had remained in Eagle Cañon ever since for his own enrichment at the expense of the claim owners and anyone else who might have something of value that he could legally seize — or illegally, although taking every precaution to appear aloof from the theft.

If Sam Ingalls was basically indifferent to theological matters — whatever appearances his current circumstances required notwithstanding — he was a believer in luck. It had been a relatively easy matter for him, to placate rigorous Puritans like Dr. Royal Logan, to chew his honey-soaked cutleaf in private, and occasionally to take a drink of rye whiskey (a couple of pint bottles of which he had picked up on his last visit to Stirrup Gap) in the seclusion of his shack in Eagle Cañon. What had been anything but easy for him was to have to give up his addiction to cards, stud poker and blackjack being among his favorite games of chance. In secret, usually when treating himself to a nip of rye whiskey, he had pulled out a deck of pasteboards that he kept hidden and played solitaire. To cheat at solitaire was unthinkable for the sheriff, since he willingly surrendered himself to the cards, and, depending on the number of times he honestly won, he believed that in some absolute, if mysterious, way the cards were providing him with a glimpse into his future.

The problem was that he had been kept so busy the last few days — what with the hanging of Yokum Bos, the jailing and subsequent escape of Ed Tyler, the search for George Steele, and securing his possession of Yokum Bos's claim — he hadn't had a chance to consult the pasteboards, and so he had been left totally unprepared for the passing of Father Matthew. He could not be sure if this was a good omen or not, in terms of his plans for the future, but his instinctive response was that it might bode trouble in the future, and that it decidedly called for an alteration of his long-range plans in the present. The meddlesome Luke Ashford had somehow gained the confidence of some of the claim owners and had even persuaded them to try to ship their gold down to the bank at Stirrup Gap, rather than wait for the Bank of Eagle Cañon to be finished. It had been the sheriff's hope that the bank would appear so safe to the claim owners that they would all surrender their gold for safekeeping. If they did that, he need only wait until there was a sizable accumulation, and then Luke Barron and his gang could hit the bank and get away with everything. In the aftermath it would be relatively easy to accuse one or two of the claim owners of being in league with the Barron gang, and, following their execution after a trial by the counsel of elders, he could add their claims to his holdings that now included Yokum Bos's and George Steele's — he wasn't actually having Steele's claim worked as yet, but that would come as soon as the man was caught by the Avenging Angels.

Now he felt he had to act, and act quickly. Very shortly after Dr. Logan arrived in camp with Neele Bos in Father

Matthew's buggy, he had secretly sent Ray Cune out to Buck Rollins's hide-out atop Rattlesnake Mesa with a message that the gang was to step up the robberies that very night, hitting no less than three of the best-paying claims, those belonging to Nels Larsen — who, after all, had managed to seize a claim the sheriff had very much wanted for himself — as well as those of Gopher Parsons and Fred Jeliff. He could no longer wait for the completion of the bank building. Repair of the jailhouse had taken precedence over the work on the bank, anyway. And he wasn't about to let Parsons, Larsen, and Jeliff send their bags of gold out of the camp on any stage. Another stage robbery at this point would again involve him as sheriff for the county and also concern the express company that insured the shipment. It would not be merely a local matter, as the robbings and killings of the claim owners had been after the first stage robbery, to be dealt with by the sheriff as a Temple member and leader of the Avenging Angels.

Sheriff Ingalls did not doubt for an instant that, come the next county election, he would probably be out of a job. The few visits he had paid to Stirrup Gap had indicated just how frustrated the citizens there and others in the county were with a sheriff who was absent virtually all the time. Holding onto that office, of course, would be meaningless in view of the wealth Ingalls was building up, both from his share of the robberies as well as what would be coming out of the Bos and Steele claims. He had a paid guard up at the Bos claim, and three emigrants from Stirrup Gap he had hired to work the claim for him on a percentage, something they had accepted once they learned that all possible claims in Eagle Creek were already taken and duly filed on at the Land Office in Stirrup Gap. As he continued annexing one claim after another, he was also aware that his need for sheer manpower would be increasing. Originally it had been his intention for the Luke

Barron gang to continue robbing claims but not to resort again to murder. The death of Father Matthew changed that. Now, with the old priest dead, the lawman did not anticipate any effective resistance to his taking over the combined Larsen claim and those belonging to Gopher Parsons and Fred Jeliff.

Dr. Logan was in no position to offer any objection. It was even questionable how long the Temple of the Redeemed would survive now that its religious leader was dead. Ingalls, willing readily to deal out death when it served his own purpose as in the case of Yokum Bos, had nonetheless been somewhat taken aback when the medical man had informed him that he intended for Neele Bos to be tried on a charge of witchcraft and, when found guilty by the counsel of elders, to be publicly burned at the stake. Ingalls had even questioned the wisdom of executing George Steele, if the man could be found and made to forfeit his claim but remain to operate his still — the improbability of George Steele's ever agreeing to such a proposition had only remotely occurred to the lawman — and in former days he surely would have balked at executing any woman, much less burning one alive at the stake. But nothing less would satisfy the medical man, and so Ingalls agreed to go along with it.

Let Dr. Logan operate his penny-ante drinking water operation — the sheriff's office was even lending him its official protection in the scheme. It had been little enough to do to keep the doctor's mouth shut, just as he and his men had given up engaging openly in any of the modest pleasures the medical man had proscribed for all who chose to live under the ægis of the Temple of the Redeemed. It had been a matter of momentary embarrassment to the sheriff when workmen, while making the necessary repairs to the jail bullpen area, had discovered the witch's chair used to extract the confession from Yokum Bos, but he had sloughed the matter off, saying it had been installed by an edict from the counsel of elders, and who was he to question Father Matthew's followers in matters of policy in dealing with the faithful?

Dr. Royal Logan had fully known about the witch's chair and the use for which it was intended. Far from being squeamish about it, the medical man had gone so far as to insist that, even with the workmen still repairing the jail roof, Neele Bos should be held secure in the chair until such a time as her hearing was convened, preferably the next morning. Sheriff Ingalls voiced no objection to the doctor's proposal. Indeed, he hoped that Gophers Parsons and the others would even come to town already that night for the trial, if not the execution, so that the Luke Barron gang could be ready and waiting for them once they returned to their claims. Ray Cune was to have Buck and his men ready to enter Eagle Cañon as soon as it was dark. His plan was for them to infiltrate upcañon to the claims. All the better if the claim owners were in town and being searched for weapons by the Avenging Angels. One thing would be certain. The claim owners would not be armed when they returned to their claims, and there would be little or no opportunity for them to get to firearms, even if they had them hidden, before they were seized and their lives forfeit.

With Pink Morgan to assist him, the sheriff locked Neele Bos's wrists into the handcuffs built onto the arms of witch's chair. A workman in what had been Ed Tyler's cell paused in nailing a connecting two-by-four to reinforce the newly installed joist beam to watch what was going on.

"Just never you mind," Sheriff Ingalls peremptorily told the workman. "There ain't any other place we can keep this woman until her trial, except this special jail-room chair. Be about your business, mister."

The workman seemed defiant for a moment and then returned to driving a nail into the connecting two-by-four.

"I reckon she'll keep safe in this chair, Doc," Ingalls said, checking the wrist cuffs. "You got anything to say, Miz Bos?"

She made no sign she heard him. Her eyes were hooded and her expression opaque. She had been passive throughout the ride into town and since.

"Why'd you figger she did it, Doc?" the sheriff asked, standing back.

"That should be quite obvious even to you, Sam," the medical man answered abruptly. "She was only carrying out Satan's work. I'm satisfied she's been a bride of the devil for some time. In murdering Father Matthew she probably thought she would destroy the Temple of the Redeemed with him. She sha'n't. We'll all be counting on the Avenging Angels more than ever before to keep the rigors of our beliefs fully in force during this time of crisis. I intend to go to the Temple after I check on the hospital patients and pray for guidance. When Nan Steele returns, I will speak to her about the ways in which she can help during and after the trial before the counsel of elders."

"I don't reckon how's she'll be all that keen on it, Doc," the sheriff replied, shaking his head slightly. "After all, she must know by this time we're after her father, and I wouldn't think she'd be any help to you or to me."

"That's where you're wrong, Sam," the physician said coldly. "You underestimate the power of faith. Did not Christ Himself say that he came into this world to divide sons from their fathers and husbands from their wives?"

"Sam, you want I should go get Mart, or do you still need me here?" Pink Morgan broke in.

"No," Sheriff Ingalls responded, "you go ahead. We're turnin' everyone back until this business of Father Matthew's death is over. I want you should go out to the Nan Steele and bring Mart Kemp back to the camp. We'll need the extra help."

"O K, Sam," Morgan agreed and, turning, walked cautiously around a pile of débris in the center of the jail bullpen and toward the office door.

"That was a wise move, Sam," the doctor said. "I'm sure we'll need every man you've got working around the clock for the time being. I think we should hold the trial very early in the morning in the Temple, say at seven o'clock. Nan Steele should be back by then, and we'll need her to provide testimony. She was an eye-witness to the murder."

"Can I get you anything, Miz Bos?" the sheriff asked the prisoner on a sudden compassionate impulse. "Water perhaps? Just a drink of water?"

"Yes, Sheriff, if you would be so kind," Neele Bos rasped in a hoarse but gentle voice.

"Before you do that, Sam, make sure her legs are cuffed in those leg irons," the doctor insisted.

Ingalls looked dubiously at the medical man and then stooped to do as he had been asked.

Timothy Kamu had entered the narrow bedroom to view the remains. It gave Nan and Luke a moment alone. Luke was standing near the table in the combination kitchen and living room. Nan, obviously distraught, her eyes sparkling with tears although she was not actually weeping, came into his arms as if it were the most natural thing for her to do. He held her awkwardly, and then, responding more honestly to her, he embraced her with feeling.

"It was terrible for you to be left here all alone," he said, his voice low, troubled. "It wasn't clear to me in camp. Why did she shoot Father Matthew? What was her reason? Surely he meant her no harm."

"Oh, it went back many years," Nan said. She stood back from him. "Dad told me something about it when we came out here to help Neele bury her husband. It seems Father Matthew and Neele once were lovers . . . back in Centralia . . . before Neele and Yokum came West . . . before Father Matthew founded his own church and came to Stirrup Gap."

"Priests don't do that kind of thing," Luke protested. "At least none I ever heard of. Preachers marry, but not priests."

"They never married," Nan said simply, bringing a handkerchief from a pocket in her Levi's and dabbing at her eyes. "I doubt if marriage was ever a question. It's just one of those things that happen sometimes between a man and a woman."

"But a priest, Nan! . . . and one like Father Matthew? I didn't get to know him very well, but he . . . he seemed a holy man to me."

"He was dat," Timothy said, standing now in the doorway leading to the bedroom. "He was de finest man Ah've ever known. Dat's why I stayed with him all dese years. He needed me, Mistah Ashford. He didn't have nobody else, really . . . not so's he could count on dem." He walked farther into the room and then paused, looking at Nan and at Luke. "Ah done tol' you dat first night as you was stayin' in the loft at the livery stable, Mistah Ashford, Father Matthew done knew he was goin' to be betrayed. Now it's done happened."

"You mean by Neele Bos?" Luke asked, confused.

"No suh, dat ain't it a-tall."

"Father Matthew loved Neele Bos, Luke," Nan said. "The last thing he told her . . . the last thing he said before he died. . . ."

"What was dat, Miss Nan?"

"Oh, he was a good man, Timothy," Nan replied, tears coming again to her eyes, "the best I'll ever know. He told Neele . . . his last words . . . that he had had to love many things in his life before he could know the one he loved most."

"I know which One dat was, Miss Nan. Father Matthew

. . . no matter what he may have done . . . always loved de Lord de most. Often was de times we spoke 'bout it together. De Lord has so much more imagination den we dat we can't know what He will do . . . not ever. Father Matthew . . . he understood dat. Before de end . . . de reason he done wanted to come out here to see Miz Bos was 'cause he done learned what dat sheriff had done to Mistah Bos. He knew dat he'd done made a mistake in lettin' dat pore man be hanged." Timothy hesitated for a moment, his own eyes, so dark and lustrous even in the dim light of the cabin, filling with tears. "He knew what a terrible wrong he done pore Mistah Bos . . . an' he knew dat it wasn't de first time. He had wronged him before . . . back in Centralia. Oh, I knew dat man of God, an' I know how much he was sufferin' inside. Only de Lord Himself mebbe could know jus' how much, but Ah felt part of it . . . Ah done felt his pain like it was my own. Dat's why Ah let him go. Sometimes de pain of jus' livin' is so much dat not even cryin' will help . . . sometimes not even prayin'. Dat's why he had to come here. He was hurtin' so much inside dere wasn't anythin' else for him to do."

"I know, Timothy," Nan said softly. "I drove him out here. Not everything he said to me at the time made sense, but it does now. I think he knew that it . . . coming here to see Neele . . . that it might be the last thing he would do. I . . . I think he felt closed off from God by what had happened. . . ."

Later, even years later, Luke Barron would say that at this moment it had happened once for always. It had been coming over him as he had approached that lonely cabin in the clearing, and it had grown to an even greater conviction when he saw Nan, when he had held her, and while they had talked. Even while Nan was still speaking, he suddenly walked forward across the room, past Nan, past the hosteler, and looked into the narrow bedroom and at Father Matthew, lying there as if asleep. Where Nan earlier had seen no shadow, Luke was consumed by what he felt. This had been no miracle, and he was no Phares with a promise that this day he, too, would be in paradise. Indeed, he doubted that he would ever be able to enter his house justified, but now the conviction was become a certainty. He dared not steal from the men in Eagle Cañon. He knew, in his heart, although he could not say how or why, that he would never steal from another person again.

He stood silently in the doorway, and then he entered the bedroom, approaching very close to the bed. That was where he remained, his gaze still on Father Matthew. Nan had stopped talking when Luke had walked toward the bedroom, and then she had followed him as far as the doorway. Timothy was standing mutely behind her. When Luke looked back toward her, there were still tears in her eyes, but a small smile played on her lips.

"I know, Luke," she said very softly. "I'm not sure how I know it, but I do. He took it with him. Into eternity."

"His soul?" Luke asked in almost a whisper.

"And his shadow," Nan answered.

Chapter Fifteen

Nothing could have unhinged Buck Rollins as did Ray Cune's report of Father Matthew's death. As far as he was concerned, this was the beginning of the end. Buck Rollins was certain of it — even if Cune were acting as if this were the furthest thing from Sam Ingalls's mind. Indeed, it seemed obvious to Buck that Father Matthew had been the mortar that had held together the entire mining community of Eagle Cañon, whether or not everyone who owned and was working a claim had been a believer in the Temple of the Redeemed. Religion meant little or nothing at all to Buck Rollins, but even he could see, from his distant perspective atop Rattlesnake Mesa, that there would be no one among those grubby miners, boomers, and claim-jumping sooners to take the place of the old priest. What authority the sheriff had had as the leader of the Avenging Angels, and through which he had kept the claim owners unarmed and prey to the supposed attacks by the Luke Barron gang, was now gone.

"Sam figures they might not really kill that woman," Ray Cune was saying in an excited voice. "But they're gonna be powerful concerned about what to do with her durin' the next few days. That's why I'm here. Sam wants you to hit them miners hard and take all you can get from 'em."

Buck looked over at Shorty Taylor who was standing alongside and a little behind Ray Cune. "Shorty, go wave Matt in. I want him in on this, an' we don't need no more lookouts nohow. This is where we make one last haul and head for parts unknown."

"Hold on, Buck," Ray Cune interrupted. "You don't get Sam's drift. . . ." He stopped then, because Rollins had drawn his Colt and now cocked it.

"You don't get it, Cune," Buck Rollins said quietly. "This here is as far as you go."

"What d'ya mean?" the deputy asked, his usually surly facial expression punctuated now by the rictus of confusion, even bewilderment.

Shorty Taylor hadn't waited. Even as Buck had pulled his gun, he was hurrying toward the near side of the sod-and-wood lean-to, still holding onto his Henry rifle. Jack Hardy was awake now and coming out of the lean-to.

"I mean," Buck Rollins told the deputy, "that we're tyin' you up an' leavin' you here. That is, if you don't make any funny moves. If'n you do, I'll drop you where you stand, an' you'll still be stayin' here, only you'll be stayin' here dead. Jack, get that rope from my saddle an' tie this feller up. Now, lift 'em, Cune."

As Jack Hardy went over to where the saddle gear was stowed to fetch Buck's rope, Rollins moved forward cautiously and relieved the Avenging Angel of his Forty-Four, shoving it in behind the buckle of his own gun belt, with the barrel pointed off to one side.

"Matt's comin' in, Buck," Shorty announced, as he came up again to stand near Rollins.

"O K, Shorty. Now you go out and start gatherin' in our mounts. Matt'll help you with the saddlin' just as soon as he gets here."

Shorty nodded and was on his own way to the saddle gear to get a cutting rope while Jack Hardy came back, with Buck's lariat, and began to bind Ray Cune.

"Do a good job of it, Jack. I don't want this feller gettin' away on us. The way I figger it, we got one more chance for a good clean-up, an' that's all."

"You're wrong, Buck," Ray Cune protested. "It's gonna be

easier pickin's than ever now that Father Matthew's gone."

Buck said nothing, but he did grimace a small and bitter smile. Jack Hardy, having bound the deputy's hands tightly behind him, kicked him behind one knee, so that Cune fell into the short grass and weeds in front of the lean-to. Hardy then bound the man's feet and secured them behind him to his hands.

Matt Geis came on the run just as the camp cook was finishing. Buck Rollins told him they were heading out and to go help Shorty bring in and saddle their horses. Geis gazed with momentary curiosity at Ray Cune, and then was on about his business.

"Drag him inside the lean-to, Jack," Rollins said. He made no effort to help in this, nor did he holster his Colt. He had a reason. Jack Hardy suspected what it was, if he did not know it for certain. After dragging Ray Cune under the shelter of the lean-to, he stepped back and out of the way.

"No . . . Rollins . . . don't . . . !" Ray Cune, who had not been gagged, begged once he heard the click of the hammer of Buck's Colt as it was pulled back.

Buck Rollins said nothing. He fired. The slug hit Ray Cune's right shoulder, knocking him, even though he was tied up, over onto his back. He was gasping in pain as the hammer of the Colt was pulled back again. This time a slug smashed into the deputy's left shoulder, little lower than where it had hit him in his right shoulder.

"Iffen you don't bleed to death, Cune, you might live," Buck Rollins assured the wounded and now bleeding captive. He laughed brusquely, motioned with his head to Jack Hardy, and the two of them retreated toward where Shorty Taylor and Matt Geis were saddling the horses.

Nan Steele was riding the horse Dr. Logan had borrowed

from the livery stable to reach the Bos cabin earlier. Luke was atop his black. The body of the dead priest, wrapped in a blanket from the Bos place, was in the wagon bed, with Timothy Kamu driving the team on the road back to Eagle Cañon. Nan and Luke rode slightly ahead of Timothy and the wagon.

"I'm afraid, Luke," Nan said, "afraid for Neele Bos."

Luke had rolled and lit a cigarette. He paused to draw on it before he drawled: "I don't reckon she's got that much to worry about, Nan, not when you make it clear that she had her reasons for what she did."

"But don't you see, Luke, both the sheriff and Doctor Logan knew about Yokum Bos's torture. Father Matthew knew nothing about it. I believe that."

"And I believe it, Nan. I talked to some of those miners today. I don't think Gopher Parsons or the others are going to hold what happened too much against Neele Bos. Even if they do, they got more against the sheriff than they do against her."

"Do you think I'm going to get the chance to tell anyone what happened to Yokum Bos?" Nan could not help asking.

"You've got Timothy and me to side you," Luke countered.

"Who's going to listen to you . . . or to Timothy? The council of elders consists of Doctor Logan, the sheriff, and two of his deputies. Do you honestly think they are going to care what we say?"

Luke drew a last time on his cigarette, snuffed it out with the fingers of his gloved right hand, and dispersed the fragments of paper and tobacco that remained to the wind that was coming up. The sun was setting behind them, and the trees on either side of the trail were bathed in red light.

"I told you and Timothy back at the Bos place that I let that horse loose on the way out for Ed Tyler. His job is to locate where this so-called Luke Barron gang is holed up. If he's able to do it, with the miners behind us, we can round up that gang."

"If that happens Luke . . . and it's a mighty big *if* . . . it'll be too late, I fear, to help Neele very much, or Dad."

"I agree with you about George," Luke conceded. "I don't reckon the plan we worked out to get around the sheriff will do us much good at this point. There's no two ways about it. The miners are going to have to go up against the sheriff and his men. If Logan is in with them, he'll have to take his chances with the rest."

"He's a doctor, Luke," Nan argued. "He's been with Father Matthew a long time. There'll be some who will do just what he tells them to do."

"Like they do about his water?"

"Just like they do about the water. If you mean robbing and killing, I don't believe for a minute Royal knows anything about that. But Lee Hop says Royal is the one who wanted the sheriff to arrest Dad, and there will be people who now will look to Royal to take Father Matthew's place as their spiritual leader. You know, Father Matthew wasn't much a believer in all those prohibitions against whiskey and dancing and the rest. That was Royal Logan."

"Nan, I suspect it won't matter a whole lot whether the doctor was actively with Ingalls in what happened to Yokum Bos, or in on the murders and robberies of claim owners. I figure Logan's going to need all the support he can get just to keep things together, and Ingalls is where he'll overplay his hand. I opine I won't stay in camp when we get back, and you shouldn't, either. We'd best head out to Gopher Parsons's claim, get Parsons, your father, and the others organized. I've had a little experience in these things over the years, and I seriously doubt that Ingalls and his men are going to wait much longer before hitting the miners, and hitting them hard. What's he got to lose? The way I see it, he wants to jump the richest claims for himself, anyway. He already has the Bos claim, and he is all set to take over the Nan Steele, if he hasn't already done it. The miners are armed . . . somewhat . . . and I'm sure Ingalls can't wait until they get any more organized than they are already."

Nan was silent for a few moments as they rode slowly ahead, keeping in front of the team drawing the wagon. Then she looked over at Luke and forward again, her eyes on the road before them. The wind was tugging now at their clothes, and Nan's right hand crept up to secure her Stetson. She said, perhaps more loudly than she intended, because she wanted to be sure he heard her: "You're certain Luke Barron and his gang aren't behind what's been happening, aren't you?"

Luke glanced at her face, shadowed somewhat in the failing light, before he answered. When he did, he, too, made certain he spoke loudly enough to be heard over the wind. "Yes, ma'am."

Before approaching the mesa, rising up out of the earth before him, Ed Tyler took the precaution of sequestering his mount out of sight of the dim path that led to the trail back toward Eagle Cañon. Of course, there was no way he could prevent his horse from whinnying acknowledgment should the deputy ride back down the wriggly arroyo that led up onto the mesa. It was simply a chance he would have to take. True, if the horse was discovered, the deputy would probably lead it away, and he would be afoot again, but Ed felt a sense of urgency inside of himself and wasn't about to wait patiently for Ray Cune to return. He wanted to know what was happening on the mesa, and the only way he could do that was to go up the worn arroyo on foot.

He was well aware that there would be moments, as he was

making his way up that narrow arroyo, that someone above, with an eye on Cune's back trail, could spot him and that he would make a clear target for a bullet. The alternative, though, would be to miss out possibly in seeing what it was that had drawn Ray Cune to Rattlesnake Mesa. One factor that was in Ed's favor was that the sun, now behind the mesa, was setting. This created deep shadows in the arroyo. Ed kept to these. When he had to come out more into the open, he did so quickly, dashing swiftly from one area of shadows to the next, then pausing for a spell to see if his presence had been noticed.

He was just coming over the lip of the mesa when he heard in the distance two reports that sounded like pistol shots. Ed ducked down behind an outcropping of rocks, removed his hat, and then cautiously raised his head slowly to see across the mesa. He could make out definite movement. Horses were being saddled. Two men were crossing the grass expanse from a squat lean-to that was dulled by shadow. If the shots had originated anywhere, Ed suspected, it must have been by one or both of the men walking away from the lean-to. At the distance and in the bad light he could not be certain that Ray Cune was not one of the four figures he sighted, but he did not think so.

When the men were all mounted and started riding in the direction of the arroyo trail up which he had made his way, Ed ducked down his head, in time he hoped not to have been seen. He diminished himself as much as he could behind the rock outcropping where, as it happened, he would not be visible to any of the riders unless someone knew of his presence and rode around the rocks, searching for him.

Apparently good fortune was his. Nothing untoward happened as the group of riders grew closer. Ed was even able to catch on the wind, blowing here on top of the mesa far more strongly than had been the case below or on his way up, one of the men saying that they must take it slow since they didn't want to get to Eagle Cañon until after dark.

Thought of this fair-haired girl was stronger than all the others quickening Luke's interest beyond anything he could remember. He honestly admitted that his feeling for her had become stronger than plain liking. At the same time he had bitterly concluded that the obscurity of his back trail ruled out the possibility of his ever taking a good woman seriously. He would never want his name to cloud that of Nancy Steele's. Even to think of it galled him, yet he couldn't stop thinking of her, looking across at her clean oval face, her smile that had the habit of bringing up a riot of emotion within him that now caused a constriction in his throat. The next time he met with Ed, they would have it out. He was resolved that anything he did from this point forward would have to help Nan and the claim owners.

He was trained to discomfort, but this day had seemed to set up an even more high-strung nervousness in him. He had become restless, and his habit of scanning what lay ahead and behind remained very strong in him now. He and Nan had been riding quietly for some time as his squinted, straining glance searched the darker shadows of the forest that bordered this trail on both sides, as though some danger lurked there. Behind them, shuttling down along this narrow corridor of the mesa trail, came the clopping of the team's hoofs and the occasional straining of the wagon with its sad burden. Timothy Kamu held the reins with a stoic resignation.

Luke was thinking about Nan, and they had just entered the slight clearing where the hanging tree stood and where he had seen Neele Bos, cutting down the dead body of her husband. He saw two riders emerge from behind the tree, when the sudden air-whip of a bullet brushed his left cheek. Instinctively his long body moved in a lunge backward in the saddle. His gun streaked from leather as he shouted: "Back, Nan!" He heard her cry and looked her way. Then the solid slam of a bullet took him hard in his left shoulder, its force spinning him around and sending him out of his saddle. The sound of the shot came a moment later, followed by another as he awkwardly streaked his gun up once more. A fourth shot sounded, and he had a swift glimpse of the paint horse Nan was riding go to its knees in a thrashing fall, throwing the girl clear. The horse got up again, shaking nervously.

The voice of one of the approaching riders called: "Drop that iron, Ashford! *Pronto,* or I bust your spine!"

Wariness, a long training in not trying to outface too-strong odds, loosed Luke's grip on his gun. He brought his hands up, turning as he moved and grimacing against the pain in his left shoulder.

Facing him on the trail was Sam Ingalls, his Colt drawn and ready to fire again. Mart Kemp, a .30-30 Winchester now at his shoulder, pulled up alongside the sheriff. Timothy had reined in the wagon team.

There was a smile of triumph on the lawman's face as he edged his horse a little closer to Luke. He called: "Bring her along, Mart! Timothy, you keep a-goin' back to camp and not a word about this, if you know what's good for you. If the doc or anybody else asks you, Ashford and the girl headed toward Rattlesnake Mesa. I figure Ashford and George Steele are in with the Luke Barron gang, but we'll know better in the morning."

The sheriff backed his horse off to one side and motioned with his Colt for the black man to continue on down the road. Timothy glanced quietly at Luke, standing now and gripping his left shoulder, and then at Nan, who was covered by Mart Kemp, then urged the team forward, proceeding past them.

He did not look back. No one could tell what he might be thinking.

Mart Kemp dismounted, caught up Nan's pinto, and gruffly ordered her to mount. He then bound her feet beneath the horse's barrel. Sheriff Ingalls also dismounted, picked up Luke's .38, shoving it beneath the left side of his gun belt. He climbed again on his horse and told the wounded prisoner to do the same.

The sheriff was in the lead when the group set out, skirting the hanging tree and heading toward the north side of the clearing into the forest. It was twilight when they began climbing a narrow trail into badlands on the far side of Rattlesnake Mesa. Ingalls called a halt near the only patch of green vegetation that could be seen in the miles that lay before them. At the western edge of this shallow basin, close in to the foot of a pock-marked sandy cliff, was a spring that bubbled to the surface of the ground, ran a few feet through a willow thicket, and then sank out of sight again, leaving only a fanning-out patch of moist sand to mark its course.

Luke was unable to stand for a moment after they lifted him from the saddle. His legs were numb below the knees. His shoulder ached like a tooth with the nerve exposed. His sleeve, the length of his arm, was crimson with blood. Nan, whose face had been etched in pain the last few miles from the tightness of the rope that bound her boots together under the belly of her horse, forgot her own misery and came quickly across to him, saying: "Lie down, Luke. Let me fix your shoulder."

Sam Ingalls drawled: "That's right, pretty lady! Fix him up. We'll shore need him later on."

The lawman had remained taciturn and aloof during the ride through the forest into this gaunt maze of badlands far west of the flanking mesa. He had ignored Luke's protest over

Nan's being roped to her animal and, when the girl once wanted to stop to bandage Luke's bad arm, he had given no sign that he had heard, only urging them on faster. It was plain that he wanted to reach his goal quickly, wherever it was.

Instead of taking them up onto Rattlesnake Mesa, the sheriff had continued swinging sharply west until they hit a wide shelf of bare rock that would conceal their sign. They had traveled this direction across a wide flat that formed the base of the Mesa's west shoulder, finally dipping down from it into this rocky, weather-eroded area. Luke judged they had ridden through a series of broken buttes and narrow cañons for almost five miles. Wind and rain and sun had eroded this land so that the soft, sandy rock had taken on fantastic shapes and colors. The beds of the washes were strewn with tall monuments where harder strata of rock had withstood the centuries-long battle against the elements. The cliff faces showed many indentations, caves of all proportions, while the reds and browns and yellows of the bare rock made vivid splashes of varied hues.

Just now the deputy set about kindling a fire, not an easy task in the strong wind that prevailed, and Nan went to the spring for water. Ingalls came to stand straddle-legged, looking down at Luke, who sat hunched over, his good hand clenching his throbbing arm tightly. "Good thing that slug was four inches out," he observed. "I won't say I've got no use for you, 'cause I do." When Luke made no reply, Ingalls glanced across at Mart Kemp and gave him a barely visible wink, continuing: "I reckon, after tonight, there'll be another hangin', or maybe we'll just turn you over to a mob of them miners. Luke Barron and his gang will be huntin' tonight, an' while I don't hold with burnin' that woman at the stake tomorrow, like the doc wants, it should help get 'em in the mood to finish off another member of the Barron gang. Might be, we'll even get lucky, an' have George Steele an' that escaped convict as well by that time."

Luke said nothing. He hoped Nan hadn't heard what Ingalls had just said, regarding Neele Bos, but she probably had. The sheriff continued to look smugly at Luke and remained tight-lipped and silent when Nan came up behind them from the spring.

Ingalls smugness was no less apparent in his voice. He jerked a thumb toward the precipitous face of the cliff. "Which room'll you have, miss? Sorry we ain't got any with bath."

Nan looked toward the cliff face, where a series of narrow ledges led upward toward a maze of cave-like openings. Luke understood immediately what the sheriff meant. Those holes were the openings to cave dwellings, occupied centuries ago by Indians who had probably cultivated this small basin when the flow of the spring was much stronger, giving them water for their meager crops.

The girl ignored Ingalls and knelt beside Luke, washing clean the hole in his shoulder just over the line of the collarbone. She made a compress of her handkerchief and bound it tightly to the wound with Luke's neckpiece. Although she didn't speak, there was a tenderness and warmth in her touch that Luke knew she intended to be encouraging.

"No bones busted, eh, little doctor?" Ingalls queried, watching her.

"No."

Ingalls gestured to Mart Kemp. "Then tie him up."

Nan said sharply: "You can't do that! He's hurt. Badly. It might . . . might kill him."

"Now wouldn't that be too bad," the lawman drawled, and Luke saw in him a changed man from the one who had once obeyed Father Matthew. Without the old priest's authority to override him, Sam Ingalls was able finally to do almost as he pleased. He added: "Better lace her up again, too, Mart, hands and feet."

Luke made one weak attempt to get to his feet, thinking that, if he could stand, he might somehow manage to get his hands on the deputy's gun. Instead, Mart Kemp pushed him roughly back again and presently both his arms were bound tightly to his sides and many windings of stout manila held his booted feet and legs together. He had to lie there and watch Nan undergo the indignity of receiving the same treatment.

They were carried up a narrow ledge to the lowest row of cave openings. Luke lay on the outer rock, watching them drag Nan out of sight through one opening. Then he was roughly carried and pushed in through the adjoining one. Either one or both of the men must have been to these caves before. There was a candle in the cave where Luke was brought, and Mart Kemp now lit it. Looking around, Luke found himself lying in a dome-shaped room. The roof of the cave was black from the smoke of long-extinct fires. A small opening high on the front wall to one side of the door was the chimney that had centuries ago let the smoke of the fires escape. In the back wall was gouged a deep niche that must have served as a shelf for food. Around the wall ran a regular zigzag pattern cut in the rock, a symbol or decoration for this crude home.

Ingalls, kneeling down and looking closely at Luke, gave a parting word of warning. "Mart, this one may try to break out. Have your rifle handy. If he shows his head outside, part his hair in a new place with a bullet." His glance swung down on Luke, who lay against the back wall. "Hear that?"

"What about Nan?" Luke asked.

Ingalls shrugged, his bearded face taking on a wry smile. "If Luke Barron don't rape an' kill her, might be the doc will want to make a deal for her," he said. He laughed softly as he saw the look of sudden rage on Luke's face and told his deputy: "Bring that candle, but keep an eye on him. Let's go."

Luke lay breathing heavily, filled with a sense of utter helplessness, for in the ten years of precarious living since he had been outlawed in Colorado he had never been in a spot like this, one in which he hadn't been able to think of even a likely chance for fighting his way out. There wasn't a chance now, he knew. Sam Ingalls would use him as another proof of the genuineness of the Luke Barron scare that had struck terror through Eagle Cañon, but he wasn't thinking of that. The fear for Nan's safety crowded everything else from his mind.

Lying there, almost blinded by his helpless rage, he was brought back to sudden sanity by the sound of the girl's voice close at hand. It seemed to be coming from the far wall of the cave, in the direction of the opening he had seen her carried into. He lifted his head and listened. What he heard brought him rigid in the grip of a faint but nevertheless real hope.

At the base of the sand-drifted wall behind him there was a narrow, slitted opening through which a sliver of light shone. The candle. The deputy had taken it with him. Luke could hear Nan's voice plainly now, saying: ". . . leave him here to die! He needs water, something to eat."

And Sam Ingalls's reply sounded through the opening just as plainly: "He'll get water. Mebbe even food. Didn't I say we need him later on?"

"But his arm! It's tied. There's danger of infection."

"Ever see a man die of blood poisonin'?" Ingalls asked. "I have. It takes four or five days. Before that ever happens we'll be finished with him."

Luke heard the girl's choked cry, then the light vanished, and was followed by the strike of boots as Ingalls and his deputy went back down the ledge.

All at once he had forgotten the pain of his shoulder. He lifted his knees and pushed himself through the sand toward the opening onto the ledge. As he worked his way across it, he was remembering the pattern of other cave-dwellings he'd seen years ago when he was a boy. They were invariably of the same pattern, one- or two-room caves, gouged into the face of soft-rock cliffs. The rooms, if more than one, were connected by low-arched passageways. The slit through which the light had shone in from Nan's cave had been the top of such a passageway, showing above the sand that had drifted in to fill the caves to ledge-height in the long centuries since their use.

It cost him a long effort and a torment of pain to push his way to the opening so that he could lie belly-down and lift his head and peer over the ledge and downward. Ingalls and his deputy were gathered below near the fire, huddled in a conversation Luke could not hear. Then Ingalls climbed into his saddle, getting ready to leave. Three horses were tied in the willows, that of the deputy who was staying behind and the two they had rode. Ingalls spoke again to Mart Kemp, pointing above toward the narrow ledge and the cave, and Kemp's answer was a significant slapping of his palm on the stock of the .30-30 Winchester he held now cradled in the crook of his arm. Presently Ingalls rode away into the surrounding darkness.

Chapter Sixteen

The wind tugged at Ed Tyler's hat as he raised his head and then crawled out from behind the rock outcropping. The blowing of the wind seemed to have become stronger with the onset of dusk, coming out like an animal of the night, sweeping across the flat mesa top, riffling the grassy meadow so that it undulated in the drafts like long cresting waves of an inland sea.

Before leaving this place, Ed was determined to approach the lean-to and learn what he could. Ray Cune's horse, still saddled, had been allowed to roam. This in itself was strange. If Ed had opined rightly, Cune had been sent to rally the gang he had seen riding off the mesa on the way to the gold claims. Why, then, would he stay behind? Then there had also been those two shots for which Ed could not account, since none of the men who had mounted horses and ridden away from this mesa hide-out appeared to be wounded.

Even though he had been responsible for getting Luke to come to Eagle Cañon, Ed was beginning to have second thoughts about how easy this job was going to be. He liked George Steele, and Gopher Parsons seemed to trust him. True, he'd got himself thrown into jail and in the shadow of a hang rope, and Luke had managed to get him out of it, but now he was going to betray the claim owners who had befriended him and who believed in him. He had begun feeling this way already last night in the wagon with Lee Hop, Nan Steele, and old George Steele. He'd even had trouble sleeping because of it, the way it kept gnawing at his viscera the long night through and this morning. His makings were almost gone again, and he didn't care. It wasn't at all like the old days in Colorado.

They had started there as miners, no different than these placer claim owners here in Eagle Cañon, and they had been fighting a combine that had jumped their claims and robbed them. Ingalls and the others were the ones they should be fighting now, not stealing from the claim owners, men trying to get ahead by their hard work, just as once had been true for him and Luke back in Leadville.

So he went on afoot, warily, hurrying across open space that didn't have any cover. He had his gun in his hand by the time he reached the lean-to and was close enough to see in the waning light the figure of a man, tightly bound. Coming closer, he recognized Ray Cune. The deputy had his eyes open and was watching him. Ed approached cautiously and then went down on one knee beside the man. He could see the dark blood that was oozing from either shoulder, staining the man's white shirt and even the rope coils that bound his upper body.

"I've got to find a knife to cut you free," Ed said, jamming the six-gun into the waist-band of his Levi's.

"What're you doin' here?" the deputy rasped.

Ed Tyler didn't answer him, but rose and went over to where the cooking utensils, air-tights, and other gear were piled against the far side of the lean-to. Rummaging about, he did come across a butcher knife. With it he returned to the wounded man and began sawing at the binding rope, being careful to avoid the places where he was wounded.

"Who did this to you, Cune?" Tyler asked, cutting through one strand and starting on another.

"Luke Barron," the wounded man muttered.

"Not possible," was all Ed said, cutting another strand. He could pull some of the rope loose now and did so before working on the rope around the man's middle.

"His name's Buck Rollins," the wounded man said and groaned. "Folks 'round here think he's Luke Barron. Forgot,

210

Tyler, that you rode with the real Luke Barron."

Although Ed had been trying his best to avoid hurting the man any more, pulling the cut strands of rope away from Cune did cause the wounds to bleed more vigorously.

"Obliged, Tyler, but I reckon it's too late fer me," the deputy did manage to say when Ed pulled the last strands of the rope free at last.

"I saw a canteen over there," Ed said. "Let me get it."

The deputy said nothing. Ed sloshed the water in the canteen, pulled out the cork stopper, picked up a tin cup from among the gear, and poured some water into the cup before coming back to the wounded man. Ed held Cune's head up so he could drink. It took a great effort, and some of the water spilled down over his jaw. Cune moaned as Ed let his head back down.

"Why'd this Rollins fella plug yuh?"

"Reckon he's decided to play his own game and cut Ingalls out," the deputy rasped.

"You need a doctor."

"That son-of-a-bitch won't come out here. He wants to burn that Bos woman at the stake. Never heard of a doctor like that one! He ain't human. Just some kinda animal."

"Your horse is still here," Ed said, looking out toward the meadow. "But I don't think you'd last the ride into camp."

"You're right there, Tyler. I wouldn't make it. I'm done fer, an' I know it. Got the makin's."

"I'm pretty low, yuh know. Thet sheriff took mine away in jail."

"Smoked 'em himself," Cune said, and laughed until the pain cut him short.

"I'll roll yuh what I got left," Ed said then, pulling out the papers and the paper wadding in which he had kept the tobacco George Steele had let him take from his pipe pouch.

211

"It's gettin' dark fast," Cune said, almost in a whisper.

"Can't light a fire," Ed said, rolling the cigarette. "Those fellas may be comin' back."

"Not till mornin'. By then, I'll be dead . . . which is what Buck planned, I guess. That bastard tied me up, shot me, an' left me to bleed to death here. I hope he has a run-in with that doc. Let 'em kill each other."

Ed was sitting cross-legged now beside the deputy. He pulled out a match, scratched it alight along a leg of his Levi's, and cupped his hands around the flame. The cigarette was dangling from his own mouth. He lit it, inhaled quickly himself, and then placed it between Ray Cune's lips.

"Thanks," the deputy said, exhaling smoke around the glowing cigarette.

"Here, let me get something to prop up your head."

There were some bedrolls lying about where the men obviously slept. Ed rose, got one of these, and stooped down to put it beneath Ray Cune's head.

"What's your game, Tyler?" the deputy repeated then, drawing again on the cigarette. "What're yuh doin' here?"

"I was watching from the side of the trail when you rode past," Ed explained, once more sitting cross-legged alongside the deputy. "Trailed you out here. Wanted to know where yuh were goin'."

Cune chuckled at that. "Lot of good it's gonna do yuh. Watchin' me die is 'bout all yore likely to get outta it."

"Maybe I can fetch Miss Nan," Ed offered. "She's a nurse. She could help."

"I'd be more obliged if yuh'd look around through thet gear fer a bottle. I know Buck and the boys keep some of the stuff up here."

The darkness was increasing, and Ed had to depend to a degree on his sense of touch as he ransacked through the cache of utensils, food stuffs, and other gear before he found a pint bottle of whiskey that sounded about half full. He brought it back to where Ray Cune was lying.

The cigarette had gone out but still clung to the right side of Cune's mouth. Ed found the tin cup he had used for the water. There was still some water left in it. To this he added a slug of the whiskey.

"Here, drink this," Ed said, kneeling now and placing an arm again behind Ray Cune's head.

The pain from the wounds in Cune's shoulders was so great, apparently, the man could not really do for himself. He gulped whiskey and water from the tin cup. He choked slightly, then looked imploringly at Tyler, wanting more. Ed gave him another drink.

"Listen, Cune, yuh gotta let me look at those arms. I don't know thet much 'bout doctoring, but I can bandage 'em, an' mebbe stop the bleedin'. We gotta do thet, or you shore as hell ain't gonna make it."

"Told yuh before, Tyler, I'm done fer. I can feel it. I must be bleedin' inside worse'n I'm bleedin' outside. I jest feel it."

Ed put the tin cup aside and then let Cune's head down slowly. "You say Rollins and his gang ain't comin' back for a spell. Well, I'm startin' a fire . . . then I'll tend to those wounds, best I can."

"Yuh wanna do somethin' thet'd really help? Go warn them claim owners thet Luke Barron and the gang's comin' again tonight. They'll have a better chance if they're ready fer 'em. Even if yuh could patch me up, I wouldn't make it to mornin'. An' don't look to Ingalls to help any. He's in it all the way with Buck and the boys. Last I heard, he planned to ride out with Mart an' waylay thet Luke Ashford an' the Steele girl. You'll never get to her to help me, an' I already told yuh the doc's worthless. All he wants is to burn thet old bitch who pumped lead . . . into . . . Father Matthew. . . ."

Those were a lot of words for Ray Cune to have said, and there was a degree of desperation driving him to say them, because, as he spoke, he was increasingly wincing with pain and finally broke off altogether. Ed set about building up a small fire at the maw of the lean-to. Not only did he need it in order to see what he was doing, but he intended, no matter what Cune had said, to examine his wounds and do what he could for him. The deputy was doubtless right, and Ed should be on his way to warn the claim owners, and perhaps even do what he could for Luke and Nan Steele. Yet, he could not bring himself to abandon the wounded man without doing something more for him. It was, after all, a long way on foot back across the mesa and down to his horse. It would soon be completely dark, and Eagle Cañon was some miles away. If he left Ray Cune here in this condition, he surely wouldn't live until Ed could bring help.

"You-all is wrong to want to burn dat woman at de stake, Doctor Logan," Timothy Kamu said, anger burning in his black eyes.

They were talking in the examining alcove in the doctor's tent hospital where Timothy had come with the wagon bearing Father Matthew's body as soon as he entered Eagle Cañon. Together they had carried the body into the hospital and placed it on a vacant bed until it could be moved to lie in state in the assembly room of the Temple. Tiny Hart was at the check point. Pink Morgan was guarding the doctor's water. According to Dr. Logan, Arlie Michaels was keeping an eye on the prisoner in the jail on which work had been going on, despite the hour.

"Don't get uppity with me, Timothy," the medical man said abruptly. "That woman murdered the finest man and greatest religious leader I've known. Only possession by the

214

devil could have prompted her to commit so heinous a crime
. . . a crime against you as much as against the rest of us. I
know how you felt about Father Matthew. You've been with
him a long time. You came West with us. I should think you'd
be the first in line to drop a burning ember on that woman's
funeral pyre."

Timothy had never been known to lose his temper, although
Dr. Logan knew that he was a solitary drinker, and felt this
compromised the man morally and made his ultimate redemption probably impossible. He hoped his words would have a
calming effect.

"You don't know how Ah felt about Father Matthew, Doctor Logan, jus' as I don't know how you feel about Miss Nan."

"What about her? Where is she? Wasn't she supposed to
be coming back with you? Did you leave her out at that
wretched cabin?"

"No, suh, she was ridin' back with me, right up front befo'
de wagon with Luke Ashford. De sheriff an' Mart Kemp done
stopped her and shot Luke Ashford off his horse. Dose two
done took dem away an' tol' me to keep muh mouth shut."

"Sam Ingalls did that! Good heavens, why, man?"

"Ah'm not sure. But Ah know one thing. Miss Nan ain't
safe with dose men, and Luke Ashford won't be no help to
her. Ah'm headin' now for Gopher Parsons's claim. P'haps he
can get word to Miss Nan's daddy. Dere's others'll want to
help, Ah'm sure."

"Help! Why, man, I'll find Sam Ingalls and force him to
release her."

"He ain't here, Doctor Logan. Ah done tol' you dat. Dey
stopped me near dat hanging' tree and took 'em with 'em."

"You just wait right here, Timothy," the doctor insisted.
"I'm going down to have a word with those deputies. They'll
tell me what's going on, or I'll know the reason why." As he

215

spoke, he shook an intimidating finger at the black hosteler and then hurried from the consulting room.

Timothy Kamu had absolutely no intention of following the physician's advice in this matter or any other at this point in his life. He waited until Logan had passed along the hospital beds and left the hospital. Then, in a hurry himself, he followed after him. The wagon was parked near the entrance. Timothy got in and turned the team down the incline and into the main street, heading in the direction of the claims. He did stop briefly, however, at Lee Hop's cafe. The place was busy now with members of the work crew, who were staying overnight in Eagle Cañon, and a few tradesmen. However, Lee Hop did insist on Timothy's coming into the kitchen so they could talk. Once he heard what had happened, he asked Timothy to wait for another moment while he went back into the living quarters. Sung Yü was busy at the stove, although she did pause to smile at Timothy and said something to him in Chinese that he did not understand but to which he responded with a smile.

What Lee Hop brought back with him surprised Timothy. It was a Remington revolver with hard rubber grips. Timothy was certain he had never seen the Chinaman with a gun at any time in the past, and he was equally certain that he could not imagine him firing it at anyone or anything.

"Loaded," Lee Hop said. "You takee care, Timotee."

"Yes," said Sung Yü, having seen what her husband had done and nodding her head vigorously at the black man.

Timothy, taking the revolver from Lee Hop, examined it for a moment and then shoved it in his pants on the right side. He grasped Lee Hop's right hand in both of his. "Ah shall do all Ah can to see dat no harm comes to Miss Nan. She loved Father Matthew as much as we did."

He said no more then, but turned and left. No one found his passage through the crowded café worthy of remark.

216

Chapter Seventeen

Shortly after the sheriff rode out of Mart Kemp's sight into the mouth of a narrow wash far across the basin, the deputy, carrying the Winchester, began making his way back up the path to the caves where Nan and Luke were imprisoned. Kemp had his orders, and they pleased him. The girl was his to do with as he pleased, as long as she was dead by dawn. Ashford was to be kept alive and brought to Eagle Cañon with the girl's dead and raped body. Ingalls figured this final outrage, committed by a Luke Barron gang member, would result in another hanging bee in which, unlike the capture of Neele Bos by the doctor, would make Ingalls appear a hero. After Ashford was brought in, tried for rape, murder, and robbery, he would be hanged by Ingalls who would then mount an elaborate search for the missing caches of gold that, somehow, would never be found. Those who had been loyal to the sheriff and had sided him would share in the spoils.

Buck Rollins and the gang would be allowed to pass through the check point after dark, but they would never get back out alive. Those among them who weren't shot, trying to escape, would be tried and hanged right along with Luke Ashford. It would be a major house cleaning. The claim owners Buck Rollins and the gang might kill in the act of robbing them would have their claims seized by Sheriff Ingalls. Mart Kemp knew his part in all this. He had seen Nan Steele, prancing about the camp, so haughty and proud, even when she was wearing Levi's as she was now. Well, she had a big lesson coming about life, and Mart Kemp was happy to be the one to give it to her. The thought of what was going to happen excited him even more when he imagined Luke Ashford, tied up in the adjacent cave, being able to overhear it.

Kemp entered the cave where Nan Steele was a prisoner and located the candle he had blown out and left there when he and Sam Ingalls had departed earlier. He leaned his rifle against a wall, lit the candle, and looked over at Nan in the flickering light. He said: "Don't fret, honey, I'll be right back." Leaving the rifle, he shielded the candle as he walked from Nan's cave the distance to Luke's cave.

Luke was back where he had been set down in his cave when Kemp entered. Stooping, the deputy made his way inside. Luke had become increasingly aware of the pain in his shoulder. The deputy's glance took in the marks in the sand. He drawled: "Been movin' around, eh?"

Luke was silent, thankful he hadn't crawled over to the opening to Nan's cave, for the telltale marks in the sand might have aroused the deputy's suspicions.

"Your partner over there is sure worried about you, Ashford. Tough you ain't goin' to be able to do nothin' about that. I got a little show planned for you, though. Wanta hear about it?"

Luke's immediate reaction was one of anger, but he suppressed it with a thought that made him smile thinly. "Sure, go ahead."

Amused, the deputy said: "Like to make a bet on that?"

Luke felt he had a rôle to play here, chiefly to put up the appearance that he was trying to find a way of escape by any means. So he went on with his first thought, saying abruptly: "You and me could take over that camp, Kemp!"

The deputy smiled broadly. It was plain that he was enjoying himself. He queried blandly: "How?"

"We know Ingalls has a lot of gold. We could take it away from him easy."

"So what?"

"I figure the two of us could bust up Ingalls's gang, throw down on the whole pack, and take over ourselves."

"Y'don't say." The deputy feigned surprise. "Just you and me, eh?"

"I could get one more man to help us. Ed Tyler, the one that broke jail a while back."

The deputy's stare widened in mock bewilderment. "Now don't tell me you busted him out?"

Luke nodded gravely. "Ed's been in with me from the beginning. I'm Luke Barron."

"The real Luke Barron?"

The awe Kemp tried to put into his expression looked far from genuine. Luke ignored that, soberly continuing this double-edged pretense. "The same."

"Then it's been you all along? Not someone else usin' your handle?"

Luke shook his head at the question. "No. Someone's been using my handle, all right. I came in here to put a stop to it. But here's my idea now. Get the gold and then get rid of Ingalls. Then we keep on with this Luke Barron idea, take the whole diggin's over and. . . ." Suddenly a loud guffaw of the deputy's cut in on his words. He looked at the man with mock anger on his face. He tried to say something more, but the deputy's laugh drowned out his voice. Then, when Kemp paused laughing long enough to get his breath, he asked flatly, "What the hell is this? You think I'm running a sandy?"

"Hell, no! You're dead serious, you poor, blind son-of-a-bitch! Think I'd take a flyer like this when I'm already in on a sure thing with Ingalls?" Laughter came again, more scornfully now.

It was hard for Luke to keep on with the pretense, to make his face take on the unaccustomed sullen look he knew should be his reaction to the deputy's derision, but he did a fair job of it.

Kemp drawled: "You must've been up against some pretty weak-minded jaspers across there in Colorado. You ain't even dry behind the ears yet, Barron. Me sling in with you? Hell, no. Now, I'll tell you my proposition. I'm goin' to give you a chance to listen in while I go into your girl friend's cave and give her a little pleasure, sort of my way of offering the condemned a last meal. You can hear her the whole time we're doin' it." He now lowered his voice to a harsh whisper. "An' after I've taken her, you can listen while I snuff her out. In the mornin' Sam'll be back. You'll be arrested for rape, murder, an' robbery. It makes it all the sweeter for us, knowin' now that you're the real Luke Barron. God, I wisht Sam was here so's I could tell him!" He moved back a step. "Anyway, that's my offer for partnership, Mister Luke Barron."

Nan could make out most of this conversation through the narrow opening between the two caves. Added to her terror at what Kemp intended to do to her was her heartsick despair that Luke Ashford, the man she had come to love in her soul, whom she knew her father and the others trusted, had actually now admitted his identity. Should she believe his proposal to Mart Kemp? Would he really have gone through with it? Hadn't he actually done something similar in Colorado before he came here?

Tears now were coursing down her cheeks as she heard the scuffing sounds of Kemp's boots when he entered her cave. He paused inside the entrance, still holding the candle, shielding it with his left hand. His wide mouth was twisted into the determined smirk of a satyr as, still hunched over slightly because of the low ceiling, he set down the candle in a niche in the cave wall. He had Luke's .38 shoved into his waistband. He removed the gun and set it beside the candle. Nan's eyes grew wide with horror and disgust, banishing the tears. Kemp removed his gun belt after pulling out a long knife he carried on it, and advanced toward her.

"Well, my little shanty queen," he said, "I'm goin' to have to cut your feet loose now, aren't I, if we're goin' to pull those britches off'n you and see what you look like?"

He bent down and with a few deft swipes with the knife Nan's leg bonds were slit, and her lower limbs were free. Kemp leaned over kneeling, putting the knife to one side, grinning. Then he crawled closer to Nan, reached out with both hands, made sure that her arms were still bound, and then undid the buttons to her Levi's. He worked quickly, his fingers deft despite his haste. Once he had undone the buttons, he straightened, moved back toward her feet, and bent over again, this time reaching for the cuffs of the Levi's. His notion was to pull them off swiftly. What he hadn't anticipated was the toe end of Nan's boot that suddenly connected in anatomical precision with tremendous impact at the point where his scrotum was located.

The pain must have been overwhelming to Kemp. His body rebounded, driving him upwards where his skull collided with the stone ceiling of the cave as his hands clutched toward his groin. Perhaps his skull had already been made fragile as a result of some physical deficiency. Whatever the case, Nan thought she actually heard Kemp's skull shatter as it hit the rock ceiling. There was a low groan, and the man collapsed, falling heavily beside her, his body silent.

As Nan stared at the man, she could see the blood drain from the surface, giving the man's face an almost translucent sheen in the diffused, flickering candlelight. She couldn't speak. She couldn't even think. It had all happened so quickly. She had seen Father Matthew die, but not like this, and not because of something she had done to him. She pulled her legs up and pushed her body away from Kemp's prone form, although, as she did it, she could feel her Levi's begin to slide down her hips.

"Nan!" Luke's muffled voice came through the narrow opening. "Nan! Are you all right? What happened? Are you hurt?"

"I killed him, Luke," she said softly, her eyes still fixed on the dead man.

"Nan! I can't hear you? What happened?"

"I said I killed him!" she nearly screamed then, and once more fell silent.

Favoring his hurt shoulder, Luke had managed to push himself across to the slitted opening to Nan's cave. His mouth was close to it as he called to her. "Nan!"

"I'm here," came her whispered answer.

"Kemp's dead?"

"Yes."

Luke heard her stir again in the darkness beyond the opening. He began a laborious effort of moving his boots around in the direction of the opening. When he could feel it with the toe of one boot, he started digging frantically at the sand with his heels, scooping it back from the opening by bending his knees. The fine sand was dry, loosely packed, and came away easily. The hardest part came with having to move the scooped-out sand to one side so that it wouldn't sift back into the widening opening. He did that by working around at right angles and pushing the sand to one side with his feet.

In the long interval that he lay there, working against the tautness of the rope that bound his legs together, his shoulder stabbed time and again with a knife-like pain that crowded in over the continuously throbbing hurt. A beady perspiration stood out on his forehead and ran into his eyes. It was a long sheer torment that he fought with all the force of his will. Many

222

times it seemed easier to lie back and close his eyes, letting the pain in his shoulder ease off. But each time he did that, he would remember the threat represented by the deputy, that Nan said she had killed him, and that she was now silent. Each time he hesitated, he could hear Nan, stirring in her cave, although she seemed to be moving away from the opening, dragging herself across the cave's floor.

"Nan!" he cried again.

There was no answer. Only the scuffing sound, growing ever more feeble.

"Nan! Can you hear me?"

He struggled on, not minding the way the rope cut into his legs and numbed his feet. Finally he reached out with his boots and thrust them through the opening. He had cleared away almost a foot of the sand now.

"Nan!" he said again.

Then he heard the scuffing sound coming closer. It seemed to be at the mouth of his cave. He craned his neck, and it was with surprise that he saw a shadow form, sidling into his cave, the form's right side edging along the wall beside the opening, as if stooping to accommodate the low ceiling. The form stopped. Were he able to see Nan's face, he would have seen it was covered with dark smudges, and that she must also have been crying because some of the smudges were darker, as from tears mixed with the grit.

"Nan?" he said, quietly, his voice filled with awe.

The form rolled over on its side and then, pressing its back to the wall of the cave, flexing its legs and pushing, it began working itself again into a upright position.

"I have to be careful about how I do this," Nan panted. "I don't want to lose my britches!"

Luke became vaguely aware from the way she moved that her Levi's must have fallen or been pushed to slightly below her knees. Perhaps it was the absurdity of the situation. Luke couldn't help it. He began chuckling at her discomfort.

"If you don't stop that bellowing, you won't get untied," she said sternly. "I'll just leave you here where you belong . . . Luke Barron!"

Luke's mouth snapped shut. "You heard me talking to that deputy?"

"Yes."

"I was just playing for time."

"So you say now."

"Nan!"

"How do I know you didn't mean it? It would have been a nice set-up for you and Ed and Kemp, to get the gold and move in on Ingalls and the other deputies."

"Nan!"

"Stop repeating my name and turn around so I can sit behind you and work at those ropes around your wrists."

"Yes, ma'am."

Luke rolled and pushed himself around in an ungainly fashion, falling over once onto his face and sputtering. He could not really see Nan from his covert position with the trace of a smile on her blackened face, her ash-blonde hair now all disheveled and drooping around her oval face.

Once he was in position, with his back to her, Luke could hear her edging along the wall and then, with a thump, she was pushing onto his back and slipping down behind him. She felt warm against his body.

"Can you move your hands?" he asked.

She was a brief moment in replying hesitantly: "I . . . I don't know. I can't feel my hands any more. My butt sure is cold, though." She shifted herself again, then said. "I'll try."

It seemed an eternity before he felt her fingers move the knotted ropes that bound his wrists. He said — "Good girl!"

— hoping this small encouragement would help.

"I don't feel much like a girl any more," she murmured.

He fell silent. Once in the long minutes that followed she paused, and he heard her breathing deeply from the effort it was costing her to work at the stubborn knot. "No hurry, Nan. Rest a minute," he said.

"He . . . Kemp . . . had a knife. I should have brought it. But I didn't. Is your shoulder hurting?"

"Not much."

He felt her hands touch his right hand and clench it with a pressure that told him the same wild hope was in her that had come to him. "I think I'll have it this time." Then her hands were working at the knot again.

Almost before he realized it, the first winding of the rope about his arms came loose, and he was bending forward in his sitting position, elbowing out of the windings of the stout quarter-inch manila. He moved his good arm gingerly at first, starting the circulation in it. Then he rubbed the other, relishing the relief of the throbbing as it eased out of his shoulder. In a moment he had twisted himself around, facing Nan's back, his hands working swiftly to untie her.

Despite Ray Cune's pained protest, Ed Tyler had cut away the sleeves of the white shirt he was wearing and exposed the wounds in his arms. It was fortunate for the deputy that both of the bullets had passed through his body. However, both wounds were bleeding, that in the right shoulder worse than the one in the left. Ed rummaged again amid the camp gear and found a discarded shirt he could cut up for bandages. He put on water to boil in the coffee pot, and thrust the knife he had found to cut through the ropes into the fire as well. He then banked the fire and went out to gather more fuel. It was now quite dark, although there was considerable starshine and a half moon that illumined the mesa top. The wind was still strong but was somewhat broken by the lean-to. It did, however, fan the fire, and soon the water was hot and the knife glowing.

Ed carefully cleansed the wound as best he could, using some of the whiskey as a disinfectant after giving the deputy another slug of it in the tin cup. The cauterizing proved so painful that Cune screamed out the first time Ed applied the red-hot knife, thrashing about. The second time Ed applied the blade, the deputy passed out.

The cauterizing stanched the bleeding, and Ed bound both wounds with bandaging from the discarded shirt. He was not at all certain of how thorough a job he had done, but in his time he had cared for injured cattle and a dog or two as well as a gunshot wound and a knife wound from the days when he and Luke rode in Colorado. Obviously, Cune would have to keep both arms in slings were he ever to move, but moving the man was something Ed didn't even want to think about. The deputy was becoming feverish, and the best thing for him, Ed felt, was rest.

Since the camp was obviously the hide-out for Buck Rollins and the gang, it was evident to Ed Tyler that it would be likely that at least some of the gold dust they had stolen would be found nearby. Painstakingly he went through all of the camp gear, setting aside appropriate victuals for himself and the deputy in the process. The search did prove rewarding. Yet, finding the cache of gold dust still in sacks also meant that it was likely that Rollins and the others would be returning after this new raid on the claim owners.

It occurred to Ed, more than once, that he ought to hurry back across the mesa and down to where he left his horse tethered. Although it was night, he could possibly find his way back to where he had climbed down the backside of the western wall of Eagle Cañon and give George Steele, Gopher Parsons, and the others some kind of warning of what to expect. The only problem with that, and the reason he rejected the urge each time it came to him, was that it would mean abandoning Ray Cune. While Ed had no especial attachment for the deputy, the man could scarcely defend himself, and to be found in his present condition would doubtless mean his death at the hands of the man who had shot him with every intention that he would bleed to death. No, the better idea would be to venture back to the eastern side of the mesa, up which he had climbed, and wait until he could see the gang returning. He would then have the element of surprise and, perhaps, were he lucky, he might succeed in getting the upper hand.

From the low opening of Nan's cave, they both looked in at the prostrate body of Mart Kemp in the flickering candle-light.

"We have to talk, Luke Barron."

"Yes, Nan, we do."

Luke, stooping slightly, stepped over to where Kemp's corpse lay. Squatting down, he examined the man. After getting back up on his feet, remaining slightly stooped, he went over to the niche where the candle stood and picked up his six-gun, placing it in the holster he still wore. He turned to where Nan was standing, just inside the entrance to the cave.

"Was it really your intention to steal the gold, or were you just trying to trick Kemp?"

Luke smiled at her. "We've got two choices when it comes to that gold. The plan I worked out with your father and Gopher Parsons won't work any more. Kemp here told me that the phony Luke Barron gang intends to raid the claim owners again tonight. We're too late to warn them about what to expect. I don't like to suggest it, and I want you to keep in the clear as much as you can, but I think the time has come for me to knock off the check point guard and work on the Avenging Angels in the Eagle Cañon camp, one by one, until I'm stopped. How far away is Stirrup Gap?"

"Too far for me to get help from there in time, if that's what you're thinking. Besides, I want to tend to your shoulder again. You're in no condition to knock over any Avenging Angel with that shoulder wound, Luke Barron. Nor have you explained to me your part in all this. It certainly can't be to help Dad and the others against Sam Ingalls."

"Father Matthew made me a special deputy," Luke said. "He wanted me to report to him alone. I don't think he trusted Sam Ingalls."

"Did he know who you really are?"

"I believe he did, Nan. He's the one who suggested I call myself Luke Ashford."

"Did you tell him why you came here? In the first place, I mean? You had to have a reason."

"Whatever reason I may have had, Nan, was lost to me forever out at the Bos cabin and . . . now, all I want to do is stop Ingalls and his gang."

"And then what?"

"Then, I reckon, it will be time for me and Ed Tyler to ride on." Somehow his saying this made Nan Steele angry. Luke walked the few paces over to where she was standing, her Levi's again buttoned and her ash-blonde hair pushed back out of her face as well as she could manage it. He could stand erect here and placed his hands on her slim shoulders, looking down into the dark, silent depths of her shadowed face. "I admit I was tempted, Nan," he said in a gruff voice. "Ed and I even planned to steal the gold for ourselves. But. . . ." He drew her to face him as she struggled to pull away. "But, Nan, I couldn't have gone through with it then, any more than I

228

can go through with it now." He dropped his hands from her shoulders and turned back toward the entrance of what had been her cave. "I can't rightly expect you to believe me, but I wasn't quite the owlhoot that Ingalls has made me out to have been. Ed and I were claim owners up in Colorado, just like your father and the others. We got cheated by a combine that jumped our claims, and we fought back. It made a lot of headlines, that's all. We sure didn't get rich doing it. Then I was on the dodge for a frame-up on a murder charge." He turned back to face her. "That's the way it's been for nearly ten years. The gang broke up . . . killed off, mostly. Ed headed north. We hoped to start a spread together, but didn't know where we'd get the money. My own funds were running pretty low when I heard from him. He wrote me about Eagle Cañon. He had wanted me to join him up here."

"For what purpose? All the claims have been taken. Father Matthew, Royal Logan, and other Temple members saw to that."

"What purpose did you have in coming to Eagle Cañon? To help your father?"

"Partly. Partly, Royal needed a nurse. We met back in Stirrup Gap. For a time I . . . I was even attracted to him. You know he asked me to marry him."

"You know him better now."

"In a way, I suppose, he's an evil man, but not the way Sam Ingalls is, or that man was, lying there, or the others who have been robbing and killing. I probably wouldn't have taken the Temple of the Redeemed very seriously, but for Father Matthew. He was a special person to me. He still is. I'll never forget him, or what he believed in." She shook her head and changed the subject. "I want to look at your wound."

"The gang got broken up, Nan," Luke said, ignoring what she had just said. "I finally had gotten sick of it and had to quit. I don't own a whole lot, except for that black horse of mine. I hoped to start a small ranch with Ed. The gold in Eagle Cañon looked like a good way to do that. Only . . . only when the cards were down, I couldn't go through with it. I couldn't cheat men I had come to regard as friends. And there was Father Matthew. And . . . and then. . . ." His voice stumbled and his mouth was dry. "And then, Nan, there was you. I couldn't do that to you. Let's settle this thing with Ingalls, and I'll be on my way again."

Nan came to him, into his arms, and he held her to him despite the throbbing pain in his shoulder. He could feel the blood trickling down his arm but wasn't about to say anything about it.

"There are things that have to be settled, Luke, but being on your way again doesn't have to be one of them."

He bent down, and they kissed for a long time, the act becoming a moment of passionate release for both of them. When they parted, Nan looked up into the dark shadows of his face.

"Luke Barron," she said. "Is that really your name?"

"I didn't lie about that, Nan," he admitted, the flicker of a smile passing invisibly across his features. "My name really is Luke Barron."

"I'm going to look at that wounded shoulder," she said, stepping back and herding him toward the candle light. He ducked his head again as he advanced. "Then we'd best be going."

"To Eagle Cañon?"

"I'm a fool, and you'll break my heart, but . . . yes."

The sun had set and darkness had enveloped the claims along Eagle Creek. A jumble of thoughts tortured George Steele. Strongest was the stark fear that he might never see his daughter again. Weakest was the devilish suspicion he had that Luke Ashford would be of little help to Nan. He was wounded and as much a prisoner of Sheriff Ingalls, according to what Timothy had said, as was Nan. They had heard nothing from Ed Tyler. Timothy had confirmed that Luke had managed to get a horse out of Eagle Cañon and turned it loose so Ed Tyler could get a mount, but that was hours ago, long before Nan and Luke Ashford had been seized by the sheriff. George could not help wondering what had become of the fugitive and if he had been successful in locating the hide-out of the Luke Barron gang.

Of course, he had to stop thinking in these terms. There was no Luke Barron gang. It had been Sam Ingalls and his Avenging Angels all the time. What Timothy had said confirmed it. Were the sheriff not behind the robbing and murders, why would he have taken Luke Ashford and Nan prisoner? What had puzzled him, though, at the time he had heard about it, and what troubled him still was why Ingalls had done it? What could he hope to gain by making Nan a prisoner? Did he intend by means of her to get her father to turn himself in? Lee Hop had left no question in George Steele's mind that the diabolical doctor intended to have him strung up just like Yokum Bos. But that was another thing that didn't make a whole lot of sense. Just how much was Dr. Logan in with Sam Ingalls and his henchmen? The doctor was a righteous man who believed in prohibiting men from drinking, smoking, gambling, and dancing, but was he also interested in stealing their gold dust? He couldn't be making a fortune from selling his supposedly *safe* water, although he was doing so under the protection of the Avenging Angels. Had he, too, grown greedy and allied himself with Ingalls?

George knew the doctor cared about Nan. He knew the medical man wanted to marry her, and he had even proposed she use this affection in order to spy on what the doctor and the sheriff were planning. But why would Royal Logan want Ingalls to arrest Nan? How could such a thing benefit him? Or had he found out, in so short a time, that she was spying for the claim owners? George didn't know, and this was only one more conundrum to assail his already besieged mind.

Gopher and Timothy should be back soon. They had both set out, Gopher on his mule, Timothy driving the wagon, heading upcreek to round up other claim owners to take the camp by force, if necessary, and to make Sam Ingalls and his Avenging Angels tell the truth. The death of Father Matthew had broken whatever peaceful unity there may have once been in Eagle Cañon. Neele Bos may have shot the old priest, as Timothy Kamu affirmed, but that didn't mean she deserved to be burned at the stake as was apparently Dr. Logan's aim. The physician had carried his righteousness too far. George had seen it happen before, fanatic reformers who presumed to care only for the common good, finally going berserk when they couldn't really control the way others preferred to live their lives.

George knew from Yokum Bos that Neele's relationship with Father Matthew went back beyond Eagle Cañon, beyond Stirrup Gap, all the way back to Centralia. Perhaps she had had a good reason for shooting the old priest. After all, Father Matthew had been among those who had sentenced Yokum Bos to hang, and he had learned the truth about the way the sheriff had elicited a confession from Yokum through torture. Timothy said the old priest had asked Nan to accompany him out to the Bos place because he knew what had been done, and that the knowledge had tormented him. Might Neele have misread Father Matthew's intentions? No one would ever know for sure if that crazy doctor were allowed to burn her at the stake.

The lighted kerosene lamp hung from the top joist over the flap door of Gopher Parsons's tent. George was outside the tent, hidden in shadow, waiting the return of Gopher Parsons and Timothy Kamu. He had been elected to stay behind, first, because he was a fugitive and some of the Avenging Angels might be out looking for him, and, second, because he had no means of riding except on the wagon with Timothy or double on Parsons's mule. When they descended on Eagle Cañon, he would be on the wagon with Timothy. Both men had chosen to go upcreek, that being a safer route than the claims toward the camp. It was from downcreek now that George heard an exchange of shots, distinct but distant on the wind. He had his six-gun in his hand and moved out in the direction from which the shots had come. There was one more, then silence.

"Git outta thet light, yuh old fool!" Gopher Parsons's voice came from behind him.

A group of mounted men were approaching with Parsons in the lead. In the starshine and light of the half moon George Steele recognized Fred Jeliffe, Bill Olds, and Nels Larsen.

"Sounds like trouble at Hopkins's claim upcreek," George said, walking up to where Gopher Parsons was sitting his mule.

"I 'spect yore right, George," Parsons said in a gruff undertone. "Reckon Ingalls and his boys have begun another night of dirty work. Git yore hosses outta sight, men. We'll hev a leetle surprise for Ingalls when he gets here."

The road into Eagle Cañon was quiet as Sheriff Sam Ingalls rode up to the check point. Tiny Hart had been in the tent behind the gun board, probably smoking a cigar from the furtive way he came out, peering toward the road, the coal-oil lamp outside the tent outlining his huge silhouette.

"It's me, Tiny," Ingalls said, sitting his saddle and smiling in spite of himself at the obsequious manner of his deputy. "Everything's pretty quiet, huh?"

"Now I wouldn't say that, Sam," Hart said as he came up to Ingalls's horse. "The doc's on the warpath, fer one thing. He heard about you an' Mart takin' Miss Nan prisoner."

"That damned nigger blabbed, didn't he?" Ingalls shot at the deputy, all at once in a rage.

"Don't know where he heard about it, Sam. He come down here all in a fit. When I told him you was outta town on business, he went over an' got Pink, took him along, sayin' somethin' about wantin' to move that dead priest over to the Temple. I understand Frank Summers has been buildin' a coffin. There's gonna be a service tomorrow mornin' for Father Matthew, and everyone's got to attend. Doc wants the Avenging Angels to summon all the miners into town, includin' families with them as have 'em. He's powerful angry about Miss Nan, an' says I'm to send you to see him soon's you get back. He'll either be at the Temple or at the hospital. I reckon he's at the Temple, 'cause Pink still ain't back."

"Arlie watching the prisoner?" Ingalls asked.

"Yeah, but strapped in that chair thataway, she don't need much watchin'. You gonna go along with Doc Logan on this witch burnin'?"

"Now that, Tiny, all depends on the doc. Things ain't gonna be the same around here, now that Father Matthew's gone. I can tell you that."

"Ashford give you any trouble?"

"Naw. I had to plug him in the shoulder, but after that he was downright peaceful."

"What you gonna tell the doc about Miss Nan?"

"The doc ain't never gonna see Miss Nan again."

"How come?"

"Because she got herself raped and killed tonight by the

234

Luke Barron gang. We even caught one of them red-handed."

"Ashford?"

"That's right, Tiny."

"There'll be the devil to pay about that, Sam, and about what's probably goin' on right now. You know, Buck and the boys rode in maybe a half hour ago. They're gonna move right upcreek, I guess."

"Yeah, well, I want to talk to you about that," the sheriff said, lowering his voice and leaning forward in his saddle. "No one is to get out of camp tonight."

"No one? What about Buck and the boys?"

"That's who I mean, most special," the sheriff affirmed. "Pink and I will be holed up in the Temple. Arlie'll be at the jail. Soon as they ride through, whenever that happens, we're gonna hit 'em and hit 'em hard. You keep up this end, in case any of them gets past us."

"What'll the doc and the others say about that?"

"I don't give a damn. Tonight is when we finish the Luke Barron gang. I sent Ray out to Buck's camp this afternoon to tell Buck that I wanted Parsons, Jeliff, Olds, and any others who get in his way put out of their misery tonight. We'll collect what gold we get from the bodies of the Luke Barron gang and impound that. Those claim owners who are killed tonight will just naturally lose their claims." The lawman paused for a moment, and then continued. "Where's Ray?"

"I don't know, Sam," Tiny said, slightly taken aback by this sudden change in the sheriff's strategy. "I ain't seen him."

"What you been doin', Tiny, sleepin'?" the sheriff demanded. "If Buck and the boys have come through, Ray must have been with 'em, or right behind 'em."

"I tell you I ain't seen Ray tonight, Sam. Mebbe he stayed out to the mesa?"

"Why would he do that? I told him to come back with Buck and the boys."

"I'm tellin' you, Sam, he wasn't with Buck and the boys, an' I ain't seen him or anyone else since they rode in. I was just takin' a few minutes out to smoke a cigar, but I would have heard him, if he had ridden in. I heard you comin', didn't I?"

"Yeah, after I called out to you. Tiny, no more of this. Ray's probably in camp and you never saw him. I want you on the job. I plan to have Ray waitin' in the bank building. That'll put two of us on each side of the street. Buck'll be caught in a cross fire." He leaned back in the saddle now. "I don't want anyone getting through. Is that clear, Tiny?"

"Shore is, Sam. No one gets through. I'll have my rifle ready."

"Your signal is when we start shooting. Think you can remember that, Tiny?"

"Hell, Sam, I'm not an idjit."

"No?" Sam said, and laughed, before nudging his horse into a trot up the street.

If Dr. Logan knew about Nan Steele, he might become hard to handle, and Sam Ingalls didn't want any trouble out of the medical man, not on this night that was so vital to his plans. He made directly for the Temple and dismounted in front, tying his reins to one of the pillars of the verandah that ran the width of the front of the building. To his surprise, despite the strong, cold wind blowing up the street, the two carved wooden doors were open, and the assembly area for worship was fully lighted.

Entering, the sheriff was disappointed to see quite a gathering around a newly hewn coffin set on sawhorses in the main aisle. He recognized Frank Summers from the mercantile store, his sister, Rebecca, Hank DeForest, superintendent of the work crew that had to interrupt construction of the new bank building to attend to repairs on the jailhouse roof, his deputy, Pink Morgan, Lee Hop, and Dr. Royal Logan. They all turned toward Sam Ingalls as he continued walking down the aisle. Seeing Father Matthew's body in the coffin, and allowing that he was inside the Temple of the Redeemed, the sheriff removed his hat.

"Howdy, folks," he said, stopping before the group that was gathered around the coffin, "I saw the doors open and the lights, and so I came in to see what was going on here."

"We are preparing the body for the funeral service in the morning, Sheriff," Dr. Logan said in a somewhat hostile tone.

The eyes of the other bystanders also seemed somewhat disapproving.

"A group of strange riders were seen entering Eagle Cañon and heading toward the diggings," Frank Summers said in consternation. "It's possible they were part of Luke Barron's gang. Tiny Hart, however, passed them right through."

"I told 'em there was nothing to worry about, if Tiny passed them through the check point, Sam," Pink Morgan said, and pulled away from the group to walk toward the sheriff.

"It may have been Luke Barron and his gang," the sheriff said. "I've been talkin' to Tiny about them. If it was, we'll be ready for 'em when they try riding out again. I would suggest all of you folks keep off the streets and stay under cover."

"We are off the streets," Dr. Logan said curtly. "I, for one, would appreciate an explanation as to why you arrested my nurse and shot the man who was with her this afternoon, accompanying Father Matthew's body on the way back from the Bos cabin."

"Who told you Nan Steele was arrested?" Ingalls demanded, anger suddenly coloring his features.

"Timothy Kamu," Lee Hop responded.

"That nigger is an ignorant fool," the sheriff said sharply. "The man who calls himself Luke Ashford, we have reason to believe, is in with the Barron gang. After we stopped him, and Miss Nan with him, he escaped with her as his prisoner."

"Come, now, Sheriff," Dr. Logan said sarcastically, "you don't expect us to believe that a wounded and unarmed man overpowered you and your deputy and managed to escape with Nan Steele as his prisoner? You are to release Miss Steele at once. Further, if those were members of the Barron gang your Avenging Angel passed into this town . . . and Frank says they were armed. . . ."

"That's right, Sam," Frank Summers interrupted. "Those men were heavily armed. The least Tiny Hart should have done was to disarm them at the check point, just as he keeps everyone in town or working the claims disarmed."

"If they were armed," insisted the sheriff, "you can bet they left their hardware at the check point. Tiny Hart's a reliable man."

"Reliable!" scoffed Dr. Logan, who had been interrupted and was pleased to be speaking out again. "I suspect Tiny Hart is secretly smoking tobacco in the tent at the check point. Smoking tobacco is against church law, and especially it is so for a man upholding the faith as an Avenging Angel. Now, I want to hear from you that Nan Steele will be released at once. Her father may be a criminal in the eyes of the Temple, but surely she is innocent of any malfeasance."

"I tell you she was taken prisoner by that Ashford gent," Ingalls protested. "She was his prisoner when we stopped them."

"I think these laws against drinking and smoking are ridiculous," Hank DeForest proclaimed. He was a sturdy, well-built, middle-aged man, wearing a brown corduroy jacket and work boots.

"No one asked your opinion, Mister DeForest," Rebecca Summers rebuked him. "We believe smoking and drinking are against the law of God. If people wish to live in sin, they can do so somewhere else than Eagle Cañon."

"Now, Becky," put in Summers, "Mister DeForest is only a visitor."

"Then he should respect our beliefs," Rebecca Summers returned archly.

"This is getting us nowhere," Dr. Logan protested. "Sam, I demand Nan Steele be released at once."

"I can't do that, Doc," the sheriff said emphatically. "I told you she was kidnapped by that Ashford gent. I'll admit the original idea was to use her to flush out her old man . . . who is now a criminal at large . . . but it went wrong when Luke Ashford took a hand. I might add he *was* armed. That man has totted a gun since he first came here. Frank, you ought to remember the run-in I had with him at your store over his carrying a gun the day he showed up."

"Sam's right about that, Doctor Logan," Frank Summers confirmed. "The sheriff did try to disarm him right in my store, but Father Matthew, bless his soul, intervened."

"I'm going to have to ask you folks again to clear out of here," Sam Ingalls said sternly. "We expect there may be shooting in the street when those men come back . . . if they are raiding the claims. You heard me! Clear out of here, all of you."

As the lawman was speaking, Pink Morgan edged closer to where Ingalls was standing, his right hand now resting on his Colt.

"If you force us to leave here, you won't be sheriff in Eagle Cañon by tomorrow morning," the doctor warned.

"Not you, Doc," the sheriff said somewhat placatingly. "I've got some things to tell you in private, so I want you to stay.

But Frank, Miss Summers, Mister DeForest, and you, Chink, I want you all out of here. Now!"

Ingalls also rested his hand on his Colt. Rebecca Summers made an inarticulate declaration of disgust but said nothing more. She began walking away from the open coffin, her brother following her. Ingalls and Morgan backed to one side of the aisle to allow them to pass. Hank DeForest and Lee Hop followed.

"Remember, you're to keep off the street. Close the doors after 'em, Pink," the sheriff ordered, and walked over to the head of the coffin where Dr. Logan was still standing, his hands now on the headboard. The lawman said nothing while he waited for the Temple to clear.

Pink Morgan closed the double doors following their departure.

"Now, see here, Sam . . . ," Dr. Logan began.

That was as far as he got. Swiftly Sam Ingalls pulled his Colt and swung the barrel swiftly, hitting the medical man along the side of his head. Logan, his eyes wide in astonishment, groaned briefly and collapsed.

"Pink," the sheriff said, holstering his six-gun, "help me carry this busybody back to Father Matthew's room."

For a moment the deputy was too shocked to move. "Sam, have yuh gone loco? The doc carries a lot of weight in this camp."

"He'll carry a lot less weight when I'm done with him," the sheriff said simply, his eyes hard and intense.

"What yuh gonna do when he comes to?"

"By the time he comes to it'll be too late."

"Too late for what?"

"To late for it to do him any good?"

"Sam! . . . What'ya gonna do?"

"Let the thinking to me, Pink. Get over here, now, and

240

help me carry the doc back to Father Matthew's room."

Shaking his head woefully, the deputy came over. Together they lifted the doctor's body and carried him to the side of the altar where a door connected with Father Matthew's room. The door was slightly ajar, and the sheriff kicked it open. The room was dark, but there was enough light coming in from the assembly room to make out the old priest's bed. It was here that Ingalls had them lay the doctor's prostrate body.

"Go out to my horse and fetch me my rope," the sheriff directed.

"What'ya gonna do, Sam?"

"You heard me, Pink. Get a move on. We ain't got a lotta time. Buck and his gang'll be comin' back through camp, and we'll catch them in a cross-fire."

"I shore as hell hope yuh know what yore doin', Sam."

"Shut up, and get that rope."

The deputy left through the door to the assembly room. Sheriff Ingalls knew the layout of the Temple well enough to know where the coal oil for the assembly room lamps was kept — in the storage room on the other side of the altar — and it was there that he went. He found two cans, one half full. He was carrying the half full can across in front of the altar when Pink returned, carrying the sheriff's lariat.

"Tie up the doc, Pink, an' gag him good. I don't want anyone to hear any screaming."

Pink Morgan went directly to do as he was instructed. He had watched the sheriff use the witch's chair, and he had been there when Ed Tyler had been tortured. He knew this fiendish mood of Ingalls's, and he knew better than to question anything the lawman decided to do. While he carelessly bound the unconscious medical man, he was surprised to find the doctor was carrying a concealed weapon, but he did not remove it. Meanwhile Ingalls was liberally dousing the walls and floor of

Father Matthew's room with coal oil. Pink gagged the doctor with his own handkerchief.

"All right," the sheriff said, setting down the empty can. "I'm going over to the jail to get Arlie and Ray ready and waiting for when Buck and the boys come ridin' through. Pink, you get that other can of coal oil out of the store room and. . . ."

"Ray ain't back yet, Sam. Leastways, I ain't seen him."

The sheriff hesitated for a moment to speculate on what this might mean, then threw his head back in a gesture of impatience. "Never mind that. Tiny's ready. Arlie's over at the jail, ain't he?"

"He was the last time I seen him."

"O K. You've got your orders. Douse that assembly room well. I want the fire to burn fast when I light it."

"When's that, Sam?"

"Soon as we spot Buck and the boys."

"Has Buck tried to double-cross us?" Pink asked, somewhat dumbfounded by this sudden change in the sheriff's attitude.

"Tonight we take over, Pink. Them as doesn't like it, can just move on. The doc is the only one that would give me trouble, and we're takin' care of him when I touch off the Temple."

The sheriff said no more, but walked promptly back into the assembly hall of the Temple.

Chapter Eighteen

Out of the darkness and in the strong wind a lone rider appeared on the road leading into Eagle Cañon. The rider pulled up near the check point. Tiny Hart had his back to the road, watching the main street in the darkness. In the distance on the wind came the sounds of shots, beyond the camp from the direction of the claims.

"Hello, the camp!" an alto voice rang out of the darkness.

Tiny Hart turned at once, the light from the lantern near the tent partially illumining his features as he peered in the direction from which the voice came.

"Who goes there?" he called out.

"Nancy Steele," said the rider.

"Miss Nan?" Tiny questioned, and then rapidly approached where she was sitting her horse. "It can't be you."

"But it is, Tiny," she said against the wind.

The deputy came closer, moving cautiously now. His hand dropped to his gun.

"I'm not armed, Tiny," Nan said.

"But I thought . . . ?" He stopped in mid-sentence, sensing something moving up behind him. He turned abruptly.

Luke Barron's .38 slashed down sharply, hitting the deputy across the face. Tiny fell backwards, and Luke was on him at once, slashing again with the .38.

"Out of the way, Nan," he said. "Ride around behind the tent. Keep out of range."

Even as he spoke, smoke, barely visible in the gloom, began pouring from the Temple doors, which stood wide open. Then flames began shooting out and upward. The gunfire was also coming closer.

"Get out of the way, Nan," Luke said again, louder, as he ran back down the road toward where he had left his horse.

Nan's inclination was to dismount and examine Tiny Hart to see how seriously he might have been hurt, but her attention was drawn, as Luke ran behind her down the road, to the Temple. Horses were running up ahead of her now, running hard, entering the main street of the camp from the direction of the claims.

Luke got to his black, untied the reins, and jumped into the saddle, urging his mount forward at the same time. He rode up to where Nan was still sitting her horse, in the middle of the road at the check point. He pulled up.

"Luke!" Nan called out. "The Temple's on fire!"

"I see it."

There was shooting now in the street as two riders raced past the half-built bank building and the jailhouse on one side of the street, Summers's mercantile and the burning Temple on the other side. One of the riders pitched forward from his running horse, while the other pulled up, looking toward the Temple and firing. Several shots were exchanged, before the rider tried to push forward again, only to be hit from a bullet fired from the jailhouse.

Luke felt Nan's hand take a grip on his arm. She was pointing up in to the sky, behind the Temple, to the western rim of the cañon. Luke's glance followed in the direction Nan was pointing, up to the far rim where, visible in the light from the flames stood Dr. Logan's huge water tank. It was a squatting bulk, held upright by sturdy timbered legs, a dark shadow hanging over the town at the head of the narrow gully down which its pipeline ran to the rear of the mercantile.

"Do you know a quick way up there?" he asked Nan.

Her answer was to urge her horse forward. "Come along."

They left the far end of the street at a run, Nan swinging sharply left toward the west wall of the cañon. As Luke rode, Nan swung farther away from him, up the steep, loose-talus slope. Luke followed, admiration filling him at the blind faith of this girl who was willing to take a desperate chance, who didn't hesitate an instant now. She pushed on, punishing her horse to keep him on his feet up across the loose rock and then threading her way between the huge slabs of rock that lay below the rim.

They climbed eternally, or so it seemed to Luke, turning back away from the camp, then swinging sharply on a line parallel with the main street, but they were gaining on those fifty feet that separated them from the rim. Once Nan's horse slipped and went to his knees. She had him on his feet again before Luke could pull alongside to help.

They made the rim with their horses badly blown, but Luke didn't stop, taking the lead now and striking down toward the towering shadow of Dr. Logan's water tank and its neighboring windmill. He drew rein close in to one of the four two-foot-thick timber supports, flicking out his rope to widen the noose. He turned to face Nan and saw that she was untying the rope from her own saddle.

"Think it'll work?" he asked, and had his answer in a nod of her head.

He spent precious moments scooping the drifted sand from the base of the nearest support with his right hand. Finally he had cleared the concrete base on which the butt end of the log rested. At that moment he saw for the first time a complication in the two long bolted rods that ran crosswise between the timbers, holding them together at a slight outward angle. The rods were of half-inch iron, capped with washers and a bolt.

Nan saw him kneeling there, looking at the bolt that held the big timber rigid, locked to the obliquely opposite support.

"Could you shoot it off?" she asked. He gave her a grateful look, drew his gun, and carefully sent two bullets crashing against the bolt. The second bullet broke the bolt end. The rod, its end released, sang with the slacked tension and pulled clear of the hole and fell to the ground.

He tied the ends of their two ropes around the butt end of the support, shaking his left arm free of the sling Nan had fixed for him back at the caves, gritting his teeth against the pain. He handed Nan the end of one, stepped into the saddle and wound the end of the other around his saddle horn. Nan wrapped her rope end around her own saddle horn.

Luke said: "When this thing cuts loose, make tracks away from here."

Nan nodded, following Luke's example and easing her horse into the pull gently, to avoid weakening the rope.

In those brief moments in which his horse strained against the dead weight of the rope, Luke glanced across at Nan and then down the line of the deep gully and at the burning Temple below. The Temple's rear wall made a gray splash in the shadows. The light from the conflagration illumined their faces as it lit the street, now filled with a mass of humanity, some on foot, some on horses and mules. Timothy Kamu and George Steele on the wagon were faintly visible. As Luke watched, he saw a sudden burst of flame become alive on the Temple's roof. There wasn't much time left.

Suddenly, his horse took a long, uncertain forward step. There was a creaking and a groaning of timbers behind. His glance swept around to the tank's huge bulk, towering high overhead. Then, with an explosion like the thunder of artillery, the butt end of the huge log support left its concrete base and shot outward.

"Run!" he shouted, but already Nan had urged her horse's flanks, lifting him to a reaching lope.

They stopped and turned their horses a hundred feet out from the tank in time to see it topple slowly inward toward the nearby rim. Its wooden seams parted, the iron rods snapped apart, and five thousand gallons of water burst outward and hit the rim with an earth-jarring drive. The water geysered upward in a tall plume, then plummeted downward.

Fascinated, they rode closer to the rim and looked downward. A raging, foaming wall of water was sweeping down the steep gully toward the back of the Temple and the mercantile, carrying boulders and uprooted stunted cedars before it. It swept onward majestically, slowly but relentlessly, with a roar that drowned out all other sound and seemed to shake the rimrock.

As the last of that rush of water drained off the rim, Luke said quickly: "Let's get down there, Nan." Then he was prodding his black's flanks, sending the animal down over the rim's edge and into the bottom of the downward-sloping gully. The black, panicked, slid and ran down the gully with a swiftness that overtook the last trickle of rushing water.

Luke saw that solid wall of water foam up out of the gully's end and smash into the back walls of the Temple and the mercantile. The thin frame walls stood up under the drive of the water for a split second only, then tore inward to let the tons of water through. Luke heard a man scream out over the thunder of the avalanche. Then he was crossing the back alley with his black at a run, aiming for the twenty-foot hole torn in the Temple's back wall.

He went through with his .38 drawn, his glance fixed on the huge opening in the front wall where the water had swept away half the Temple's face. A deputy, Pink Morgan, was barely visible, struggling knee-deep in water, holding to the torn end of a two-by-four wall support. At that moment his hold broke, and he was swept out of sight in the rush of water onto the street. Off to Luke's left, a gun lanced a crimson stab of flame that nearly hit him. As he vaulted from the saddle, he targeted that flame-stab and thumbed a single shot. He heard a choked cry of pain, then the mad scampering of the man as he side-stepped toward one darkened wall. It was Sam Ingalls. Luke ran out of the charred and still burning rubble.

Men were milling around in the flooded street, some still mounted, others running along the opposite walk. A lantern was lit in the half-formed structure of the bank building. Another was being carried along the street by Lee Hop. Ingalls was now running toward the check point.

Luke laid his sights on the sheriff's wide back, then lowered his gun. It would be cold-blooded murder, even if the man he was killing deserved no chance. He started after the lawman, trying to think of a way of taking Ingalls alive, when all at once he saw that the sheriff, dimly visible in the lantern light from the tent at the check point, had stopped and was lifting his gun into line with him. Luke lunged as Ingalls's gun exploded. Then, arcing up his own weapon, he slammed into the man, bringing his six-gun hard against Ingalls's shoulder. The sheriff yelled in pain and dropped his .45.

"Hold it right there, Ingalls," Luke warned.

All at once a lantern's flickering light moved forward along the street. At the corner of his vision Luke sensed the presence of men, several men. But he was watching Ingalls as the light from the lantern held by Lee Hop fell fully on him.

The sheriff stood there staring across at Luke, eyes wider than Luke had ever seen them. Luke was certain that his blow could not have mortally wounded the man. Yet there had been firing while he was riding down from the rim, and the sheriff's gray-shirted chest was torn by two holes that could have been covered by the spread of a man's hand. It was stained darkly with crimson. Then he tottered sideways, slowly, reminding

Luke of the ponderous fall of the water tank on the rim a few moments ago. He fell stiffly, face downward, in the street.

Someone behind Luke said: "Goddlemighty! It's Luke Ashford!"

He turned slowly to face the men near him now in the front of whom were George Steele, who had spoken, and Lee Hop, holding the lantern.

"I didn't shoot Ingalls," Luke said. "I wanted to, and maybe would have, but I didn't."

"No, I did," said a voice coming forward in the darkness. It proved to be the disheveled figure of Dr. Royal Logan. "Ingalls gun whipped me, had me tied up . . . not very well . . . by Pink Morgan, and would have had me burn to death in the Temple which he set on fire. Morgan's back there in the rubble, badly hurt from a falling beam and not a gunshot wound, as nearly as I could tell in the dark."

A flurry of activity had occurred. Pink Morgan had been carried to the tent hospital accompanied by Fred Jeliffe who had incurred a bullet wound in the running fight with Buck Rollins and his gang, both attended to by Nan Steele. The bodies in the street had been placed temporarily inside the bank structure along with the two gang members who had fallen in the battle at Gopher Parsons's claim. It was then that George Steele asked dismally of Timothy Kamu: "Where's Nan?" He was looking at the blanket-draped shapes nearby against a completed wall.

"Aftah she finished at de hospital, she helped let Neele Bos out of de jail and that terrible witch's chair and over to muh room. Miz Bos is ovah dere with Rebecca Summers, 'cause the mercantile was done washed out with de Temple. Father Matthew's body is also ovah at de livery stable where we moved him."

Steele and Parsons had been out to the claims in the wagon, bringing back two bodies, and had just carried the second one in and laid it beside the others in the bank structure.

"I don't get it," George Steele said. "Ain't Neele the one who killed the old priest?"

"She loved dat man more'n any of us," Timothy replied softly. "Miss Nan says it was an accident. Most believe her, an dat doctor is being held with dem deputies that were captured. Dey say he's gotta stand trial for his part in de murder of Yokum Bos."

"And well he should," George Steele affirmed. "But the doctor bein' out of commission, so to speak, do you reckon, Timothy, you and I should have a drink?"

"Waal, you cain bet I'm a-firin' up my pipe," Gopher Parsons said, and proceeded to bring it out of the shirt pocket in which he had kept it hidden. Once he had it going, he looked around at the blanketed bodies. "Which one of these d'you reckon's Luke Barron?"

Lee Hop was there also, having originally supplied the lantern that now stood on a sawhorse. "Seems likee sheriff man was Lukey Barron."

Parsons looked surprised and then disgusted. "Waal, I don't s'pose it matters one way or t'other, now."

In the shadow of the open front doors of the livery stable, Luke was standing beside his black horse, Nan near to him. The wind tugged at them.

"I talked to Tiny Hart when he came to," Luke was saying. "Tiny figures Ray Cune is still out on Rattlesnake Mesa. That's where Ingalls sent him and where the Luke Barron gang was hiding out. I figure Ed's out on the mesa, too. Maybe they had a shoot-out. I don't know, but I've got to ride out and see."

250

"What are the chances you'll find Luke Barron there?" Nan asked quietly.

Lantern light from inside the livery stable made her blue eyes seem luciferous in deep, dark sockets. She was aware of him as being outside herself, but she was, in this look and this question, uttering a command that was not to be broken. From now on, on this one side, between her and him, who had shared so much in the past two days, and on the other side, encompassing the rest of the world, what had not been there before was now drawn, an insurmountable line to last forever.

Peter Dawson is the *nom de plume* used by Jonathan Hurff Glidden. He was born in Kewanee, Illinois, and graduated from the University of Illinois with a degree in English literature. In his career as a Western writer, he published sixteen Western novels and over 120 Western novelettes and short stories for the magazine market. From the beginning, he was a dedicated craftsman who revised and polished his fiction until it shone as a fine gem. His Peter Dawson novels are noted for their adept plotting, interesting and well developed characters, their authentically researched historical backgrounds, and his stylistic flair. His first novel, *The Crimson Horseshoe,* won the Dodd, Mead Prize as the best Western of the year 1941 and ran serially in Street & Smith's *Western Story* prior to book publication. During the Second World War, Glidden served with the U.S. Strategic and Tactical Air Force in the United Kingdom. Later in 1950 he served for a time as Assistant to Chief of Station in Germany. After the war, his novels were frequently serialized in *The Saturday Evening Post.* Peter Dawson titles such as *High Country, Gunsmoke Graze,* and *Royal Gorge* are generally conceded to be among his masterpieces although he was an extremely consistent writer and virtually all his fiction has retained its classic stature among readers of all generations. One of Jon Glidden's finest techniques was his ability after the fashion of Dickens and Tolstoy to tell his stories via a series of dramatic vignettes which focus on a wide assortment of different characters, all tending to develop their own lives, situations, and predicaments, while at the same time propelling the general plot of the story toward a suspenseful conclusion. *Dark Riders of Doom* (1996), *Rattlesnake Mesa* (1997), and *Ghost Brand of the Wishbones* (1998) are his most recent titles.